The Landlord's Ex-Fiancée

TERRY JOE GUNNELS

Inquiries and Book Orders should be addressed to:

Gunnels Publishing
Email: terrygunnels51@cox.net
Phone: 757-930-1596

ISBN: 978-1-960939-21-0 (sc)
ISBN: 978-1-960939-22-7 (ebk)

Contents

Acknowledgments

To my wife, Shirley Jean (Cookie), for encouraging me through 45 years of marriage in all projects I have undertaken. And for spending untold hours proofreading this manuscript for errors.

To my editor, Donje Putnam, whom I have known since she was a teenager and my daughter's best friend. She always nails me to the wall with corrections and suggestions. I thank her.

To all my BETA readers who gave me valuable feedback.

To Sterling Norris Monk for reading, giving feedback, and finding errors I missed.

To Debby Groome Wilkerson for her insight on storyline.

To James Dove who pointed out many errors and shortcomings in my writing. And added valuable criticisms.

To Carl Yaddow who read the manuscript and added some interesting comments.

To all others, for exciting me to move forward with the story and encouraging me to publish.

I give my heartfelt THANK YOU to every person involved with this book.

Prologue

"You need to take care of her," Grant said as he loaded another bag into the back of the van.

"Why? She doesn't know anything. I agree she's curious, but so are a lot of people," Amir stated.

"We can't afford for her to see something she shouldn't see. Get rid of her," Grant insisted.

"Okay, but I don't like it. If she knew something or threatened us, it would be a different story, but she's just an excited young lady that wants desperately to be a chef," Amir said sadly. "I like her. She's sweet."

"You like every girl that smiles at you, Amir. Now, help me with this last bag."

Amir grabbed a bag, threw it into the van, and shut the door. "Can we have a drink before I pull out?"

"Sure, come on into the office. We'll have a drink, and I'll tell you how to get her out of the way," said Grant.

"When do you want me to do it?"

"Tonight. We can't wait much longer. Besides, she just paid her tuition last week for the coming semester. If we can find someone to take her place, then we get another tuition-paying student."

"That doesn't give me much time to prepare."

"You don't need time to prepare just to crack her on the head," Grant said. "Make it look like a break-in gone wrong. It isn't rocket science."

"Man, I can't believe you're making me do this. You have no heart!"

"And you do? Just do what I tell you. I'm just protecting my business," Grant said calmly, "and so should you."

They sat there drinking a glass of Kentucky bourbon straight up, each lost in their own thoughts. Grant owned the culinary school Valerie was attending, trying to become a certified chef. Grant was in his mid-forties, light-skinned with a pock-marked face left over from his teen years of severe acne, a 1980's style mustache, and a bit over-weight. He had started this culinary school over ten years ago with a reputation for training excellent chefs around the country.

Several years ago, he had started shipping some of the popular desserts around the country labeled as "gourmet" sweets. Some were ready to serve. Others were combined ingredients ready to add things like water, cream, and eggs, making a fresh, delightful dessert served by many high-end gourmet restaurants all over the continent. They were gourmet desserts that could be whipped up like a traditional cake mix. When the economy took a dive, so did their business. Grant had gotten into trouble when he took in some investors to help keep them afloat. As it turned out, the investors were, in fact, drug dealers looking for ways to distribute their products that regular government agencies don't usually scrutinize.

Amir came to this country illegally to work for Grant. In his mid-thirties, he was a cold-blooded killer, running from the authorities in his native country. He was small, wiry, and could make almost anything he picked up a deadly weapon. He could shoot but preferred a knife.

They trained chefs by day and ran drugs and occasionally guns at night. Grant Littleton found it very profitable and had built a sizable network of distributors. He had curious students in the past but had taken care of them in a similar way that Grant wanted Amir to take care of Valerie.

"Grant, are you sure there isn't another way we can get rid of her other than killing her? I don't like killing a woman," said Amir. "Can't we just fail her, and she'll leave?"

"No, we can't do that. She's doing well, and she knows it. So that in itself would look suspicious."

"What do you want me to do with the body? Bury it like I did the other two guys?"

"No, I said earlier, make it look like a burglary gone wrong. Or if you can think of something better, do it. Now, go," Grant said, getting up and wiping off the glass, and putting it back into his desk drawer.

"Fine. But I don't like killing a woman."

"I know. I'm not too fond of it either. I agree, she's a sweet girl, but we don't want anything or anyone to get in our way. A few more years of this, and we'll have enough to retire. Just wait until late at night, and knock on her door. She knows you, so she'll answer. When you get inside, do what you need to do and leave quietly," said Grant.

Amir got up and left. Although he had killed men before, but never a woman, he was Grant's hit man. If someone didn't follow Grant's explicit instructions, Amir would make him disappear. Reluctantly he would do the same with the young girl Valerie.

It was going to be a long night for Amir. One he would not forget until his dying moment.

CHAPTER 1

The Late-night Phone Call

The buzzing in his ear wouldn't stop. It buzzed and buzzed and buzzed. He put the pillow over his head, but it wouldn't stop. Finally, he realized that his cell phone was on the bedside table.

Mickey reached over and knocked it off onto the floor. He reached down, picked it up, and pushed the answer icon as he put it up to his ear.

"Hello," he said groggily.

"Hello, Mickey Ray?" asked the voice at the other end of the phone.

"Um, yeah?" he answered.

"It's me, Valerie," she said.

"Oh, hi, Val. What time is it?" he said, turning to the clock on his bedside table and trying to focus.

"I don't know. I think it is around eleven-thirty, I guess. Oh, Mickey, I'm scared."

He looked at the clock and said, "Valerie, it is almost two-thirty in the morning here. What's so important?"

"Someone outside my apartment is just sitting in a car. I can't see who it is, but they keep looking up at me in the window."

"Maybe they're looking at you because you're staring at them, Val. I'm sure it's nothing. You're on the second floor, looking out the window. That, I'm sure, looks strange to anyone walking by," he said as he sat up and tried to clear his mind.

"They aren't just walking by. They're sitting in the car looking at me, or at least this window. It creeps me out. I'm scared."

"Okay. Calm down. Call the police. Tell them they should send someone out to check out the area. Okay?" he said.

"Yeah. I'll do that. Can I call you back if they don't come?"

"Sure. You can call me anytime, day or night. You know that. It'll be okay. I guarantee it."

"Thank you. I still love you," she said.

"I know that, and I still love you, too," he answered.

She disconnected, and Mickey got up to make a cup of coffee. He was wide awake now. After pouring a cup of coffee, he sat thinking of Valerie.

Valerie Green was Mickey's high school sweetheart. A couple of years ago, they were engaged to be married, but she was abducted by human traffickers. Mickey and his best friend James Bower had rescued her, but she was traumatized by the event, which changed her. She left Bridgeton, a small town between Williamsburg and Richmond, Virginia, and enrolled in culinary school.

Valerie called Mickey on a regular basis and always on edge and nervous with stress. He'd talk to her and calm her down. He suggested she get professional counseling, but she refused to go.

When they'd talk, he would convince her that she was concerned about nothing. He didn't know if this was another one of those occasions, but he always tried to help.

He had to go to work tomorrow, and he needed his sleep. After finishing a cup of decaf, he crawled back into bed. He'd call Valerie on his way to work.

A few hours later, Mickey got up and started getting ready for work. He looked in the mirror and realized he hadn't shaved for several days. He didn't care. He raked his hand over several days of stubble. Heading for the shower, he passed the full-length mirror and looked at himself. He worked out with James several times a week and had pretty good abs, but he still didn't have good muscle tone in his upper arms. At almost 6 feet, he was toned and fit, but he knew he needed to work harder. He was in and out of the shower in minutes and on his way to work.

James Bower, a disabled, disfigured military veteran, married Mickey's sister. Valerie, Mickey Ray, his sister Darcy Jean and James had all gone to Bridgeton High. He would meet James later this afternoon for a much-needed workout at the gym.

When Mickey was a teenager, he worked as maintenance on his father's apartment complexes. When his parents were in an auto accident, he stepped in to help run the apartment management and construction business with his sister, Darcy. When his father decided to retire, he took over.

He was now 30 years old, single, and the CEO of the largest construction firm in lower eastern Virginia. He dialed Valerie's number as he drove to work.

When there was no answer, he thought that maybe after calling the police, everything was fine, and she was no longer upset. He disconnected and threw the phone on the seat of the car.

That was okay. Mickey knew Val would call again in a few days. If she didn't call him, he would give her a call. No problem.

He had a lot of office work today to keep him busy until after lunch. He had to meet with a finance officer from one of the banks. Then he had a staff meeting with the maintenance crew at one of the apartment complexes he owned. It would be a busy day.

When he got to his office after a late morning meeting with the bank, there was a message on his desk to call Detective Veronica Morgan with the Florence, Oregon, police department. The phone number was written at the bottom of the note. He looked at his watch and shook his head as he dialed. Florence, Oregon, is where Valerie lived. He wondered why the police were calling him. Valerie couldn't be in any trouble.

At the other end of the line, he heard a voice say, "Detective Morgan."

"Detective Morgan, this is Mickey Christianson. I have a message to give you a call?" Mickey said into the phone.

"Yes, Mr. Christianson. Thank you for returning my call. Do you know a Miss Valerie Green?" she asked.

"Yes, I do. Why? Is something wrong?"

"What relationship did you have with Miss Green?" she asked.

"What's wrong, Detective. Is she in some kind of trouble?"

"Please answer my question, Mr. Christianson."

"I will as soon as you tell me why you are asking them!" said Mickey Ray.

"I'm sorry to tell you this, Mr. Christianson, but Miss Green is dead."

Mickey had been looking out the window at his desk as he dialed the phone. When he heard this, he immediately sat down and took a deep breath. He continued staring out the window as the voice at the other end of the line called to him.

"Mr. Christianson, are you still there? Sir? Are you on the line?" she called to him.

"Um, yes. I'm sorry. I never expected to get a call like this," Mickey said into the phone.

"I understand, sir. No one expects to get a call like this. Would you like to take a few moments to compose yourself and call me back? I'll be here," she offered.

"No. That's okay. I'll be fine. How did she die?" he asked as he felt a lump swell in his throat.

"What relationship did you have with Miss Green?" she asked once more.

"We used to be engaged. She broke it off and moved to Florence. What happened?"

"For now, I'll ask the questions," she said.

"Okay. How may I help?"

"Before she called the police, your number was the last one she placed before her death last night. Why did she call you at eleven-thirty last night?" the detective asked.

Mickey answered, "She called because she was concerned that someone in a car was watching her apartment."

"Why was she so concerned?"

"Val would get that way sometimes. She had something happen to her a couple of years ago, and she sometimes gets upset over insignificant things like people watching her. Most of the time, it's nothing. I told her to call the police, and they would send someone to check it out."

"What were her reasons for the breakup?"

"I told you, something happened to her, and she had problems with it. When she could no longer deal with it, she left town."

"Was that problem you?"

"No. Look, Detective. That's a long story, and I don't have time to explain it over the phone. Now, if you don't mind, tell me what happened to Valerie," Mickey said, getting exasperated with the detective's questions.

"At this time, it looks as though it may be an accident. But we are investigating it."

"What kind of accident?" he asked, trying to calm himself down.

"She'd been drinking, fell, and hit her head on a coffee table in the living room of her apartment."

"No. That couldn't happen. Valerie didn't drink. She called me around two-thirty this morning. I told her to call the police, and she would call me back if they didn't come. When I didn't hear from her, I went back to bed."

"That's why I'm working the case. A glass was on the floor beside the table with a rum drink spilling onto the carpet."

"How do you know it was rum?" he asked.

"An empty bottle was sitting on the table," the detective said.

"I'm telling you, Detective, Valerie didn't drink. One drink and she would get violently ill. You need to check other reasons why she hit her head."

"We got your name and number from the building manager as her contact in case of an emergency. Also, as I said, your number was on her phone."

"Yes, we kept in contact. We'd call each other every few days to talk."

"Is there someone else we can call to identify her and claim her body when the autopsy is complete?"

"No. She was an only child, and her parents died a few years ago. If someone doesn't claim her body, what will happen to it?"

"There are several avenues that we use. One is to bury or cremate the body. Medical schools are sometimes willing to accept bodies for use by medical students. The last one is the potter's field."

"Potter's field? You mean, you throw her body in a field and leave it to rot so someone can pick her apart to study? That's so gross, Detective," Mickey said, getting sick at the very thought of it.

"I'm sorry, Mr. Christianson, I didn't mean to upset you, but you asked. Those are our only choices."

"Can I claim the body so I can bring her home and give her a proper funeral?" he asked.

"Since she has no other family, and you are listed as her point of contact, I'll do my best to make that happen for you. You'll have to come here in person to sign papers to release her body. We still need time to complete the autopsy and get the report. Give us a week or two," the detective said sympathetically.

"That long? It doesn't take that long to do an autopsy, Detective."

"True, but we have other cases pending. We autopsy most people that die in situations like this."

"Like what?" Mickey asked.

"When someone is found alone in their home, like Miss Green. We need to find out why. If you excuse me, I have other cases. If I need more information from you, I'll give you a call," she said curtly.

"Wait a minute, please. That seems like a long time. Maybe you can speed up the process if I come there to claim her body?"

"I don't know, but I doubt it, sir," she said.

"Will you call me as things progress on the case?" he asked.

"I'm sorry, but I can't give you daily reports. I can only say that some things about her death don't quite add up. I will call you when my report is complete, and you can pick up her body."

"I'll take care of a few things here and come out as soon as possible."

"That won't be necessary, sir. I'll call you when my report is complete."

"Thank you, Detective. I'll catch the first flight out," he said. He politely ended the conversation and began making other calls to clear his calendar for the balance of the week.

He called his sister, Darcy, and told her about Valerie. "Oh, Mickey. I'm so sorry. I'm sure you're devastated to hear that."

"Kind of. I'm not devastated, but I am down about it. I never thought about something happening to Val," he said sadly.

"She was around in some way or another most of our lives. In school, around the house, when you were dating, and then you were engaged. She was such a sweet person. I know you'll miss her," Darcy said.

"Yeah. I will, but I've moved on, and I think, on some level, so did she. But I still cared for her. And it will take a while for my feelings for her to dissipate."

"I know. Do you want me to make reservations for you to pick up her body and bring her home?"

"If you don't mind, I would appreciate it."

"Okay. Done. I'll call you back as soon as I can make arrangements for you," Darcy assured him.

Arriving in Florence, Oregon

Mickey Ray looked out the plane's window, and the setting sun gleamed in as it descended over the horizon. He thought of the times he and Valerie had sat on the front porch of her little house and watched the sunset. The sweet memories of the evening rides they took through the town's main street in his Rolls Royce Corniche.

Mickey had eaten so many meals at her house that she would use him as her guinea pig for some special recipe she found in one of her many cookbooks. He thought of the many meals she had served him when she worked at the diner.

Memories swirled in his mind of Valerie until he fell asleep. When he woke up, the plane was on the approach to the airport in Oregon. Even though he had slept, he was still tired, but he got off the plane, headed to the auto rental counter, and drove to the hotel.

The following morning, he dressed in casual clothes, khaki cotton slacks, and a polo shirt. He stopped briefly at the hotel breakfast area, got some coffee, and made a breakfast-type sandwich to eat as he drove to the police station.

Florence was a typical small town. The police station was a modern building surrounded by a short wall with the words *Florence*

Justice Center. He later found out the police department had only twenty-four staff members, including the police chief, a handful of officers, and two detectives.

When he got to the police station, he asked for Detective Veronica Morgan.

When she came into view, Mickey took a deep breath. She was about his age, and her long auburn hair was tied up in a bun with clips. She wore a dark business suit perfectly tailored to fit her petite frame, and the gold chain hanging around her neck glistened in the sun. She pulled the suit coat around her and buttoned it tight around her tiny waist. Her dark brown eyes shown bright as she looked at him with approval and flashed him a smile.

Putting out her hand, she said, "Hello, Mr. Christianson. I'm sorry to meet you under these circumstances."

"Thank you, and please, call me Mickey," he asked with a smile.

"Won't you come back to my office?" she said, turning and directing him to the back hallway of the building.

He stepped aside and turned to allow her to lead the way. The station was bright, modern, and airy. Suitable for a seacoast town. When they got to the back, her office was a desk in the corner of a large room filled with several other desks similar to hers. She had a panoramic view of the ocean and the Florence Marina.

As they walked down the hallway to her office, they passed pictures on the wall of officers killed in the line of duty. Most were old black and white pictures, and the last one he noticed was the name Sergeant Alfred Morgan.

"Was the person in the last picture back there any relation of yours?" Mickey asked.

"Yes. It was my father. Killed three years ago," she answered.

"I'm sorry," he said sincerely.

"Thank you."

He looked around the room and out the expansive windows at the Marina. "What a beautiful view you have!"

"Thanks, and I agree. We all have a great view from here. We share the building with the Florence Marine Patrol. Since we have a small town, this building is also home to the Municipal Court. We provide services to the city jail and dispatch center for police, fire, and ambulance services throughout an area of over 500 square miles."

"Very impressive for a small town," he said.

"Now, Mickey, have a seat and tell me whatever you feel may be helpful in our investigation," she said as she pulled out the chair to her desk.

Sitting down in the chair on the other side, he started with a question, "Why do you say investigation? Will you tell me what you have so far?"

"I'll tell you what I can. It's an...."

"Ongoing investigation. I know the drill," Mickey said, shaking his head, "Look, I'm not here to interfere with what you're doing. I came here to claim her body and take her home. That's all."

"I understand, but we can't let her go for a few days. First, we need to do a complete autopsy, and then when we get every bit of evidence from her, we'll let you have her body. You said that you were engaged to her?" she stated.

"Yes, but that was a long time ago. She left Bridgeton, and we both moved on. We were still friends. And we kept in touch. That's all."

"If you moved on, why are you here to collect her body?"

"Now, you're getting a bit personal, but she has no one else. I owe her that. We were in love at one time, but as I said, it was long ago."

"I see," she said as she took notes. "Do you know why someone would want to hurt her?"

"No? Why do you ask that?"

"Just covering all the bases."

"Can we go to her apartment so I can see it? Who actually found the body?" he asked, getting up from the chair.

"As you assumed, she called our department the night before last after calling you. It seems that she carpooled with someone named Janice," Detective Morgan said, thumbing through notes on her desk. "When Miss Green didn't come by to pick her up, Janice called her. When Miss Green didn't answer, Janice called the building manager. The building manager noticed that Miss Green's car was still parked outside, so she went inside the apartment. She found the body and called us.

"It's a crime scene now. You aren't supposed to be there until we release it."

"You go with me and watch every move I make so I won't contaminate anything."

"I guess we could go together. It shouldn't be a problem," she said, then closed her notebook. "Are you ready to go now?"

"Sure, I've got nothing else to do."

She said they could take her police car. Since, technically, no one but police and prisoners are supposed to ride in the cars, she had to stop at the captain's office to get permission.

As they took the scenic tour to Valerie's apartment building, the detective pointed out some things that might interest Mickey while he was there. Making small talk, he told her about digging up a dead body when they started construction on the last project and how he and James had assisted the Bridgeton police in solving the case. By the time they got to Valerie's apartment, she had told Mickey that he could call her by her nickname Ronnie, instead of Detective Morgan or her first name, Veronica.

When they got to the door, it had a padlock and was crisscrossed by yellow crime scene tape. She pulled the tape off and unlocked the door.

"Okay, Mickey, you can look at anything, but you can't touch," she said.

Mickey walked around the room, stopped, and looked at the corner of the glass-topped coffee table with dots of dried blood. He looked up at Veronica quizzically.

"Yes, it's her blood, and a broken drinking glass was lying on the floor next to her. We think she may have been drunk, stumbled, and fell. She hit her head on the corner of the table, which caused her death."

Mickey shook his head. "I told you, Valerie didn't drink."

"Maybe she didn't drink when she lived with you, but people change," said Veronica.

"We weren't living together just because we were engaged."

"It's just a thought right now. We'll know more when we get the autopsy report," Veronica said. "You two didn't live together?"

"Nope."

"But sometimes you would spend the night together, didn't you?" she asked.

"Nope. Never."

"If you say so," she said unconvincingly.

"I say so. Can we go into her bedroom?" he asked as he walked toward the back of the apartment.

Mickey walked to the dresser, opened the top drawer, and took out a journal.

"Hey, Mickey, I said you couldn't touch anything!"

"I gave it to her just before she left Bridgeton."

"If you didn't stay with her, how did you know where she kept it?"

"Because she told me that she kept it in her top dresser drawer. For some reason, she thought it would be safer there. Most people put private things in their bedside table, so she put it in a different place."

"I guess that sounds reasonable. But you still can't take it."

"I know, but you can, and we can look at it together," said Mickey with a smile.

"I can take it to my office, and I'll look at it there," she said.

Mickey thought for a moment, then said, "Why don't we take it to your office and look at it together. Sometimes she used a code to write."

"A code? What kind of code? And why would she do that?" she mused.

"Long story, Ronnie," said Mickey as he smiled, knowing the entire story. He remembered the time they had to crack an email code.

"Have you seen enough now?"

"Yep, let's get back to the station and figure out this code."

"You can do that? Figure codes and stuff?" asked the detective.

"This code I can figure out in minutes," Mickey said as he handed the book to her.

They took a detour by the culinary school that Val attended. It was time for lunch, and Mickey suggested they stop and get a sandwich. Detective Morgan stopped at a coffee and sandwich shop, and while they waited for their food to arrive, Mickey took the detective's tablet and began decoding Valerie's journal.

He had a section decoded in a matter of minutes, showing Ronnie the decoded messages. It said:

> *At school today, I saw something strange. I went to the back area to look for some flour for one of the classes. I was supposed to go to the supply closet, but I turned wrong in the hallway and went into the loading dock area. I saw some men dumping what looked like sugar out of cloth bags and replacing it with another white powder. When I asked them why they were doing that, they told me to get out and never return. It was strange that they wore rubber gloves and what looked like gas masks. I didn't get near them, so I don't know who they were.*

Some journal areas were written cursive, others were printed, and some had coded messages. Mickey knew that Valerie would write depending on her mood, but never in code unless she was concerned that someone might read her journal.

"Why would she use a code, and where did she learn to do something like that?" Veronica asked Mickey.

"It's a long story, and right now, it isn't important, but I can tell you this, at one time, we worked a case where the men we were looking for used a code. It was difficult but just simple enough that my brother-in-law figured it out. He's very keen on things like that. This code's so simple, but many people couldn't do it. It's a simple two-step over solution," said Mickey.

"What's a two-step over solution?"

"It's a simple matter of moving over two letters in the alphabet. Think of it like this. Take the letter A, for example, and substitute C. The letter B becomes D, and so it continues."

"What happens when you get to the end? What are Y and Z?"

"Then you start over. Y becomes A, and Z becomes B. It's simple. There are no capitals and no spaces or punctuation. Valerie told me she puts private things in a slide-over code. Trying a couple of different slide numbers was simple to get the entire code. Anyway. We got the message. Now, all we need to do is find a way to get inside that culinary school and discover what's happening."

"We can't do anything. And I can't do that without a warrant, Mickey," she said. "I can't get a warrant on your girlfriend's third-grade diary code."

"It's a journal, not a diary. There's a difference," he said.

"Not to a judge or me," she said.

"Okay, it's time to call in help."

"What do you mean, help?" she asked suspiciously.

"As my brother-in-law would say, don't ask."

"We better get back to the station and put this in evidence," she said as she took the last few bites of her sandwich.

Mickey reached over, took the journal, and began turning the pages and snapping pictures of each page. When he finished, he handed it back to Veronica.

Veronica pointed out some landmarks and gave him information on the city on the way back to the station.

"Florence has a population of over fifteen thousand and sometimes grows to almost twenty thousand people and has miles of beaches, many little antique shops, and the most delicious seafood on the country's west coast," she said as she drove.

"You sound like a tour guide, Ronnie," as Mickey looked at the various places she pointed out to him.

"I was, for a while, when I was in high school. I wanted to be a marine biologist."

"And why didn't you become one?" he asked.

"I was in my second year of college when my mother was diagnosed with early-onset Alzheimer's. Daddy was taking care of mother and still working part-time on the police force but was killed in a drive-by shooting. I had to leave school to take care of my mother. She died about a year later, and by that time, it had taken all my college funds to pay for all the treatments and doctor bill co-pays, so I couldn't afford to go back to school. So, here I am, on the Florence police force."

"I'm sorry to hear that. It must have been hard to give up your dreams and move back here."

"No, not really. Sure, I wanted to finish my degree, but Mother and Daddy were some of the greatest parents a girl could have, and it was my pleasure to take care of Mother. I wish now that I had been home for the last days of Daddy's life. He was gone quickly. I miss them both."

"I understand. What kind of case was your father working on when he was killed?"

"I don't know. He worked on many cold cases. He had just started an in-depth investigation on a case when he was shot. The Department investigated it but found no clues, so it's now officially a cold case," she said. "But it was CIOF, the same school that Miss Green, I mean Valerie was attending."

Mickey hesitated momentarily and said, "I lost my mom a few years ago in a car accident. It was also sudden and unexpected. Pop was injured in the same accident, but he recovered and did well." Mickey didn't explain further.

They rode the rest of the way back to the station in silence except when Veronica pointed out another possible area of interest. When they pulled into her parking space, she told Mickey she would call the coroner and determine when the autopsy would be done.

"We don't have many cases involving possible foul play. Most autopsies are done at the hospital because the police department doesn't have a lab. They're done by a doctor on staff there. I did ask him to put her on top of the list since it was suspicious, but it still may take him a couple of days to get it done and get us the report."

"Thank you. I appreciate it. The sooner you close this case, the sooner I can take her home and have a proper funeral."

"Not a problem."

"Hey. Ummm, I'm a stranger in town, and all I know about it is what you pointed out to me on the way. When you get off work, are you free to show me around a bit more?"

Mickey looked straight into her black eyes that, at that moment, sparkled as she blushed. He had embarrassed her by asking her out. He smiled at her knowing what he had done.

He tried to help her out by saying, "I'm sorry. Maybe you're busy or have a boyfriend."

She looked at the pavement to hide her blushing face. "Oh, no. I'm not busy, and I don't have a boyfriend. You just kind of caught me off guard, that's all. I thought that maybe you might feel awkward since you're here to pick up your girlfriend."

Mickey said, "No. She broke off our engagement when she left. Yes, I still had feelings for her, but as a friend. I would still ask you out if she were standing here beside us."

"Okay then. I know a great little seafood place downtown that caters to the home folks here. It's small, but the portions are large and delicious. Since you're here from out of town, it's my treat," she said, smiling.

"Sounds good. How and where should we meet?" he asked.

"I can pick you up at your hotel, and we can go from there. That's easier since I know the town and you don't. I get off at five unless a call comes in, and I'm assigned to investigate."

Mickey gave her the hotel's name and his phone number, got in his rental car, and drove away.

When he got to his room, he phoned James.

"Hello, James?"

"Hey, Mickey. What's up?" came the answer.

"I'm here in Florence. It's a nice little city, and I've met with the police. They're doing an autopsy and suspect foul play but won't know until that's complete. So, I'll be here for a few days. Can you have Dee run a background check on the school Val was attending?" asked Mickey.

"Sure. What's the name?" James asked. "Dee should be able to do that first thing in the morning. I'll be there in a few hours. I'll catch the red-eye as soon as I can get one out of here tonight."

"You don't need to do that. I've got enough to keep me busy here. I'm having dinner with the lead detective in the case this evening."

"Dinner? I didn't know that detectives got that friendly with out-of-towners on a case," James said.

"The detective's a woman. It's just dinner."

"Uh, huh. What does she look like, Mickey?"

"Oh, she's attractive," Mickey said.

"Just attractive? Mickey, you've been there just a few hours, and you've already met a woman and arranged for a date with her. She must be more than just attractive," James chided.

"Alright, enough of that. You don't need to come here. I'll call if I need help," Mickey said into the phone.

"You've said enough in those words, 'possible foul play'. I'll be there as soon as I can get a flight out. No arguments. No more discussions. We'll be back home with her body soon enough if it's nothing. Until then, I'm sticking by you as a good brother-in-law should. I'll ask Darcy Jean to make the arrangements. Later, Bro!" James disconnected before Mickey could object further.

Mickey took a long hot shower. He let the water roll down his back and invigorate the tense muscles in his back. It was early afternoon, and he was exhausted. His former fiancée was dead, possibly murdered, he's here to pick up her body, and he's going out on a date. Nothing was wrong with what he was doing, but it felt strange, like cheating on Valerie. He wasn't, but it felt like it. He needed to get over that feeling. She broke up with him long ago, and she's dead now. He had every right to move on.

"How messed up is that?" he thought. He stood under the flowing water, thinking of his past with Valerie. After all, they had known each other for years. Those feeling don't just go away. He got out of the shower, lay across the bed, and dropped into a restless sleep.

His phone buzzed. He woke up and reached to grab his phone. "Hello, Mickey. I'm in the front of the hotel, and I'm hungry. Let's take a ride before we get something to eat," Veronica said when he answered.

"Sure, give me five minutes," he said, still waking up. After disconnecting, he sat on the side of the bed for a few moments to collect his thoughts. He got dressed quickly, went downstairs, and headed for the front doors of the lobby area. Parked outside the doors in a fiery red corvette was Detective Veronica Morgan.

Upon seeing her, his mouth dropped open. He stood there, paused and enjoyed the vision, and finally moved to the car and got inside. He saw a completely different woman. This woman's long auburn hair was flowing down her shoulders over a skin-tight bright flower print shirt that was low cut in the front. She wore shorts that accented perfectly shaped long legs and wore a huge smile with gleaming teeth and oversized dark sunglasses. Around her neck was a gold necklace with a small cross hanging at the end.

"Hi, Mickey. I didn't think you were going to answer your phone. I was about to hang up and go back home," she said as she put the gear shift into drive and pulled out of the hotel lot.

"Wow, you don't look like a cop," Mickey said, returning her smile.

"I'm not. The second I clock out, I'm just a private citizen, like you," she said as she pulled out for a drive along the coast highway.

"How does a cop afford a car like this?"

"I told you that my parents died. Momma and Daddy left a little life insurance and a house with no mortgage. They had a few investments that bring a small amount of money each month. I have no house payments, and the investment account pays the taxes, insurance, and monthly utility bills, so my paycheck from my job is pretty much mine to spend on extravagances like this car."

"We should all be so lucky when our parents die. Most people I know have parents that don't leave them anything but debts, and what little they do leave, it takes to bury them," he said.

"You're also one of the lucky ones. I did some checking on you this afternoon," she said without taking her eyes off the road.

"You did a background check on me?" he asked, somewhat concerned.

"Sure. I didn't know anything about you. You fly in town and want to pick up a body and pay for a funeral out of your own pocket. Then you're so forward as to ask me out when your fiancée's body isn't even cold. I may be a woman, but I'm not stupid or gullible. So, yes, I checked you out. And if you didn't check out completely, I would have called and canceled this evening."

Mickey then laughed. "I guess you're right on all points. I called my brother-in-law and told him that you were pretty sharp. Most men detectives would have called Valerie's death a home accident and moved forward. I understand that the autopsy is protocol, but you gave Valerie the benefit of the doubt. I appreciate that. So, what did you find out about me?"

"I found out that your parents were involved in a car accident that was an attempted murder and that your mother was killed. You were working for your father, who had built a small real estate rental business and was a building contractor. You also have a sister with two children, and she married an ex-military town hero. Just as you told me, you and your brother-in-law helped the police solve a murder case concerning a dead body that was uncovered on one of your building projects. You are now the CEO of the very profitable family business. And you're single."

"You were very thorough. I'm impressed. You'll get to meet my brother-in-law James because he's on his way here as we speak."

"Is he coming here as moral support, or does he think he'll help with the investigation?" she asked.

"Whatever's needed."

"While you're here, I'll work this case. You may tag along, but you'll not interfere. Do you hear me? I don't need your help," she said emphatically.

Mickey looked at her profile as they rode down the road with the ocean on his side. Her skin was silky smooth, with just a whisp of makeup, just enough to disguise a few freckles sprinkled across her cute little nose. She had pierced ears with little stud earrings the shape of a tiny cross to match her necklace.

She began pointing out things to him that she liked. The ocean was crashing against the shore in some places, and there were beaches with people lying in the sand under umbrellas in others. Her hair was waving behind her as the wind flowed over the windshield of the convertible. He thought she had the life. The sand, the sea, and beautiful weather. She was a beautiful woman. She reached over and turned the radio on.

Out of the speakers blared some golden oldies. Old songs of the 1960s. Just his style.

"You like oldies?" he asked.

"Yes, that's what Mother and Daddy played all the time, so I got used to it. You don't like it?"

"I do. My Pop used to play it all the time. We have a huge garage, and Pop would go to his 'man cave' and play that music and work on restoring old cars."

"So did my Daddy. He didn't restore them. He would buy them already restored, but he did maintain them. He said life was too short to spend restoring a car. He liked to tinker, but he loved to drive them. I have a couple in the garage behind my house. If we have time and you are here long enough, we can go by, and I'll show them to you."

"I would love that," Mickey said and turned back to the road. He liked this woman. After taking a ride down the coast, she turned around, and they went back to town for dinner.

He insisted that she order for him at the restaurant since she was familiar with the menu. She ordered him a large seafood sampler platter and a small one for herself. As they ate, they talked. There was so much that Mickey couldn't tell her. He couldn't tell her about Valerie's abduction or when he and James had rescued a little girl's parents because it had to be done without the help or knowledge of the authorities. He found it difficult to speak of his past without telling these dark stories.

"What's it like running a large construction business?" she asked, taking a bite of fish.

"It's not all that hard."

"Tell me about it," she said.

"It's nothing, really. Mom and Pop started buying single-family homes. Then Pop traded up to a couple of apartment complexes. I'm sure you know that we took in some investors and built an entire complex in Bridgeton. I run that, but it isn't that hard. The trick is to hire competent people to do different aspects of the business. One person's in charge of renting apartments. Another department handles maintenance, and another is accounting, and so on. I just kind of supervise and make sure it all gets done."

"And that leaves you free to jet around the country."

"You make it sound glamorous, but it's not," he said. "It does give me a bit of freedom."

"I'm sorry that you felt you had to come here to bury an old girlfriend," she added.

"Thanks, but I felt I owed it to Valerie. It's difficult on some levels, but I don't know. Life goes on," he said thoughtfully.

Strolling down the street after dinner, Mickey and Ronnie window-shopped and, after some debate, decided on items for Mickey's niece and nephew. After stopping for coffee and sharing a dessert, they walked until sunset, comfortable in each other's company.

Veronica's cell phone rang, she picked up the phone and pressed the icon.

"Hello, Detective Morgan," she said into the phone. "Oh, hello, Tom. Aren't you calling a little bit later than your normal hours? Sure, I understand. Tonight's fine. I'll be over first thing in the morning to pick it up. Is there anything particular that I need to see in person? Thanks, Tom, for doing a rush job for me."

After putting the phone in her purse, she said to Mickey. "That was Tom Weinberg in the morgue at the hospital. He said he's just starting on the autopsy, and I can pick up the report tomorrow morning. He's doing it now as a favor to me."

Mickey said, "I've had a good time this evening, but I still have some jet lag, so I think you should take me home. Also, James should be here in a couple of hours. I want to meet him at the airport."

"I've enjoyed this evening, but I've got an early day tomorrow. On my way to the station tomorrow, I'll detour by the hospital and pick up the report. If you can meet me then, we can go over it together. Is that good with you, Mickey?"

"That would be great!" he said.

Veronica took Mickey back to his hotel and drove off with him standing in front of the hotel, watching her drive away. He saw her lift her hand in a goodbye wave and returned the wave with a smile.

He got to his room, turned on the TV set, laid back on the bed, and promptly fell asleep.

CHAPTER 3

James Arrives

Mickey woke up to someone knocking on his door. He opened the door, and James walked in.

"My gosh, you look like you slept in those clothes," James said, looking up and down at Mickey's disheveled appearance.

"Actually, I did," said Mickey, yawning. "Ronnie dropped me off last night, and I fell across the bed thinking you would call when you landed at the airport. I didn't intentionally spend the night fully dressed on the bed. When did you get in?"

"I got in around two-thirty and took a cab here. I didn't want to disturb you. And by the look of it, I didn't," James laughed.

James Bower, Mickey's best friend, and brother-in-law was disfigured while on a military mission several years ago.

Because of multiple burns and scars on his face and most of his body, he was discharged on full disability. When people got to know him, his facial scars became unimportant. In the face of an enemy, James was a frightening monster that would strike fear in them immediately. He was devoted to Mickey's sister Darcy, Dee, as they called her, and her kids from a previous marriage.

"Give me a few minutes to wash my face and change my clothes. What time is it?" Mickey asked.

Looking at his watch, James said, "Six-thirty. I'll wait for you downstairs."

Micky yawned, and James walked out. Ten minutes later, he went downstairs, got a cup of the hotel coffee, and sat at a table across from James in the breakfast dining area, and started reading the local paper.

"Now, tell me what's going on," James ordered.

Mickey filled him in on what he knew so far, which wasn't much. He had to see the autopsy report.

"Okay, there isn't much to do until we talk to the detective. Tell me about your date with her."

"Well, her name is Veronica Morgan. But she goes by Ronnie. She's very attractive," he said and continued to tell him about the evening.

"Sounds like a very pleasant evening. I guess we should meet your new detective friend and look at the autopsy report," said James. "And on the way, let's go by the place where Val was going to school. Kind of scope it out," said James.

Mickey drove slowly by the culinary school so they could get a good look. It was brick and painted white with a large metal sign attached to the front that gave the name of the school. They noted that the signage also advertised that it was also a bakery that packed prepared items and packaged bakery product kits. It was unassuming, with a chain-link fence eight feet high, a loading dock, and several delivery trucks parked around the loading dock area.

"Hey, Mickey, I've got an idea. We know that there's an opening in the school now. Maybe if we find someone to take Valerie's place, she could go undercover," suggested James.

"We could do that. Who do you suggest?" asked Mickey.

"We could call Marie Sanchez or Alyssa. Either one could do it for us," answered James.

Marie had gone undercover for them in a previous case. Alyssa owned a company that hired out mercenaries. Alyssa had helped Mickey and James rescue a little girl's father.

Mickey thought for a moment, then said, "Alyssa may be good, but we don't need a group of mercenaries for a job like this. Marie might be better for undercover work, but what if she got caught? Could she take care of herself?" Mickey wondered.

James assured him they were both up to the job and could take care of themselves in any situation. Marie was a free spirit and didn't want to be tied down with a regular job to run a company like Alyssa. He also told Mickey that Alyssa would only bring what and who she thought they might need and agreed with Mickey that they didn't need a group of men. He and Mickey could be her backup.

"Why don't we wait until we find out the autopsy results," suggested Mickey. "We need to get to the police station and talk with Ronnie."

When they got to the station, Veronica had left a message with the front desk to give them visitor passes and have someone escort them back to her desk. When they got there, Detective Morgan was working on paperwork concerning another case she was trying to pass off to another detective in the office.

She looked up, and Mickey and James saw the look on her face as she saw James. Her mouth dropped open for only a moment, and she regained composure. His disfigured face sometimes had that effect on people.

Detective Morgan rose from her chair and put out her hand to shake James' hand.

"Hello, I assume you're James. I've heard wonderful things about you," she said, clearly embarrassed by her reaction to his appearance.

James smiled. He shook her hand. "Apparently, he didn't tell you about this," he said, waving his hand around his face.

"No, he didn't tell me about it."

"Don't worry about it. I'm used to it now. A lot of people do the same thing. You should see little kids run away like I'm a monster."

Mickey butted in and said, "James, that's because they don't know you. Now that you've gotten acquainted with the detective, let's look at that autopsy report."

"I have the report right here. I've read over it, and I've found some interesting things you might want to see," Ronnie said, handing the report to Mickey.

She pointed out several things to them. "Look at this," she said, pointing to the paper in Mickey's hand. "It says that she had cocaine in her system, but there was bruising around her nostrils. Tom said that indicated that somebody forcefully put it in her nose. You don't get those kinds of scratches if the addict does it himself. Next, there was alcohol in her stomach but not much in her blood system. And she had bruises and lacerations inside her mouth, also indicating that something was forced down her throat. Last thing. The wound on the side of her head didn't match the pattern that would have been made if she had fallen against the table. She was hit with something, but not on the coffee table. She was murdered, and they tried to make it look like she had sniffed the coke, got drunk, high, and fell against the coffee table. In another day or so, we'll release her body to you, and you can take her home to bury her."

"We aren't leaving until this case is solved, Detective," said James.

Mickey was shocked. Why someone would try to kill Valerie.

"James, I told Mickey that he could be around some of the investigations, but he cannot assist in any manner. I'm so sorry. I will do everything in my power to find her killer. But neither of you can interfere."

"We aren't officers and aren't bound by the same rules you are. We have resources that you don't have," said James.

"Rules?" she asked. "We have rules and procedures that help us solve cases like this. And what resources do you have that we don't?"

"Don't ask!" said Mickey and James at the same time.

Mickey pulled up a chair, sat in it, and stared at the opposite wall. He said nothing but his mind was racing. James and Ronnie silently stood by, leaving him to his private thoughts.

After several minutes of silence, he looked from Detective Morgan to James. "Ronnie, we'll be going now. We have a job to do. We have a killer to find and make him pay."

"Mickey, don't interfere. I like you, but I will lock you up if you get in my way or break any laws. I'll do it to protect you from yourself, the law, and whoever's out there that killed your girlfriend. To help me out here, will you tell me why she picked Florence to live?" she asked.

"She enrolled at the culinary school here. She wanted to be a chef. Maybe open a restaurant. I told her if she did, I'd help her by being a silent investor."

"Do you think it was something related to the school? By the way, it is the Culinary Institute of Oregon and Factory or CIOF. We pronounce it as kee-of."

"I don't know if it is related, but it gives you a place to start. Also, she worked part-time at a local restaurant as a server," Mickey told her.

"Do you know the name of the restaurant where she worked?"

Mickey thought for a second, "I think it was the Golden Bull."

"Yes. I know that one. It's the premier steak restaurant at the edge of town! I go there quite often. Maybe I knew her," she said as she wrote in her notes.

"James and I'll find Valerie's killer. Please, don't get in our way," Mickey said. He turned to James and said, "Let's go."

"Mickey, will I be seeing you again?" she asked. "I had a very nice time last night. I don't want you to get hurt."

"Of course. I was hoping that the three of us could have dinner tonight," Mickey answered.

"Keep me out of this. I've got a lot to do. The two of you go out and have a nice dinner without the third wheel. I'll wait in the car for you, Mickey. Nice to meet you, Ronnie," James said and walked toward the hallway to the front of the building.

Mickey turned to follow James. Veronica called out to him as he walked away. "Mickey, please be careful."

James was on his satellite phone when Mickey got back to the car. He had a tablet on his knee and was taking notes. He disconnected and made another call. After about ten minutes, James disconnected. James always took his satellite phone with him when he went out of town. He could get service when there were no cell towers.

"Let's get back to the hotel. I need some rest so I can go out tonight while you and Ronnie are having dinner."

Mickey pulled out of the station parking lot, "I'll call and cancel dinner tonight."

"Nope, I have to do a few things and make arrangements you can't help me with. Go. Have a good time. When things get hot, you'll need to be at the top of your game."

"Are you sure, James?"

"Yep, I'm sure. You haven't dated or had any female company since Francine Braydon. You deserve some company. One thing you can do is pick up four or five burner phones," James said.

"One other thing, I took pictures of the pages in Val's journal. I'll email them to you. They're on a two-step slide code, and you'll have it translated in a few minutes. I'll drop you off at the hotel," said Mickey.

After dropping James off, he drove around the city limits to familiarize himself. He went by the culinary school and took several roads leading out from there to get bearings if he needed to make a quick exit. He drove for hours, crisscrossing roadways in all directions. He timed his routes so he would know where he was in relation to the hotel and the school. He looked for dead-end streets and small hidden road entrances to hide if necessary if anyone followed them. Finally, when he felt comfortable, he returned to the hotel to shower, shave and get ready for his date with Ronnie after having a strategy meeting with James.

He and James met at a corner table in the breakfast area. James had a small notebook type of computer and some google map printouts. He sat looking at the prints and had a list of things and supplies they would need.

Mickey sat across the little table and looked at James' list.

"Why do we need all this stuff?" he asked James.

James took a deep breath, "Let me start at the beginning. I looked at the pictures of the pages in Val's journal. I translated it. As you said, it took only minutes. Here are the translations of all her coded notes."

He slid several handwritten notes for Mickey to see.

The first coded note was the one that Mickey had decoded and shown to Ronnie. The rest were shorter and didn't make much sense to either Mickey or James. They only made sense to Valerie, and she couldn't help.

> One. *I saw the two men loading more stuff. I don't know what it is. But they were sealing the containers with a coating of wax before putting on a lid. They cook in another part of the building but don't use this kind of ingredients.*

> Two. *The men had some guns this time. I know a gun when I see one. There were two cases, and they covered them with what looked like flour. I don't know why.*

> Three. *The men mixed the sealed cans in with other stuff and were meticulous when they packed it so it wouldn't be noticed.*

That was the end of the coded messages, and they spanned a time period of two weeks.

Mickey looked at James in confusion. "I'd say that it's possibly drugs. That would be easy to pack in with the other shipments of food mixes. But why the guns? What do you suggest we do to find out?"

James smiled at Mickey, and Mickey knew that he wouldn't get a straight answer to whatever James had planned. As James had said so many times, when Mickey asked about what James had done, he had gotten a standard reply, "Don't ask."

"I know by now not to ask how, but I will ask 'What!'"

"Good conclusion," said James. "Usually, I'd say you and I could handle it, but if they are running drugs and guns, it might be too big for us. We need help."

"What kind of help?" asked Mickey.

"Professional help. We don't know how organized they are, but we don't want to assume anything. We did that in the past, and look what happened."

"I remember you almost got killed. What do you want to do?" Mickey asked.

"This culinary school that Valerie was enrolled in is involved in some pretty nasty stuff. They could be a bunch of local street thugs or serious arms dealers. We need to be super careful. They have a contract to hire ex-cons. First, I put in a call to Marie Sanchez. We can see if we can put her in place undercover in the cooking school. I'll have her call and inquire about admission requirements.

"Next, I'll give Alyssa a call. We'll want to get some type of surveillance on the premises. She can do that and give 24/7 monitoring. If we need to go in, she can be oversight."

"That sounds great, but they're all the way across the country. Can they or will they come? We don't need an entire team of men to help us," said Mickey.

"Yes, they'll come because they go all over the world. Also, at one time, I was part of the team. I'm not calling for the entire team, just Marie and Alyssa. Don't forget the burner phones while you're out. Now go, my brother, and have a good time."

Mickey left and again took a quick tour of the town to make sure he remembered where he was and time-lapse from one point to another. After his mental test of the city, he headed for the police station as Veronica was walking out. She saw him and walked up to the car.

"Hey there, Mickey. I didn't expect you to be so punctual. We're not in any hurry, so why don't we detour back to the hotel and drop off your car, then stop by my place so I can clean up and change clothes," she said with a wink.

"We can do that," Mickey said. "You go your way, and I'll go mine, and we'll see who gets to the hotel first. No cheating like speeding or using your police privilege."

"You're on, buddy boy," she laughed and headed for the unmarked police cruiser issued to her by the department. When she pulled out of the lot, Mickey turned the opposite way she went. Ronnie pulled beside him as he got within a few blocks of the hotel. She gave a quick wave and passed him with a smile.

When he pulled into the hotel lot, he got into her car as she pulled beside it.

"Well, that was fun. I've got a feeling that you had some reason behind asking me to race you here. Especially when your only rule was to observe all the laws," Veronica said.

"No reason. Just curious," he answered.

"Uh-huh," she said as she pulled out of the lot. "What are you and James planning?"

"Nothing," he said as he looked out the window on the passenger's side of the car.

"Whatever it is, it's illegal, isn't it?" she probed a bit more.

"Have you checked out the CIOF?" Mickey asked her avoiding her question.

"Not exactly. Should I?" she answered.

"Yes. You should check them out," he said casually. "What have you done on the case so far?"

"I can't say too much, but I did go by and talk to the school owner," she said.

"And?"

"His name's Grant Littleton. He said she didn't show up for classes for the last few days. Other than that, he doesn't know anything about her personally."

"What about where she worked?"

"We can go there tonight for dinner. Two birds with one stone, as they say."

"That's a good girl," he said, laughing.

"I also ran some checks on James T. Bower," she added.

"How did you get his last name?"

"It was on the form you filled out to get your visitor's badge at the station."

"I forgot about that. And?" Mickey said, now interested in what she found.

"He has no background. It's almost like he's not a real person. You and he did go to school together, and as you said, he's married to your sister. That's all there is about him. No police records, no work records, and nothing shows up on his military background. As I said, he's a non-person. He exists, but he doesn't."

"That's James."

"Would you care to elaborate?" she quizzed.

"Nope."

"Are we going to get along, Mickey?" she said with a smile.

"That depends on you, Ronnie. I've enjoyed our time together so far, and I plan to continue having a wonderful time with you, but my past is just that. In the past, and so is my brother-in-law. Let's enjoy each day as the sun rises. You're pretty. I assume that you already know that."

"Wow, you know how to put a lady in her place and brighten her day all in one sentence, Mickey Christianson."

"Why, thank you. That was my intention," he said with a smile.

"We're going to get along fine, Mickey," she said, slowing down to pull into her driveway.

As they pulled up to the two-story, Cape Cod-style home, she parked in front of the double-wide garage to the right of the front door. She pressed a button, and the door opened. Inside, he saw several pieces of gym equipment on one side and her corvette parked on the other.

They got out and entered the kitchen from inside the garage. She threw her briefcase and purse onto a chair near the door.

"Make yourself at home. There is the living room," she said, pointing. "Help yourself to a drink from the fridge or the bar in the living room if you want something a bit stronger. I'm going to shower and change."

Mickey went over to the fridge and took out a bottled soft drink. When he entered the living room, he looked around. It had a distinct masculine feel to it. He noticed several pictures of a man and a woman, who he assumed were her parents. Most of the wood trim was stained dark, and the fireplace was simple and functional, with more family pictures on the mantle. The furniture was fashionable, but he could tell it was decades old. She hadn't redecorated the house when her parents passed away. It was a way to keep the memories of a wonderful childhood alive. He liked it. It felt comfortable and inviting.

"What do you think?" he heard her say as she padded into the room.

"I like it. It's very comfortable. I bet it hasn't changed since your parents moved into this house," he said, not turning around.

"That's true, but that's not what I was talking about. What do you think of how I look?"

He turned around, and he loved what he saw. "Well, I can say that you make that t-shirt look great. Who poured you into those skin-tight jeans?" he gasped.

"This is my driving around town in one of daddy's cars outfit. Are you a Chevy or a Ford fan?" she asked with a giggle.

"Right now, I'm a fan of whatever car that's on the front of your shirt, little lady," he smiled back.

She was hitting all his buttons. She worked out. She liked cars, and the icing on the cake, she was pretty and fun to be around.

"Let me show you daddy's cars. They're in the garage at the back of the house. We'll go out the back door."

The garage had a massive sliding door like the one at Pop's house. She slid it aside, revealing three immaculate cars. She stood at the opening, waiting for his response, and after a few moments, she continued inside.

Once they were both inside, she continued over to the first black, plain-looking car from the 1930s. "This car is a genuine bootlegger's car. Did you know there's a difference between a moonshiner and a bootlegger?"

"Okay, you must know that I'm from Moonshine country. And yes, I know the difference. A moonshiner makes the whiskey, and a bootlegger smuggles it. There are variations, but that's the gist of it."

"Most of the moonshine came from North Carolina," she said, propping her hand on her hip, cocking her head, and looking him straight in the eye.

"Yes, true, but Virginia had its share of them, too," he countered.

"I guess so. Daddy got this one from an auction when he and my mother took a vacation in the North Carolina mountains. This car doesn't look like much, but it could outrun any police car in the county at that time. It's got the original flathead V8 motor. It's stripped out inside to make room for the liquor. Let's move to the next car," she said, walking away toward the next one.

"This little baby is a 1965 Mustang. It has a 289 V8 engine with a four-barrel carburetor. It puts out 225 horsepower with 10.1 compression and the optional four-speed manual transmission. Daddy got it when I was a little girl and paid two thousand dollars for it.

He did some essential work and kept it in its original condition. It's worth a lot more than that today."

She left the Mustang and walked over to the car that had Mickey salivating. She spread her hands out. "And this is the queen of the collection, a 1963 Jaguar XKE. The sexist car ever produced. This is my favorite one in the collection. Let's take it out."

She threw him the keys and said, "Here. You drive," she smiled and winked at him.

Mickey stood looking at the car as he caught the keys. The Jaguar was beautiful, with a silver-blue metallic color and white interior. He was almost afraid to touch it.

"Mickey? Earth to Mickey!" she said and laughed at his open mouth.

"Wow. I've seen them in magazines but never been up close to one. Are you kidding? I couldn't drive this. What if I scratched it or if we got into an accident?"

"It all depends. If you're at fault, I'll kill you. If the other person is at fault, I'll kill them," and she laughed.

"You know you could sell any one of these cars and pay a huge chunk of your tuition to get your college degree," he said as he regained his composure.

"I know, but that part of my life's in the past. I like what I have now. I don't want it to change. Let's go for a ride," she said as she opened the passenger door to get in the Jaguar.

Mickey got in the driver's side and fired it up. He sat and listened to the engine purr like the proverbial kitten. He also liked it and was going to enjoy this afternoon! He pulled out onto the road, as Ronnie pointed the direction to take. When he revved the engine, he felt the power and the slight vibration of all cylinders. To get the feel of the car, he drove slowly at the posted speed. Being overly cautious as he drove, his heart raced with excitement and pleasure as he floated down the road. Ronnie silently pointed at various intersections until there was nothing on either side of the road but empty, bare land.

She tapped him on the arm, put her thumb up, and said, "Fly this machine, Mickey Ray!" He noticed it was the first time she had addressed him, including his middle name.

"How fast do you want me to take it?" he asked without taking his eyes off the road.

"All the way up…make her fly!" she said.

He gently pushed down on the gas pedal and watched the speed increase. She touched his arm again, "I said, make it FLY!"

Mickey pushed the pedal all the way to the floor and felt the gentle increase in speed. Higher and higher, the speedometer climbed. So far, the road was straight and level. He pushed it. 100…130…135…140. The needle began to slow down the increase as it reached 148 and topped out at 153. His heart was racing. Sweat flowed down his face from the adrenalin rush. He didn't dare remove his hand to wipe the liquid flowing down his face. He began easing off the pedal. He watched the needle back off to a slower speed. The shot of adrenalin was wearing off now as the car slowed down. As they slowed down below 100 MPH, he glanced over at Veronica. She was also dripping in sweat. She loved this. Her head was back against the headrest, and she was almost hyperventilating. Her breathing slowed as the car decelerated.

She opened her eyes and looked over at him when he got back down to the speed limit. "That was the most exhilarating thing I've ever done, Mickey. Thank you. It was wonderful." She was almost breathing normally now.

"You've never taken it up like that before?" he asked.

"No, I've never had the nerve to do that. It was fabulous. I think it was almost as good as…let's just say it was good, Mickey."

Mickey pulled in and shut the engine off when they got to a pull-off area. He was exhausted. He had never been that fast in a car, either. And while he agreed, it was exhilarating, he wasn't sure he liked it.

"I would never expect that from a cop," he said.

"I'm a cop, but I'm a person too, Mickey. I know this road, and no one ever comes down here. You can drive for miles and never see another car. So, no cops, and very little chance of another person. It was as safe as it can get to drive like this," she said, taking a tissue out of her purse and wiping her forehead. She took out another and wiped Mickey's forehead, also. "That was the rush of my life!"

Mickey leaned over, and she met him in a passionate kiss, or as passionate as possible, sitting in a sports car on the side of the road. When they broke apart, she sat for a few moments, looked at Mickey, and said, "I'm starving. Let's get something to eat."

He started the car, turned around, and headed back the way they came doing the exact posted speed limit. He parked the car where she directed him at The Golden Bull Restaurant.

As they walked inside, she took Mickey's hand in hers. "Mickey, I'm really sorry about your girlfriend, but we wouldn't have met if she hadn't left Bridgeton. Do you have any idea how long you'll be here?"

He squeezed her hand and looked down at her. "I don't know. A few days, maybe a week. It's hard to say. I do have responsibilities back at home." He opened the door and ushered her inside.

As the hostess stood behind a small booth, she greeted Ronnie as if she knew her.

"Good evening, Miss Morgan. How are you this evening? Just two of you?"

"Yes, Susan. A table in the back, if we may ask."

"Of course," she said as she took two menus and started toward the back of the restaurant.

"Is Valerie Green working tonight, Susan?" she asked, knowing the answer.

"No, ma'am. Valerie hasn't shown up for several days. Lisa will be your server tonight. She is excellent also," she said, placing the menus on the table. "Enjoy your dinner, Miss Morgan."

Soon a young lady showed up and introduced herself as Lisa. "How may I be of service to you tonight?" she asked.

They ordered and began a quick inquiry into Valerie Green.

"Yes, ma'am. We don't know what happened. She just didn't show up. No call or notice to quit. No one knows what happened to her," Lisa offered.

"Was she friends with anyone here? Anyone like another server or any employee?" asked Ronnie.

"No, ma'am. She was going to school at the CIOF, so she didn't have much time for socializing. She was nice but not social, if you know what I mean."

"Yes, we understand. Lisa. Did she ever mention anything about her school or classes?"

"No, not really. She really liked it. She said it was fun, but some things were going on there that didn't seem right. I don't know. Is she alright?" asked Lisa.

"It's nothing. I was just wondering where she is. That's all," Ronnie said, smiling.

"She was one of our best servers. She always got the biggest tips. Every one of our customers liked her. The only thing was she would get upset over the tiniest things."

"Like what," Mickey cut in.

"If someone asked her something personal. She would get upset about it like they were spying on her or something," Lisa said.

"Spying? What do you mean?" Mickey asked, hoping she would clarify her statement.

"I don't know what I mean. It's hard to explain. She didn't like people asking her anything personal. It's like she got scared if someone asked her about what she did out of work."

"I see," said Mickey.

"We never asked her what she did over the weekend or anything like that. All we felt we could say was, how was your weekend and left it at that. She was kind of strange like that. But she was always nice. Sorry, but I have to get your order in and serve some other tables."

"Sure. Thanks for your help, Lisa. If you think of anything else, give me a call," Ronnie said, handing her police business card.

They ate dinner and talked about life in a small city. Even though Bridgeton was small, it was still like a larger city. It was close to Hampton Roads, which is a conglomeration of several cities, and the town of Williamsburg, which drew so many tourists year-round. Then on the other side was Richmond, the capital of the state.

Florence, Oregon, was small compared to most cities, and the crime reflected it. There were many uniformed police, but only two detectives. For the most part, it was a great town to live in, and she liked it here. After having dinner, complete with a couple of glasses of Merlot, they left and walked down the street hand in hand.

They stopped at some of the shops to look at souvenirs and popped into a little coffee shop for dessert. Henry Oswald, the owner, insisted on Veronica trying his newest bakery delight. It was a new recipe for a cinnamon roll with special strawberry icing. Henry named them "Ronnie Rolls" in honor of her.

As they sat, drank coffee, and talked, Henry came over to their table and asked her how she liked the rolls.

"It's great, Henry. I would never have thought of strawberry and cinnamon together."

"I know. It's so sweet, and the red strawberry gives it that pretty but sweet flavor, just like you!" he added delightfully.

"Who's your friend here, Ronnie?" he asked.

"This is Mickey Christianson. He's visiting here from Virginia. He won't be here but a few days."

"Nice to meet you, Mickey. You know my son has had an eye on Ms. Veronica for quite some time."

"Is that so?" Mickey said, sneaking a glance at Ronnie, who was rolling her eyes at him.

"Yes, he's working in the back tonight. Someday when I retire, I'll turn over the business to him, and he'll make some woman a great husband."

"If that happens, Henry, maybe she'll send me an invitation to the wedding."

"Will do, Mr. Mickey. You take care now, enjoy your stay here and have a safe trip home," he said and walked back to the counter.

"Sounds like you have an admirer," Mickey said.

"His son's a nice guy, but not for me. He's not all that bright and about seventy-five pounds overweight. As the expression says, only in his dreams, Mickey."

"I noticed that your house seems to be stuck in time."

"I admit, it is. When I came home to take care of my mother, I couldn't change it because it was one thing that she was familiar with. She was comfortable there. And when she was gone, I couldn't bring myself to change anything. The same goes for cars. Daddy loved those cars, so I keep them. I have a friend who comes over every month to look over and help maintain them. He says that cars are made to be driven, not sitting in someone's museum or garage."

"He's right, but if you like the Jaguar and the Mustang, why did you buy the Corvette? Why didn't you just drive one of them?"

"I take it out sometimes. It's sexy to look at, but I like my Vette better. Newer, flashier. I can't explain it."

"As a car guy myself, I know the feeling can't be explained. It's like faith in God. You either believe, or you don't."

"Do you believe in God?" she asked.

"I most certainly do! I believe with all my heart. He's alive and well and hears every prayer and concern we have."

"If there is a God, why's the world in such shape?"

"That's the question of all time. I don't know. I can say that he doesn't force us to believe in him or obey him. It's our choice to follow or reject. Do you believe, Ronnie?"

"Yes, I do, but I don't go to church as often as I should, and I still have many questions about Him."

"I can't give you any advice but try to read the Bible. It might help, but I need to warn you, in spite of what some preachers say, all the answers aren't in the Bible. All the essential ones, like how to get to heaven, why people go to hell, is all there. You just need to look for it."

"Maybe I'll try that," she mused.

Mickey's phone rang. He took it out of his pocket and pushed the answer icon. "Hello, James. Okay, I can pick them up at the airport. When will they be in? A van? I guess so. I'll ask Veronica. She'll know where to get one. When will you be back? That late, huh. Okay. That's way past my bedtime. I'll see you in the morning. Later," he punched the end button.

"That was James. I need to go and pick up two people. And I need a van. Do you know where I can get one today? Most likely, they'll not have one at the airport."

"Sure. We have an auto rental right down the street. They usually have a couple of vans and small trucks. What do you need a van for?"

"To haul some equipment."

"What kind of equipment," she asked.

"I don't exactly know. Whatever we might need."

"Oh, no. You're getting a bit fuzzy here, and as a cop, I don't think I'll like it."

"You're probably right. Maybe I should take you home after we pick up the cargo van. Will you drive the car home after I get it?"

She smiled at Mickey, "I don't suppose I have a choice. You can't drive both at the same time. Let's go."

They went to an auto rental down the street a few blocks, got an extended van, and drove back to Veronica's house. They had a couple of hours to kill before he had to go to the airport.

"How did you get into this kind of stuff, Mickey. Your father was in construction. It isn't detective work?"

"It's hard to explain, but it all started when Mom and Pop were in a car accident. The police refused to investigate it, so James stepped up, and we became a team."

"There's more to the story than that. I know it."

"Yes, but that's all I can tell you."

"You're a real man of mystery, Mickey Ray Christianson!" she laughed.

"Maybe I am, but it isn't something that I can always be proud of. I've done necessary things that were wrong in the law's eyes."

"How's that?"

"Don't ask," he said to Veronica as a tiny voice in his head said, "You're sounding like James now."

He got up and looked out the window at the garage. "You know you could get a tidy sum for those cars, don't you?"

"Yes, I do. But those cars belonged to my father, and I don't want anyone else to have them. Maybe someday I'll part with them but not today."

"I guess I had better get to the airport and meet my people," he said, turning for the door.

"Want some company? As long as I'm not out all night. I need to work tomorrow. I have a murder to solve."

"I don't think you should come with me. Why don't you stay at home and do a background search on Grant Littleton and the CIOF."

"Who can you trust if you can't trust a cop?"

"I agree, but I have stories about cops, too!" he said.

She furrowed her brow and said in an accusatory tone, "and you don't think you can trust me?"

"It's not that I don't trust you. I'm trying to protect you. You know, give you plausible deniability."

"I don't want plausible deniability. If it helps catch a killer, I want to be part of it."

"Okay, but there may be a point when you have to leave."

"When it gets to that point, I'll call a cab," she said sarcastically.

"Come on. I'll drive."

They got to the airport, and Mickey checked in to find where they unloaded the chartered jets. They proceeded through security with the van checks and pulled up in front of a small business jet.

As he pulled to the hanger door, the folding steps dropped, and Marie and Alyssa stepped down the ladder dressed in jeans and flannel shirts and carried a duffle bag over their shoulders.

As Mickey approached them, Veronica lagged behind, but she definitely noticed them. Alyssa gave him a big hug, but Marie held back a bit more reserved.

Marie Sanchez was Latin with coal-black hair, straight and flowing halfway down her back. She wore the jeans like she was born in them, and just like the last time Mickey saw her, she was stunningly beautiful. Marie was still as sultry and demure as she was two years ago when they first met. Her dark eyes looked straight into Mickey's eyes, and she still made him feel uncomfortable.

Alyssa was also a Latino, but she had bleached her hair and had other enhancements to fill out her figure. Her dark skin made the blonde hair even sexier swinging to and fro as she came down the airplane steps. She was short, only five feet tall. In the last mission, she helped Mickey and James when she brought a team of mercenaries and several drones and performed as their overwatch during the mission. She was a wizard with electronics.

Mickey hadn't seen either of them for a year or more. They hadn't changed and were just as sexy and exciting as he remembered.

After a few words of greeting and "how have you been" statements, he motioned for Veronica to come to meet the girls.

Marie and Alyssa, this is Veronica or "Ronnie" Morgan. She's working on the case as a detective for the police department.

"Wait a minute, Mickey Ray. You know we don't work with the police. We have an entirely different set of rules," Alyssa said, and Marie nodded in agreement.

"Hold on, ladies. Let's talk about this over there," he said, pointing at the plane. "Ronnie, if you will excuse us for a minute, please."

Veronica turned and walked back to the van, and got inside.

Mickey and the ladies boarded the plane and sat down inside.

Alyssa started. "Mickey, you know that we work outside the law. They have rules that we don't abide by. She can't be a part of this."

Marie shook her head in agreement. "You don't understand. What we do is morally right but legally wrong. If we get caught doing ninety percent of what we do, we'll end up in prison. We can't take the chance of someone like her even knowing about us."

"You shouldn't have even bought her here," Aly said. "How long have you known her?"

"Two days," he said, realizing that they were right. He had messed up, and if Ronnie did turn them in, they would be in serious trouble.

"You decide to bring someone in on a mission that could put us all in prison for the rest of our lives, and you didn't even consider consulting with us first?" said Marie.

"You screwed the pooch on this one, Mickey Ray. We're leaving right now," Allyssa said as she got up and headed for the cockpit.

"Wait a minute, Aly. Give Veronica a chance. Neither of you knew me, but you gave me a chance, and it turned out okay."

"That was different, and you know it. James has known you most of his life. You've known this girl for TWO days. TWO days, Mickey Ray, and you're willing to risk all of our lives on it. Nope. Aly, fire up the engines. We're going back home," insisted Marie.

"Wait a minute!" Mickey called as Alyssa started for the cockpit.

"What. Why should we wait?" Marie said.

"Let's call James," he pleaded, pulling out his phone and dialing. When James answered, he handed the phone to Alyssa.

She took the phone and said, "James. Mickey has pulled a real stunt this time. Marie and I are firing up the engines to leave and go home."

Mickey saw her roll her eyes.

She started talking again. "He brought this woman cop to the airport as we landed. And we almost started unloading our equipment when we realized that he had only known her for two days. I'm putting you on speaker."

James' voice sounded loud and clear inside the plane. "Mickey, what were you thinking, doing a stupid thing like that?"

Mickey spoke up, "I didn't tell her anything. She knows they're here to help us find Val's killer."

"Unless she's a moron, and I don't think she is, it'll take her about thirty seconds to figure out that some of the stuff we do is illegal. If she doesn't report us, she could lose her job. If we follow the law, we'll never find Val's killer. We might as well pack it up and let the local yokels find who killed her. Do you want that?"

"No," Mickey answered.

"Then take her away and let Marie and Aly unload that equipment," James said. "Aly, are you still there?"

"I'm here, James," she answered.

"Please don't leave until I get back. Did you fly your own plane in?"

"Yes."

"Okay. Unload the equipment into the van and take it all back to the hotel. Just let Mickey take you to the hotel and check-in. I'll be back as soon as possible, and we'll talk about it."

"What do we do about Miss Muffet?" asked Marie.

"Hello, Marie. How are you, my dear?" asked James as nicely as he could.

"I'm fine and don't 'my dear' me. I don't like what Mickey did. I don't like it one bit."

"I know. We'll work something out when I get there. I'm on my way as we speak. Okay, ladies, check in and get a good night's sleep. I'll see you all in the morning. Deal?"

They all said, "Okay," and James disconnected.

They got out of the plane, opened a cargo door on the side, and unloaded several boxes into the van. Marie and Alyssa sat on the floor, and Veronica sat in the only other seat in the van on the passenger's side as Mickey drove them back to the hotel. They rode in silence as thick as a tar pit.

When they got to the hotel, they left the equipment in the van, and the ladies checked into the hotel.

After unloading the boxes, Mickey took Veronica home. On the way, as they talked, Veronica expressed her dislike for both women.

"I don't like them. They were rude and made me feel totally rejected, Mickey."

"I know, and I'm sorry. They're great at their jobs and usually don't have civilians around as they work."

"I must say, they're a couple of beautiful ladies. But I don't get exactly what you mean by 'civilian.' They definitely aren't in the military. At least not the military I'm familiar with."

"Yeah. It's kind of hard to explain. You'll have to trust me on this, Ronnie. And just for the record, you'll not be allowed access anywhere we'll be operating. Trust me. It's for your own good," he said.

"I don't understand why you're going to all this expense for a simple murder. And why you need all that equipment and a team of people. What is that stuff anyway?"

"I can't explain, but Valerie was the love of my life at one time. Even though, as I said, I'm over her, she was an important person in my life, and no one, and I do mean no one, hurts a person that is or was close to me. As you call it, this team always deals with situations like this. How many murders have you worked?"

"Florence is a small city. This is my third," she said.

"Those ladies have lost count of the number of missions or situations they have been in and solved. They're experts. This is what they do."

"So, they're part of a government agency, like the FBI or CIA?" she asked.

"I didn't say that. No. They're neither one. And for your information, legally, the CIA can't work inside this country. This is where the FBI comes in. That's all I can say. Now, can I count on you NOT to tell anyone else in the police department about this?"

"Can I tell…."

"No. I mean NO ONE," he said emphatically.

"I need to report that someone else is working on the case."

"NO. I mean it, Ronnie. If you do, that'll blow our entire operation. Give us a week. And if we don't get it done, we'll leave, and you can do whatever it is you do."

She sat with her own thoughts. "But, Mickey, I'm assigned to this case. I need to send in progress reports."

"We'll give you information that you can report. Don't tell anyone anything. I mean it, Ronnie. We'll do it, and you can have all the credit. We don't want credit for anything. We only want justice. Promise me. We'll protect you and your investigation if you cooperate with us. PLEASE," Mickey almost pleaded.

"Well, I need to think about it."

"No. I need your word NOW," he insisted. "Look, I had someone do a background on you too. I know more about you than you know about me. I know your father was a police detective and didn't retire to take care of your mother. He retired because he was wounded in the line of duty. At that time, your mother was sick, but she could care for herself. In his spare time, he worked on unsolved cases. He was killed working on a cold case on his own time. You want to find his killer, and working for the police is one way. You want justice for your father as much as I want justice for Valerie. I can't get you justice for that, but you can help me get justice for Valerie by letting us do our job."

"It's not your job to get her justice, it's mine, Mickey," she added.

Mickey drove, and Veronica looked out the passenger's window in thought. Finally, she turned back to him. "Okay, Mickey, I'll not tell, but you must let me in on whatever it is you're doing. I mean full disclosure. I want to be part of the team."

"I can't promise that. I need to talk it over with the rest of the team," he answered as he pulled into her driveway. He got out to walk her to the door.

She whispered in his ear as he leaned down to kiss her good night. "You don't have to go back to the hotel tonight, Mickey. You can spend the night here."

"I've got a long day tomorrow, Ronnie. I need to get back and get some rest. Go to work tomorrow and help us find Valerie's killer." He walked back to the van and drove back to the hotel.

CHAPTER 4

Reading Veronica in on the Plan

Mickey got up at five o'clock, went downstairs to the gym, worked out for an hour, and then went to the hotel breakfast area. When he arrived, Marie and Alyssa were already eating a sweet roll and having coffee.

James was standing over a table, looking at some maps and making notes on the borders. He looked to make sure no one was in the area to hear what he was about to say.

"Good morning, everyone," he called out to no one in particular. They all moved together to a large table and acknowledged his greeting.

"James, what're we going to do about Veronica. She already knows we're here to help you and Mickey. Anything out of the ordinary, she'll know it's us. We'll almost be in the police's way and on their radar if she reports us."

Mickey stood up. "I didn't tell Ronnie anything particular, but she promised not to report us if I promised to keep her up to date on our progress."

"You promised to give her progress reports! Are you crazy? We might as well just walk into the police station and announce ourselves," said Marie.

"We don't exactly give her progress reports on what we do. Only on the information we get," Mickey said.

"That's one step from the same thing, Mickey," said James. "If we give the police information, they'll know that we got it illegally, and they can't use it. So, we're at square one."

"And if she reports any information, someone will want to know how she found out. Same results…," said Aly.

"Let's set this aside for now," said James. "We need a place to set up base. Who wants to go out looking for a good place to set up?"

Alyssa raised her hand. "Mickey and I'll go. Mickey can drive. He already has a basic knowledge of the area."

"Okay. What're we looking for?" Mickey asked.

"We need a recently vacated commercial building outside the city limits," she said.

"Why do we need a commercial building?" Mickey asked.

"If it's been recently vacated, it'll still have power-active electrical boxes. All we need to do is install a jumper in the box to get power. Same with water connections, we can install plumbing jumper pipes, and we have water. Commercial building walls have better protection and are easier to secure," James explained. "Aly and Mickey can find one and call us so we can get the necessary tools to get utilities and set up the equipment. Let's go, people!"

Mickey and Alyssa got up, headed to the rental car, and went building hunting. After several hours of driving around back roads looking for a vacant building, they found one they felt had the things James said they needed.

When they got back to the hotel, James and Marie were sitting in James' room, looking at pictures of satellite photos of the CIOF.

"Okay, people," said Mickey, "we've found a place that might be good for us to use as the command center."

"Great, Mickey. Lead the way," said James.

As they walked out the door, James said to Mickey. "Hey, man. I got us another Humvee."

"That's where you went?"

"Yep. It's fully outfitted too. I'll show it to you later, bro!"

Mickey just shook his head and continued outside to load up the vehicles.

They left with the van and the Humvee that James had gotten. When they got to the building, they agreed it was adequate for their needs.

In the rear of the building was a large roll-up door. After cutting the locks off with bolt cutters, they pulled the vehicle inside. It was dark in the area, so they got out flashlights and scoped out the building inside. They found several rooms that they felt sure were once used as offices. The rooms had numerous electrical outlets that would be useful as soon as they hooked up the power at the power connections outside the building. And as they expected, it had bathrooms but no shower facilities. There were numerous rooms that they assumed were storage areas. Many rooms had large thick glass windows that would be excellent security against the average burglar.

Moving equipment into one of the interior offices, they arranged it semi-circularly. They found some old wooden boxes and set the equipment on them. It was dark and dirty, but it would suit their needs.

Mickey volunteered to go out and get the additional supplies to hook up the power and plumbing. They covered the windows with black paint so no light would filter out in case anyone wandered into the area.

While Mickey was shopping, he picked up some personal items. They would live in the building, so they needed bedding and toilet items. A small dorm-style refrigerator, a small camping stove, and sleeping bags was some of the items he got in addition to enough food to last a couple of days. He hoped they wouldn't be here any longer than that.

The plan was to get in, get the information they needed to find Valerie's killer, and go back home. Mickey never expected to have to go to this much trouble and expense. After all, the police would also be working on the case. He didn't understand why James had gone to so much trouble and expense for all this drama.

That's what the police did. They solved crimes. James had assembled an assault team. The team was comprised of soldiers, not detectives. The only thing he could see is that they could bring swift and total justice, whereas the police could take months to do it, and even then, a high-powered lawyer might get the guilty ones free.

He pulled back into the new command building and everyone set about hooking up facilities and picking out sleeping areas. The ladies stayed in one room, and the men picked another, but all within sight and hearing distance of the command room. Within two hours, they were set up and had all equipment up and running. They had power, running water, and temporary home comforts.

It was nearing time for Veronica to leave work, so Mickey headed to meet her. When he left, Aly and Marie were both sitting on boxes in front of the computers, looking on the internet, printing out satellite photos, and researching Grant Littleton and the Culinary Institute of Oregon and Factory.

Mickey drove up to the police station just as Veronica came out. She broke into a huge grin when she saw him and walked up to his car.

As he lowered the window, he called out to her, "Hello, young lady. Would you like a ride?"

She opened the door and dropped down into the passenger's seat. She took a deep breath and leaned her head back against the headrest. "Oh, Mickey, what a day. My Captain says we need to close the case of Valerie Green and move on."

"What did you tell him?"

"I said that it should be closed in a few days."

"And?"

"And I told him it wasn't that simple. I believe that Valerie Green was killed, and it wasn't an accident."

"And, what did you tell him?"

"What do you think I told him? I'll do my best, but I need time," she said exasperatedly.

"Didn't you insist that he give you more time?" Mickey asked.

"He's my boss. You don't insist on anything with him. If I don't get at least a suspect, he will insist I close it."

"Do you have any suspects?"

"No. You know I don't. I know you'll say that the code from Valerie's diary is something, but it isn't. It isn't enough to get a warrant to search the premises. All I know now is to go back and talk to Grant Littleton. Pressure him to let me look around his facility."

"Do you think he'll let you do that?" Mickey asked.

"Would you, if you had something to hide?" she retorted. "And besides, if I did, it would tip him off, and he would move anything he might have."

"Can't you put surveillance on the building to get information?" he asked.

"No, it costs money to set up surveillance, and without a warrant, the department won't spend the money on it, and I said we don't have enough evidence. I believe Valerie was murdered, but I don't know who or why, so it's dead."

"That's literally your job, to find out who and why, isn't it? That's what detectives do!"

"I know, Mickey. I'm so mad at the captain right now. I'll do what I can the next few days, and then you can take her home when her body is released."

"Yeah. You're right. Let's get something to eat?" Mickey said as he put the car in gear and pulled out of the station. They pulled into a public parking lot and parked the car.

Walking down the street, they discussed why Veronica had decided to become a detective.

"I don't know. I guess it seemed the thing to do since Daddy was a cop."

"Do you want to help people?" he asked.

"Yes. I guess so. No, I mean, it really is about Daddy. I don't know. I don't want to talk about it."

He put his arm around her. "Well, we're here about Valerie. I want to get justice for her! It's true, I don't love her anymore, but she was a good person. Sure, she had her personal demons, but she didn't deserve to be killed."

"I feel the same way about Daddy. He was good to Momma and me. I want justice for him too."

"Did you find out any more about the school? Or Grant Littleton, the man that owns it?"

"No, I didn't. Why is it that important?" she asked.

"You don't think the code I found in Val's journal was important, but it was. It led me to give a copy to James to decipher. He deciphered the rest of it."

"Did it tell you anything?" she asked, now interested in what he had found out.

"Not anything that could be construed as evidence. Probably not enough to get a warrant or permission to order surveillance on the business. But we don't need a court order to get surveillance installed."

"Mickey, if what you're doing is illegal, don't tell me. I don't want to be any part of it."

"Fine. I just thought maybe we could work together. That's all," he said as they walked on.

"No. We can't do that. I'm not allowed to share any information with you. My captain made that especially clear."

Mickey smiled at her, "So you admit that you were talking about me?"

She gave him a slight jab in the side, "Yes, but don't let it go to your head. All I told him was that you wanted to help. And that you and James had helped the police solve a case last year when you dug up that girl's body."

"That sounds promising," he said.

"He said definitely not. And he forbade me from talking about the case to you. I thought he might even tell me we couldn't see each other while the case is open."

"And if he had ordered you not to see me?"

"I don't know. He's my boss, and I need this job, but he has no authority over my personal life."

"I like that answer," said Mickey as they strode down the street. He continued talking as he dug a piece of paper out of his pocket and handed it to her. "We aren't talking about this case. I am, so technically, you are not violating his order. I'll add that this is a copy of the deciphered code. You have the original copy because it's in Val's journal. Check it out and check if it's evidence enough to get a search warrant."

She took it, looked it over, and put it in her pocket, and they continued walking silently down Main Street.

At the new command building, James, Marie, and Alyssa conducted deep searches on Littleton, finding nothing technically illegal. His operation was, for all intents and purposes, clean.

James called and talked to the admissions officer of the culinary school. He phoned as Marie's uncle about midterm admission to classes. The gentleman said they had a recent dropout, and they did have an opening. They didn't usually allow mid-term sign-ups, but what she had missed she could take up at the beginning of the next session.

James stepped over to Marie, "You'll be Marie Alvarez from California. The cover name that we've assigned you. You'll go in and start classes tomorrow. You'll wander around during breaks and between classes to get your bearings. Try to set as many bugs as you can near phones and places where people or workers might gather. If you can get cameras in areas, then do that too. You'll wear an earbud that Alyssa will give to you. I don't need to tell you that if someone sees or notices you are wearing it, tell them it's a hearing aid. You'll plant some bugs daily as you gain access to more areas until we flood the place with eyes and ears."

Marie listened intently. When she spoke again, she had a slight Mexican accent. "I see, Mr. James. I will not let you down. I will study and make perfect grades to be a top chef in your restaurant."

James let out a big smile. "Excellent accent Marie. And you'll become a world-class chef, I'm sure," he said with a slight bow.

Marie began brushing up on her cooking skills or at least doing some speed reading on the subject to be ready.

Finally, Mickey walked in the door. "Hey, guys, what's up?"

"Glad you're back. I've gotten Marie enrolled in school tomorrow," said James.

James was sitting at the table, looking at the aerial printouts of the plant. "We should get a camera with lenses here and here on the rooftops of the other buildings," he said, pointing to neighboring buildings.

Mickey looked, "I agree. We can see trucks going in and out and get a good shot of the license plates and drivers. Also, with that camera over there," he pointed, "we should get a shot of the people on the dock loading the trucks. I hope that Marie can get audio on the dock."

"If she can't, we can go in after closing and do it. We can get the long-distance cameras placed anytime someone is not in those buildings across the street."

"Why were you gone all night last night, James?" asked Alyssa.

"I got some transportation," he said

"That's where you got the Humvee," she said.

"Yep. And I got it loaded with munitions," smiled James.

"We don't need munitions. That's overkill," Mickey said.

"You don't know that. We need to be prepared if these slimes are moving guns and drugs."

"I guess so, but I don't think it's that big," Alyssa added.

"I know, but what set me off was when Val said she saw them putting guns in cases. And sending out drugs packed as cake and dessert mixes is a perfect cover for running drugs. Those smells could possibly confuse a drug dog. Cake mixes and drugs, they won't know what they're trying to sniff out. And remember this location. We're right on the coast. It isn't a big seaport. Boats come and go from the marina every day. A small shipment here, another there, no one'll notice," said James.

"You've convinced me. When do you want to set those cameras?"

"How about in the morning," James added.

Mickey walked back over to Aly's makeshift desk. She was pulling up one tab after another on multiple monitors, printing out sheets of paper, and moving items from one screen to another to keep both in view.

On another wall sat several boxes with numerous computers and six monitors sitting on top. Alyssa had run cables and plugged them into distribution boxes.

Marie was quietly sitting in a chair reading cookbooks. "Do you think you can remember what you're reading?" Mickey asked, strolling over to her.

She smiled and nodded. "I have an almost photographic memory. I can speed read hundreds of words a minute. Did you know that President John Kennedy could read at 1200 words a minute? I'm not that good, but I could give him a run for his money," she said in her Mexican accent.

"That accent's impressive," Mickey said.

"Thank you, Mickey, but I'll have it from now until the mission's over. I need to stay in character," she said as she gathered her things and left for school.

Since there was nothing he could do, he returned to the warehouse area where the vehicles were and called Darcy. "Good evening, Dee. How's everyone going?" he asked when she answered the phone.

"Did James ask you to run a background on Veronica Morgan?" he asked.

"Yes, he did. She's pretty good. I hope the two of you get along. I'll send you the report that I got."

"Yes, we're getting along very well. I don't need to read a report on Ronnie. I trust you, and especially Ronnie. I'm still not sure we aren't going overboard in bringing everyone out here for this. James and I could have taken care of it," Mickey said.

"Maybe so, but James wanted to help, and he's pretty sharp about picking up on small things. I'd listen to him, Mickey. I'll send the report on Morgan anyway. I'll send it to your phone. Read it. It's always a good idea to know someone you might be involved with, Mickey Ray."

"Yeah, I guess you're right. I just wanted to check in. Say 'Hi' to the kids for me." After disconnecting, he went to his area to lay down until they went out to place the cameras. There was nothing anyone could do right now.

He checked his email on the phone. As he looked at the report on Veronica, he saw her entire education levels, her credit ratings, and even her medical records. She was in a severe car accident caused by a drunk driver. She sued the driver, and a doctor had to give testimony in her case, which included her blood type, and that she was allergic to Sulfa drugs.

Wow, he thought. How does Dee find out all this stuff about people? She's a legal assistant, not a background fact checker. She even got some basic medical background details about Ronnie. It's amazing what private information is recorded in a trial transcript.

CHAPTER 5

Setting Cameras Across the Street

The next morning, James and Mickey drove to the parking lot in the middle of town.

As James drove to the school and bakery, he kept in touch with the girls at the command room. Mickey took stock of the Vee, his nickname for a Humvee, and its contents.

"James, show me what we're driving here. What features and special equipment are installed?"

"To start, it has a remote starter just like your truck to prevent us from getting inside and getting blown up. It's fully armored. Not quite as heavy armor as a military Vee, but as close as civilian specs will allow. It has run-flat tires and bulletproof glass that'll take small arms fire. The engine is turbocharged for speed and has an extra-large armored gas tank for distance."

"I'll bet you also got more equipment than the ladies brought," Mickey said.

"I did, but they did pretty well. I didn't get a lot more. I did get a couple of rocket launchers with several extra rockets to reload and smoke grenades to add to the flashbangs they brought."

"Wait a minute. You bought rocket launchers? Do you mean like Bazookas? What in heavens name are we going to do with one of those?"

"I don't know. We could have used one of those in New Jersey a couple of years ago on those propane tanks. Bazooka is an old term. We like to call them rocket launchers today."

"We did just fine without them! James, if we get caught by the authorities with those in our possession, they'll put us under the jail," Mickey said.

"Simple answer to that. We don't get caught," James said calmly as he continued driving.

"I don't believe this. We'll end up in jail trying to catch a murderer!"

"Calm down, Mickey. It's going to be fine. I promise. You and your new girlfriend can drive off into the sunset in her red Corvette," he said as he laughed. "Now, the school's right up ahead. I wasn't sure, but the building across the street is a multi-level parking garage. It'll be a piece of cake to mount a camera up there. All we need to do is find a way to get up on the roof of the building beside it and mount the second camera."

James pulled into the parking garage and continued going until he got to the roof area. The other end had an open view of the bakery building. They parked away from the edge so the Vee couldn't be seen from adjacent buildings. James walked to the edge and looked over. He motioned for Mickey to come over. They stood behind a metal shed room on the top floor that may have housed the elevator machinery. James pointed out the bakery building and then pointed to where they could mount a camera across from it. He pointed to an area where Micky could leap from the garage to the roof of the adjacent building.

"Getting over there, James, may be easy, but how do I get back after setting the camera?" Mickey asked.

James pointed a bit farther over to the next building. "Look over there. It's flat, and you can jump to it. There's a door that leads to the roof, and you can go through that door. I'll meet you at the bottom at the street," James said.

When James started mounting the first camera on the top level of the building, Mickey descended to a lower level equal to the roof on the building adjacent to the parking garage. Standing mentally measuring the height and distance, he wasn't sure if he could make it, but he would die trying. His heart started pounding just thinking of the distance from the ground to where he was and the distance from the garage to the other building. It was about four feet lower than the level he was standing, and he hoped the lower footage would allow him a little more glide distance.

Securing the camera tight to his waist, he started running, but as he neared the edge, he stopped. He couldn't do it. His heart was racing, and nervous sweat dripped from his forehead. It was done in the movies all the time. Stuntmen would run and jump from one building to another until they reached the ground. Yes, he thought, but that was Hollywood, and there were nets below, and usually, these stunts were done by professionals, not by the stars themselves. He couldn't do it. Yes, he could. James said he could do it, so he could. He rubbed his hands on his pants to dry them.

Mickey backed up again. This time he ran. He ran for his life. Launching himself off the ledge of the parking garage, it seemed that time stood still. Gliding across the chasm, he looked down between the buildings and then felt his feet touch the roof. He dropped and fell, then rolled to a stop. Laying there for a while, he checked his body. Arms, okay. Legs, okay. Head. He didn't hit his head. It was okay. He got up. When he did, he looked up, and James gave him a thumbs-up sign. Mickey moved to an area not easily seen from the bakery and mounted the camera. It wasn't easy to pick out from a distance, but it could see the entire loading dock.

After mounting the camera, he turned to the building behind the one he was on. It was also a few feet lower than where he was standing, but there was more distance between them. The only way off was to jump to the next one. It was farther. Could he do it? No, he couldn't. It was too far. A good five feet more distance. He couldn't do it. Turning back looking up at James, he saw no moves. No encouragement. Just a human statue. Mickey shrugged his shoulders at James. No movement. James just stood and watched.

Mickey walked to the edge and looked over. He could see trash. Old rotten pieces of wood and broken bottles were lying on the ground between the buildings. His heart began racing faster than the first time he jumped. He did it once. He could do it again. It was a long jump, but he had to do it, so he backed up once more. He wiped the sweat from his hand onto his pants again. Then he took several deep breaths. Mickey looked back at James one last time. James was still a human statue. Mickey ran. He ran like the frightened man he was and jumped as high and hard as he could. He sailed through the air but didn't look down this time. Finally, he felt his toes touch something. It wasn't the roof this time. It was the edge of the building wall. His body slid down and slammed against the wall. He put his arms out and hit the roof's edge, closing his fist to grab the edge. All at once, his entire body hit, and he was hanging onto the wall, but he knew he couldn't hold on to it long. His body ached. He hurt from head to toe. When he fell, he knew the debris would break his body on the ground. The glass would slice his body open. Hanging there, he waited for the end to come. It would be here soon enough. He thought his aching chest would burst with the beating of his heart.

He closed his eyes and started praying. "God, now I lay me down to sleep." It was a childhood prayer, but that was all he could think of at that moment. "I pray to the Lord, my soul to keep." Yep, he hoped God would be merciful and make it painless. "And if I die before I wake…Wait." What was that thing grabbing his collar? Was it God picking him up by His own hand.

Then he heard the familiar voice of James.

"Come on, man. Hold on. You're going to be okay. I've got you now. You're my brother. Brothers, don't drop another brother," he said as he pulled Mickey up by the collar and dragged him to the rooftop.

Mickey laid there getting his breath and letting his heart slow down. After several minutes, he opened his eyes and raised his head. He saw James looking at him from several feet away.

"I thought you were God pulling me up, James," Mickey said between breaths.

"Believe me, God and I were constantly communicating when I was pulling you up," James answered calmly.

"How did you get here so quickly?"

"I did what you did. I jumped from the garage to that building, then from there to here. I made it. You didn't. You need to work out more, bro. When we get home, I'm going to put you into training," he said and got to his feet. "Let's get back to the command building before someone sees us on this roof and asks questions."

As they rode back to command, Mickey said to James, "What do we tell the team when we get back?"

"About what?" James answered.

"About me missing the roof."

"I don't know what you're talking about."

"I mean, you had to jump over there and pull me up."

"That's not how I remember it. I put the camera on the parking garage, and you put the one on the other building. End of story."

"Thanks. I appreciate it."

"Appreciate what? We had a job to do, and we did it. Like I said, end of story. Let's go home. Call command and check-in to make sure they have video now."

Mickey punched the buttons on his phone, and when Alyssa answered, he put her on speaker. "Hello, Mickey. We've got good clear video from here. Everything's good, and we're getting audio from Marie. She's in class, doing well, and fitting in comfortably. We all have to admit, she's a babe and is getting quite the attention from a couple of the male students in class. The teacher has taken special notice of her also."

"That's good. If Marie gets in good with the teacher, she may get some chances to go deeper undercover. A little alone time in an office or other 'off-limits' areas."

"We're hoping that happens. How did it go with you and James? Anything notable?"

Mickey looked at James, and James spoke up. "Nothing worth reporting. We're coming back to command. We're out." He reached over and touched the end icon, and ended the call.

"James, I'm still wondering what use we may have for a rocket launcher," Mickey said, leaning back in his seat.

"You never know," James said as he continued driving.

They stopped on the way and picked up some sandwiches for everyone. When they were on a mission, the monitors were never left when someone was in the field. And until Marie got out of school and back to the command center, someone would be watching and listening.

When they returned to the room, they let themselves in. Alyssa was laughing at what she heard coming over the speakers.

"Why, Jack. I don't need your help. I can do it myself," said Marie.

"Hey, Mr. Hamilton said we could work on this part together," the male voice said.

"I know, but I don't need help," she replied.

"Come on, Marie. I'll hold the bowl while you stir it. It won't be as messy that way."

"Alright, but the bowl's all you can hold, understand?" said Marie.

"Got it," came the answer.

They could hear knocking, sounds that might have been moving things around, and finally, what sounded like scraping. Mickey thought it sounded like stirring in a metal bowl.

"Here, we brought sandwiches," Mickey said as he took them out of the bag. And they each got up, went over to the small refrigerator, and took out some water bottles.

Mickey looked inside the fridge and made the comment, "There aren't any sodas in here."

Alyssa answered. "That's right. Soda's bad for you."

"I forget. You're a health nut," he said.

"You could use more water and fewer sodas. You'd be in better shape," she said.

Mickey and James exchanged glances.

They could hear the teacher going into other ways to change flavors with simple spices, and he advised the class to make notes. They could also hear Marie mumble to herself. "This is boring. I already knew this even before this stupid class. It's a class for culinary idiots. I don't like to cook, but it would be boring even if I did. All the while, I'm here, smiling and pretending to be enthralled with this moron they call a master chef."

James shook his head. "I don't think she's enjoying her undercover work," he spoke as he downed an entire bottle of water.

They sat around the audio speakers and video monitors.

"We have to take turns monitoring the monitors at night when everything's shut down. Who is going to do that?" Alyssa asked, looking at the others.

Mickey volunteered to do it. He asked, "Are we recording things 24/7?"

"No, unless we see something that might look out of place. Anything that goes on after closing will be suspicious. If you see anything, hit the button right here," she said, pointing to a button on the main keyboard. "If you think we need to act on something, pick up the phone and call James or me."

"What about bathroom breaks?" he asked. "I know I should limit drinking, but eight hours is long without a break."

"Mickey, that is a part of our human makeup. Yes, you can limit breaks by not eating and drinking. But when it is absolutely necessary, start the recording when you leave. Make it quick and get back. If nothing's happening when you get back, leave the screen and look at the recorded time on another monitor. If it was quiet during that time, then delete it. If something happened while you're gone, keep it, and make the call to one of us."

"Got it," he said.

Alyssa continued. "Later this evening, we'll let you go grab some sleep before your shift begins. We'll give you a wake-up call-in time for you to get down here and take over. We'll do five-hour shifts. That way, we get enough sleep to function, still have time to meet and exchange thoughts and ideas, and go in the field and get away from this room for a break."

Mickey shook his head in understanding.

They sat quietly talking until they heard Marie say to herself, which translated to her earbud. "Okay, guys, we're taking a short break, then back for one last lesson for the day. Everyone's leaving the room. I'll take off my apron, and you'll see the layout from the button camera. As I looked around during class, I saw a camera on the wall in a corner. I'll try to place one next to it so you can see what they see. I don't know if the camera has audio or not."

As she talked, they saw one of the screens light up as Marie took off her apron, uncovering the camera she was wearing. The room was long and narrow, with posters on the walls showing delicious foods photos of recent students. Marie moved close to the picture so they could get a good look and then run facial recognition on the staff in the photos. After a few moments, she moved to the next one until she had stood in front of each photograph long enough for command to get a screenshot of them. She then left the room and tried to find the rest of the class. She opened doors on the right and left of the hallway on the way out. A coat closet for staff. A utility closet. When she opened the door to a private office, she saw an overweight man sitting at a desk, writing in a large ledger.

"Oh, excuse me, sir, I was looking for the ladies' room," she said, looking embarrassed and moving her body so the camera would get a good shot of the man.

He looked up, moved his hand outward in a pointing motion, and said, "Down there to the right. This door is labeled 'Private.' The ladies' room is labeled 'ladies.'"

"Yes, sir. I'm sorry. It won't happen again," she said and closed the door. In command, they all laughed as she walked down the hall and whispered to them, "A-hole."

She continued down the hall opening other doors. At the end of the hall, the door opened into a large room stacked with boxes. She made a mental note as she slowly walked around so they could record what was there. After a quick walk-through, she returned to the hall-way and turned in the direction the man in the office had directed.

After the restroom visit, she returned to the classroom for the last class. As the teacher droned on about the importance of spices and which flavors mixed well and which ones to avoid, she continued to grumble so only command could hear.

"I hate this. I'd rather be fighting an anaconda in the jungles of Africa than listen to this man any longer. I'm going to call in sick tomorrow!" she said.

James leaned over into the microphone. "Sorry, pretty lady. You'll be there again looking beautiful and sexy as you always do, and to add insult to injury, you'll pretend to enjoy those instructions on culinary perfection."

She quietly said, "Oh, God, please spare me!"

"Only one more hour today, and you can come home!" Mickey said into the mic.

Later James and Mickey drove around the city to get more familiar with the landmarks. It's one thing to see an ariel view, but another to see it from the ground. They wanted a ground view, travel times, possible shortcuts, and hidden driveways. They drove by the school several times from different directions. They stopped at the corner and watched a couple of trucks come and go from the loading area of the school. Just to be sure they could run vehicle checks, they snapped pictures of the license plates of the trucks and sent them back to the ladies.

They parked in sight of the entrance and snapped anyone who entered and exited the building.

"Mickey, you think you'll ever get married?"

"Sure, when I find the right woman. Why did you ask that?"

"Was just wondering. You've been engaged twice."

"The second time didn't count. I didn't ask her."

"You were going to ask. If she didn't…well, you know," James said.

Mickey turned to James. "You sure pick the strangest time and oddest topics to discuss when we're on a stakeout."

"Stakeouts are boring. You pick something to talk about," suggested James.

"Okay. I want to know why you got rocket launchers. We don't need them. Can we get a refund if we don't use them?" Mickey asked.

"Are you crazy? What do you think they're running there. There's no money-back guarantee with an arms dealer. Geeze, Mickey!" James said. "When you buy it, it's yours. Forever!"

"How am I supposed to know? I've never dealt with people and things like that before."

"If I have my way about it, you'll never have to know about it," he said.

"I'll say it again. You scare me, James."

"I know. You've said that many times before. I'll say it again to you. People like the team and me keep people like you safe."

"I know. I know. Still…." said Mickey.

"It's about time for Marie to get out of school. Let's crank up and get back to command," said James.

As they started the vehicle, Marie walked out. Shortly after that, a man walked out behind her. Mickey and James sat and watched as the man approached her. For a few minutes, it seemed friendly enough until he reached out and took her arm. She gently took his hand from her arm and moved toward her car. As she did, he grabbed her arm again and clamped down tightly.

When this happened, Marie drew back and slapped him hard across the face knocking him back, and he let go. He regained his composure, approached her, grabbed her arm again. He then raised his other arm in a gesture to hit Marie.

Mickey and James watched all of this sitting in the car, but when the man raised his arm to hit Marie, Mickey grabbed the door handle and get out of the car. James reached over and grabbed Mickey's arm. "Whoa, bro. Trust me, Marie can take care of herself. Hold off for a bit. Let's see what happens."

When the man raised his arm, Marie reached up and clamped down on his raised arm. She pulled it down and spun him around, pinning his arm against his back. She kneed him between the legs from behind, connected with some delicate male organs, and the man went down. As he went down, Marie held his arm tight against his back. She also went down and placed her knee square in the middle of his back. She bent down and whispered into his ear as she held his arm. When he didn't respond, she pushed his arm higher up his back, and he let out a loud "Yes!" that Mickey and James could hear from across the street.

James just turned to Mickey and smiled. "I told you she could take care of herself," and he raised his hand for a high five. James and Mickey slapped palms in pure delight!

"I wish we had a video of that," said Mickey.

"We do. Command should have a video and audio from her button cam. Call them, Mickey."

Mickey called Alyssa, and when she picked up, he put the phone on speaker, "Did you get the latest development there?"

"Yes, Mickey. We did. Wasn't Marie awesome?" Alyssa said.

Mickey and James could hear Alyssa laughing out loud.

"Aly, can you shoot the audio to us so we can hear what they said?" asked James.

"Be glad to do that. The video wasn't so great because it was too close to get a good view, but we heard it all…Coming to you as soon as I can. Are you coming back home?" Alyssa asked.

"Yeah, as soon as we hear the audio. We don't trust ourselves to drive and laugh at that poor jerk. Send the audio ASAP."

Mickey clicked off, and they sat waiting for Aly to call back with the audio.

After a few minutes, the phone rang again, and they answered it, and Aly connected them to the recording.

They heard the door close as they imagined Marie leaving the building. They heard the door close in the background in a few moments.

"Hey there," they heard a male voice say.

In their mind's eye, Marie turned around. "Yes, may I help you?" she asked in her assumed Mexican accent.

"Um, I noticed that you're new here. Are you new to the area?" the voice asked.

"Yes. I am."

"Great. I'd love to show you around the city," he said in a friendly tone.

"No, thank you. I have to go home now."

"Come on, beautiful," he said. "It won't take long. We could drive around and get to know each other a little better."

"No, thank you. I need to get home."

"Do you have family around here?" he asked, still being polite.

"That really isn't any of your business. Now I want to leave."

"Hey, don't be in such a rush," he said a bit more persuasively.

"Don't touch me. I don't like for strangers to touch me."

"Hey, I didn't mean any harm. I'm no stranger. I'm Rollo. I work here," he said.

"I don't care where you work. I want to go home. Now please leave me alone and let me leave."

"Hey, girl. All I want is a couple of drinks. That's all. You don't have to be such a little snob to me. You think you don't have to go out with me because you're good-looking, don't you!" He was getting obnoxious this time. "Maybe you think I'm not good enough for you, stupid Chiquita."

"I never said that. I just want to go home. Now, please let me go," Marie is almost pleading now.

"Come have a couple of drinks, and then you can go home."

"I don't want to go anywhere with you. Now let me go."

Then they heard the slap.

They both grinned at each other at that sound.

They heard other movements as they knew he had raised his hand, and she took him down.

After a few moments, they heard her whisper in his ear, "I do not want to have a drink with you today, tomorrow, or ever. And don't ever raise a hand to me again. You were going to hit me. Weren't you?" she said.

No sound from him.

Then they heard him call out the word, "Yes."

"I'm not a stupid Chiquita, as you say. If you so much as come within ten feet of me, I will tear your arm off and ram it down your throat. Understand?"

More movement sounds. They assumed it was the man trying to nod his head. More rustling as Marie got up. They heard her brushing off her clothes, getting into the car, and closing the door. End of transmission.

Mickey and James laughed until tears flowed down their faces as they drove back to the hotel.

CHAPTER 6

Command After Marie's Encounter

James and Mickey walked into the command room. The video and audio of Marie's encounter were playing in the background on the computer monitors.

James and Mickey stood and watched it all play out once more. They shut it off and decided to take a much-needed break from the shut-in status of the group in the small room. They decided to go somewhere in the outskirts of town and celebrate the evening. They all piled into the car and went to a small seafood restaurant at the edge of town that overlooked the seashore and had a stunning view of the water. They all went inside and sat near a window facing the water.

As one would expect from a seafood restaurant, it was decorated in a marine motif with pictures of sailing ships, harpoons hanging from the walls, fishnets draped from the ceiling and a statue of a pirate in the corner of the room.

James spoke up first. "Marie, when Mickey saw that guy raise his hand to strike you, he jumped to get out of the car. I stopped him and told him that you could take care of yourself. I knew you'd take him down and make him regret even thinking about hurting you. I was right!"

Mickey blushed a bit and shook his head. "Yep, I was ready to rescue the damsel in distress, but James was spot on. You nailed that guy's butt to the pavement. You were a sight to see."

The ladies raised their glasses to toast themselves, "Here, here!"

The evening went well for a deserved break. After a delicious dinner, they returned to the command building. Aly stayed up to watch the cameras Mickey and James had placed facing the loading dock while the others went to their sleeping rooms. During that time, Aly played the recorded video taken during their time at the restaurant. Nothing that looked suspicious happened. She deleted that video.

The following morning Marie got up and went to class. During the first class that morning, she was summoned back to the office she had entered the previous day that had the man doing paperwork. When she knocked, he called to her to come in and sit down while he finished writing in a notebook. Finally, he looked up and addressed Marie.

"Miss Alverez. We have something we need to talk about," he said, leaning back in his chair with folded arms. He stared intently at her.

She sat, then looked down at her lap, pretending to be intimidated by his gaze.

He finally spoke to her in a tone reserved for a disobedient child. "Miss Alverez. We saw what happened yesterday as you were leaving the building. Do you realize that you almost broke that man's arm?"

She, head lowered, arms crossed, shook her head. "No," she said.

"Well, you did. He was taken to the emergency room after you left. His shoulder is severely sprained, and if you had moved it higher, it would have fractured. Also, he's on painkillers for the pain in his groin. He's one of our workers and will be out of work for several days."

"How did you know, sir?" she asked.

"We have a very secure facility here. We have cameras all over the entire facility. See that box up there against the wall?"

Marie turned her body so the button cam could face the security system box, hoping that Alyssa at command could see the printed label in the front of the box.

"I didn't know you had that," she said.

"We saw everything. Would you like to see the video?"

"No," she answered. "Did you hear what he said and tried to do to me?"

"We have video, but no audio. We saw enough to know that what you did was not necessary."

"He threatened me. And when I refused to go with him, he insisted. If you saw what was happening, why didn't security come out to help me?"

"We don't keep a man in an office 24/7 monitoring videos. We didn't see it until early this morning."

"Don't you have an internet hook up to monitor the facility remotely?"

"No, it's CCTV. That means it's closed-circuit television. Why are you so curious about our security?"

"Because I thought I was going to be beaten or raped by that man. You tell me that you don't have anyone here to monitor it. If I had not defended myself, you would have come in this morning and found me beaten, maybe dead."

"You're blowing this entire thing out of proportion. I'm sure he meant you no harm. He probably found you attractive, and all he wanted was to spend a little time with you."

"I didn't want to spend time with him. When I didn't go out with him, he called me names, and I was afraid that he might hurt me. If you saw the video, you saw that he raised his hand to hit me."

"That was after you slapped him, and he didn't hit you, did he, Miss Alverez?"

"That was because I took him down before he had the chance."

"If he had hurt you, you could have come to us. We would have taken care of it."

"So, you're saying that I should let him hit me, or beat me first, then you would have stepped in? I won't let any man touch me that doesn't have permission!" she said, now getting angry at this man's attitude.

"You don't know that he would have hurt you."

"When anyone raises a hand to me, he has nothing good on his mind. I came from a family with six kids. We lived in a poor crime-ridden neighborhood. As a girl from the 'hood,' I don't wait to be hit or raped. I'll not be threatened or be disrespected by anyone. May I go now, sir?" she said with an emphasis on the word "sir."

"Okay. We understand where we stand on this point. Because you're new here, I'll let it go this time. Now, we have one more item to talk about."

"What is that?" she said, still in her deep Mexican accent.

"As I said, we have cameras around the facility. We saw you looking into and wandering around rooms you are not authorized to be in. Would you like to see those videos?" he asked.

"No, I know where I went," she said.

"Why did you go into those areas?"

"It was my first day. When I opened your door, I was looking for the ladies' room, as I told you. I was just curious and wanted to see what else was there. No one told me I couldn't look around," she explained.

"Okay, I'll accept that. But in the future, you go to and from class. That's the extent of it. We have a lot of different things going on here. We have food manufacturing, packing, and shipping, as well as the school you're attending. There's a lot of dangerous equipment. You could get hurt if you aren't careful.

"I'll speak to the employee you injured, and he will be dealt with. Do you understand?" he asked.

"Yes."

"Now, you may go back to class, Miss Alverez," he said and returned to his paperwork.

Marie got up and walked out of the room. "Did you hear that, guys? Video, but no audio. We can discuss that later when I get back to command," she said softly so that only command would hear her from her earbud comm unit.

An answer came over her earbud. "We heard. He's an A-hole."

"Yep," she said as she opened the door to the classroom and re-entered it.

She finished out the day. As she walked out the front door of the building to her car, she raised her arm and extended her middle finger.

CHAPTER 7

Mickey Meets Toni

They all sat in a restaurant that evening and talked. Veronica joined them after she got off work. They also agreed that certain things were not to be discussed in front of Veronica because, at this point, they still didn't completely trust her.

Marie said, "I guess you heard it all. I'm not tech-savvy, so Aly, you take it from here."

"We heard everything, Marie. We see some advantages but also some problems," Alyssa said. "The good news is that they already have cameras in the building. The bad news is that it's CCTV, and they aren't connected to the internet, so we can't hack into the system."

Veronica spoke up at this time. "I may be able to help here. I'm not tech-savvy either, but I know someone who is. I can give her a call."

"No," came a resounding answer from the others in the room.

She gave a sly smile and said, "I understand that you haven't let me in the group. But I also know some people due to my time in the PD. She is a CI, that's...."

"We know, confidential informant," said Marie.

"Yes, and she's spent time in jail for hacking into bank accounts and making withdrawals. I have some things on her that'll send her back to jail if I tell the proper authorities. Oh, and also, she's my niece."

"You trust an ex-con?" said Alyssa.

"She's your niece?" asked Marie.

"You guys deal with ex-cons and illegal people all the time. James just got an armored Humvee that isn't street-legal," Veronica countered sarcastically.

They all exchanged glances, nodding, "Are you sure you can trust this girl just because she's your niece?" James asked.

"Yes, and if she ratted you out, I'd probably be in a cell beside her."

"Fine, what would you suggest?" asked Alyssa.

"I'll go see her and see what she suggests we do," Veronica said.

Mickey said, "I'll go with you, Ronnie."

James said, "Okay. When can you get in touch with this person?"

Veronica said, "I can try to call her now if that's okay." She got up, walked to the restaurant's waiting area, and called her niece.

While she was gone, the others began talking about who this person was.

"Why should we trust her?" asked Marie.

"Why not?" said Mickey.

"Because we don't know either one of them. They could land all of us in jail, that's why!" Alyssa added.

"Dee ran an exhaustive check on her. She comes up clean in every case. She's trustworthy," said James.

"Trustworthy to whom? Us, or the police?" questioned Marie.

"That's a good question, James. If we let her know what we are doing, she has to be disloyal to someone. I'd rather it not be us," said Aly. "And we know nothing about this CI she has. She even admitted that her CI is an ex-con. Ex-cons are loyal only to themselves."

"Ronnie also said that if her CI is caught doing something illegal, she'll go to jail with her CI. That's a pretty good reason not to rat us out or turn on us."

"Okay, I agree, but we still keep both of them on a need-to-know basis," said Marie.

They all agreed on that.

Veronica returned to Mickey and said, "Okay, let's roll."

They took Veronica's car, cruised into town, parked, and walked to the public park.

"This's a pretty little town in the evening, The weather's nice, and it's relaxing walking around like this. How old is this girl, Ronnie?"

"Early twenties. She got into computers in high school. She's kind of a rebel. A geek. She's a whiz on a computer, and the high school computer club accepted her because she was way more advanced than anyone in the club. Social outcasts, especially computer nerds, tend to bond.

"How did she end up in jail?" he asked.

"That's a story for another time, but when she got caught, she refused to talk, rat anyone out, or make a deal, so she went to jail. She took the heat for the entire bunch," Veronica said as she looked around for her niece.

"A teenager in jail for computer crimes seems like a pretty stiff sentence."

Veronica gave a small laugh at that one. "That's true, but the entire group stole half a million dollars from various bank accounts."

"Did the authorities get it back?"

"Originally, the club members were going to split the money. But Toni kept her mouth shut when they started talking and making deals with the district attorney. They got probation, and she got time. She did give in on one point, and it reduced her time to one year."

"What was the one point?"

"She returned the money to the original account holders."

"It still seems rough," Mickey said, shaking his head.

"She did spend time, not in a real jail, but close enough. It was in Juvie. She spends a lot of time on the internet, but I don't tell on her because she's going straight. Her name is Toni."

"Okay, but how will Toni take it when you show up with me?"

"I don't know. I'll get it straight." Veronica looked down at her feet. Not exactly sure how it would go down with him and his team.

After walking around for another ten minutes, Veronica's phone buzzed. She looked, and it was a text from Toni. She texted back.

"It was Toni, and she wanted to know why you're with me. I told her, you're good. She doesn't like it, but she'll come over if I vouch for you."

Mickey smiled.

"What are you grinning at?"

"There is a lot of 'vouching' going on around here. I vouch for you. You vouch for me, and so it goes."

Veronica vouching for him was a similar response by his team when he wanted to bring Veronica in on the mission. They sat down on the wall of the community fountain and waited. Finally, a young girl walked up to them and stood silently, looking from Mickey to Veronica. No one spoke.

The girl was butch with short dark purple hair, cut like a boy's haircut. Her short-sleeved t-shirt revealed tattoos up and down her arms. Completing her outfit were camo cargo pants and high-top work boots, laced halfway up, the laces untied and dragging the ground.

Mickey looked at the boyish girl, then back at Veronica.

"Hello, Aunt Ronnie," she said. "I thought we agreed never to meet unless we were both alone," she said in a matter-of-fact tone.

"Yes, we did, but these are extenuating circumstances."

"That doesn't explain why he's here," Toni said, nodding toward Mickey.

"He's my boyfriend, and I wanted you to meet him, and we both know that you're my only family. It's a bit like bringing my boyfriend home to meet momma and daddy, dontcha think?"

"Come on! It's nothing like that at all! You don't have a boyfriend. So, what's the deal. Why do you need my help?"

"Okay. Mickey's not exactly my boyfriend, but he's the closest thing I have to one right now."

"Fine. I'll buy that. That doesn't explain why you need my help."

"Here's the scoop. Mickey here came from Virginia to pick up his girlfriend's body and take her home."

"Ex-girlfriend," interjected Mickey.

"Okay, ex-girlfriend," she said sarcastically, then she continued. "We believe she was murdered and want to find out who and why."

"If she was his ex, then why does he care?" still talking as though Mickey wasn't sitting next to Veronica.

"Because, at one time, he loved her. She was a good person, and so is he. He wants to get justice for her and get closure for himself. The biggest thing is that he cares about people, Toni. Just like I care about you. I believed in you when no one else did. Now he believes in his ex-girlfriend. Last, of all, he's not my boyfriend, but we have had a couple of dates, and I believe in him and want to help him."

"Are you sleeping with him?" Toni asked.

"That, young lady, is none of your business, but no, for the record," Veronica said.

"Okay. I'll help. What do you need?" Toni said.

They sat at a nearby picnic table. Toni sat across from Mickey and Veronica. Veronica took out a photograph of the front of the security box and told her the entire story, except the place's name. When she finished, Toni smiled.

"That's simple enough for a high school retard to fix. You unplug the camera feeds into the back of the central input on the security systems main panel. Then plug an inline transmitter to put it online. It's a simple fix. I can do it in two minutes."

"No. You can't do it. You give us what we need, and we'll send one of our team in to do it."

"I do it, or it's no go," she said defiantly.

"I can't let you go in. The rest of the group won't agree to it. Right now, even I don't know everything they're doing," said Veronica.

"I don't care. Either I go, or you can go to someone else."

Mickey spoke up, "We'll give you a thousand dollars. Cash."

Toni looked at Mickey, furrowed her brows, and said stubbornly, "I don't care if you offer me ten thousand dollars. I don't need your money."

Veronica turned to Mickey and said, "She's right. Her parents are rich. They made something like ten million in bitcoin a few years ago. She doesn't need the money."

"Come on, Toni. Please help us out. We need your help. I'm sworn to secrecy. I can't tell you anymore."

"I can't meet your group?"

"Absolutely not, Toni. We've told you more than we should have already," said Mickey.

"Who's going inside to do the job?" she asked

"Can't tell," said Mickey.

"Can I at least go along and stay outside?"

"You going in?" said Toni to Mickey.

"I'm not trained for that, and I'm not tech-savvy," he said.

"You don't have to be. Are you sure you two aren't sleeping together?" she said.

"Yes, and as Ronnie said, none of your business," answered Mickey.

"So yes, you are sleeping together," Toni said.

"I meant to say, I'm sure we aren't sleeping together."

"Okay, but I would if I were a guy. She's pretty, don't you think?" Toni knew she was getting Mickey a bit flustered.

"Yes, she's pretty, but get off this subject. That's off-limits to you!" Mickey said.

Toni laughed a bit for the first time. She continued. "First, you need to cut the power to the security system, and most likely, they'll have a backup battery power pack, which will kick in about 45 seconds after the power goes out. Many businesses don't do regular maintenance and replace the batteries yearly as they should. They can be a bit pricey, like fifty to one hundred dollars, so they let that slide. Taking a chance like that is like playing Russian roulette. You may win, or you may lose, and bang! You're caught on candid camera. If you get out soon enough, they still won't know who you are, but they'll see that you tampered with the system. So, if you lose, they know, and you still lose. Get my drift?"

"Yes, we see," they both said. "Can you cut the power to the building?"

"Nope, I'm not an electrician. Suppose you can find which individual electrical circuit it is on from the main box. If you can overload the circuit and blow the entire main security panel…then there is no security system."

"That won't do. We don't want to put it out of commission. We want to piggyback on it and see what they see through their cameras."

"Okay, it's back to plan A. That is to hook up a transmitter to the main panel in line with the incoming camera feeds."

"What if all the cameras are wireless feeds?" Mickey asked.

"It's a little more complicated. It all depends on how old the system is. What makes me think it's hard-wired is that you tell me it is

CCTV, which by definition means a closed circuit. But some newer systems are wireless and on frequencies that still provide a closed circuit. Now, can I go in so I can see it?"

"No," said Veronica.

"Okay, but I'll stay outside where it's safe, but I'll be close enough that I can help if needed."

"We can arrange that," Veronica said.

"No, we can't," said Mickey adamantly. "Since you know what we need, I assume you can provide the equipment?" Mickey asked.

"Yeah, but it'll cost. Upfront. No credit here. I ain't no bank."

"What if it doesn't work?" Mickey asked.

"It will."

"But what if...." Mickey started.

"I said it will. Do you want my services and equipment or not? Take it or leave it," she said smugly.

"We'll take it. When can we get it?" Mickey asked

"Give me till nine-thirty this evening. Now, I said cash up front."

"How much? And it's payable on delivery," said Mickey.

"No, I said upfront! Or no deal."

Mickey said, "I don't carry cash around."

Toni also got up, "I don't care. I already told you I don't need the money. See ya. Take care, Ronnie," she turned to walk away.

Ronnie was still sitting on the picnic table bench. She called out, "Toni, how much do you want?"

Toni turned and looked at both of them. "Five grand, if it's for him. I'll give you the friends and family discount, so three grand."

"If I give you three now, you'll promise me delivery tonight?"

"I said I would," Toni said.

"Deal," said Veronica as she reached into her handbag and started counting out money. She put the money into another bag that was also inside her handbag. She took the one with the three thousand dollars and discreetly handed it to Toni. "What time can we pick up the equipment?"

"Around nine-thirty. As I said, I also go on this thing with you guys, so I'll keep the key piece of equipment until we go, then, when we get there, I'll give it to you."

"It might be dangerous. I think you should leave it to the pros, Toni," said Veronica.

"I go, or I give you the money back."

"Fine. We'll meet you at nine-thirty this evening. I'll give you the time and place for installation placement," said Veronica.

"Thanks, Toni. I appreciate you agreeing to help us," Mickey said with his hand outstretched to shake her hand.

"Yeah, right. I'm doing it for Ronnie. I still haven't made up my mind if I like you. You hurt her, and I'll come after you," she said and walked off without shaking Mickey's hand.

Veronica laughed softly when Toni was out of range. "She doesn't have a clue who she's dealing with, does she, Mickey?"

"That's okay. She doesn't need to know as long as she helps us. Her parents are rich?"

"Yep, they dote on her and give her everything she wants. But she does have an overall bad attitude. She likes me, so I guess I have to give her some slack."

"And," Mickey added, "she doesn't play well with others."

"Toni can't go back and meet the team, so this arrangement insulates them and their anonymity."

"I can see that working out. By the way, you carry around that kind of cash?" Mickey asked Veronica.

"Normally, I don't, but I know Toni. She wouldn't sell something to God Himself without upfront payment in cash."

"Did you know how much she was going to charge?"

"Nope. So, I brought ten thousand."

"In cash? You came here with ten thousand dollars in cash?"

"Yep."

Mickey just shook his head. "Women, I'll never understand them. We still need to run this thing by command."

CHAPTER 8

Placing Audio and Video Equipment

"Y̶ou promised what?" asked Alyssa. "Are you crazy? First, you agree to buy something from someone we don't know. Then you agree to let her come along. Have you lost your mind, Mickey Ray?"

"Ronnie knows her. And she even gave Toni the money, so we need to re-reimburse her for the payment."

"We don't pay a dime until we get the equipment. But when she delivers, if she delivers, see James for the money. I just handle equipment, not money. Now let me get back to my audio equipment and the monitors. At least Marie has her button cam on until we can get the cameras hooked online. We also need to place microphones everywhere so we can get audio. Pics may be worth a thousand words, but audio can be more important in surveillance."

James entered the room, and Mickey filled him in on everything. He also didn't like that Mickey brought in another unknown person and agreed to let her come on the mission. Even if it was outside the facility, in relative safety, he felt it was bad business.

"If we get this equipment, we can go tonight," he said.

"How do we cut the power? Toni said that we need to do that to shut down the security system," said Veronica.

"Hold on a minute," said Alyssa. She turned to the monitor and moved the camera by remote control over the backside of the building near the loading dock area. She panned the camera and zoomed in on a large metal box mounted on the side of the building.

"See?" she pointed at the monitor to a grey box. "That's the outside shutoff. That's where the fire department can shut off the power to the building in case of fire. If for some reason, that's disabled, we can also pull the meter. Not a problem. I can add that they may have a backup power pack built into the security system. So, we still need to be careful. A bonus is the shut-off is outside the gate on the backside of the building. At least it's out of sight of their camera. You'll need to carry bolt cutters to cut the lock off."

"Now, we all need to go in and place the equipment and get out. Even in the case of power failure, some old systems may have enough power in an old battery to dial out a response number. They're often connected either to a monitoring company or the police."

Alyssa turned to James. "We'll need to go in to place the audio and microphones. We all go in simultaneously to light up and get out before anyone gets there to check things out."

James took over from there. "I got the floor plans of the building online, but over time, companies move walls and make additions, and so they could be outdated. I suggest that we all get acquainted with them as best we can.

"Toni will stay in the van. Assuming that she is the tech-smart person you say she is, she can stay and ensure the audio is working. I can't emphasize enough how fast we need to be. I'll install the transmitter that Toni gets for us. Marie, Mickey Ray, and Aly can go around, locate cameras, and set as many mics in places where we may feel things happen or in an office or meeting room. Everyone got it?"

They all nodded their heads.

"Okay, we move out at midnight. And Mickey, call Ronnie. She needs to ask Toni to meet us there at twelve-thirty hours. It should be late enough for everyone to be gone. We don't want to stay there more than ten minutes. If something goes wrong, we don't have a response time. Do we have any idea of a police response time?" James asked.

"The closest precinct is ten minutes away, but cars are patrolling all night long, so we can't say who or where anyone will be at that moment. In other words, I don't have an estimate of response time. Sorry. Just be quick," Aly answered.

"It's about time Ronnie and Mickey go pick up the equipment and get instructions on installing it. We'll only get one shot to do this. Let's do it right. Justice for Valerie might depend on this."

Mickey left to meet Veronica and Toni, pick up the equipment, and tell her where and when to meet them. They also told her that she would not be meeting the rest of the team and would remain inside the van at all times. Aly and Veronica would be there to help direct the team, and when the cameras came online would watch for possible threats. Toni accepted those terms. Mickey and Veronica returned to her house so Ronnie could select some suitable clothes to wear later that night. Even though she would remain in the van, they both felt she should wear dark clothes. They took some time to relax and talk while they were there.

Veronica poured two glasses of wine, and as Mickey sipped the wine, he looked out over the room. "I know what you said about this room, but do you think you'll ever remodel it or at least get new furniture?"

Mickey understood what she meant about not being ready to remodel her house. It wasn't the same thing but was he prepared to replace another girlfriend with this one? First Valerie, then Francine. Now, it may be Veronica. Furniture and girlfriends. It wasn't the same, but in a way, it was. You get comfortable with the look and feel of your favorite chair. Then you get a new one, and you have to get used to the new one. It was the same with girlfriends. Mickey also felt a bit ashamed that he was mentally comparing girlfriends with furniture.

He looked at Ronnie and felt feelings he hadn't felt since Francine. He liked Veronica. However, it's easy to get caught up in emotions when things are topsy turvy like they are right now.

They might not even be compatible when things get back to normal. He knew this, so he tried to reel in his feelings.

Enjoy the moment. He admitted that he was enjoying himself so much right now with this girl. Even so, he did feel a bit uncomfortable that he was here because of Valerie. Where was his feelings for her, he wondered. He knew he should move on. Valerie did when she left Bridgeton. He did when he fell for Francine. It was different now that Valerie was not just gone but dead. Val was gone forever, never to return. There was no going back, he thought, as he sipped his wine.

"Hey, Mickey. Earth to Mickey Ray!" Veronica was saying to him.

"What?" he said as he came back to the present.

"You were off in La-la land. I could see it. You weren't here," she said, also taking a sip of wine. "Do you want a refill?"

"No. One is enough. We don't want to be impaired when we go out. I wouldn't have had this one glass if we were going now. Yes, you were right. I wondered how right this is that I'm here with you, and Valerie's body is in the hospital morgue."

She looked down at her glass and hesitated before answering him. "If you were engaged to Valerie just before she was killed, I'd agree with your misgivings, but she left you. She moved here and made another life. You said yourself that you were no longer in love and only friends. You're here as a friend with a strong sense of loyalty and a past relationship. But it's nothing beyond that. There's no indication that she had found someone else, but she cut ties with you. You need to cut those emotional ties with her. There's nothing wrong with us being friends, or even more if it progresses to that level. We still have a bit of time before we need to get back. Would you like to take the Jag out for a spin again?"

"No, but thanks. Maybe when this murder case is solved, we can see where we lead. Let's relax until it's time to meet at the CIOF."

"Okay. I'll put on some music. What kind do you like?" she asked, getting up and heading over to an impressive sound system.

"I'll bet you don't have any old sixties rock, do you?"

"I'll bet I do!" she said. "I have a fantastic collection of old CDs that Daddy played all the time."

"Oh, my goodness. So did my Pop. Your choice. Anything's fine with me," he said.

They talked about their lives growing up while the CD player blasted old music. Finally, after a couple of hours, they knew they had to leave and get the equipment.

CHAPTER 9

Late Night Raid on the School

When Mickey and Veronica returned, they discussed what Toni had told them to do and how to hook it up, loaded everything into the rented equipment van, and left for the school.

They pulled into a dark area across from the school that was difficult to see from the street. Everyone wore dark clothing, gloves, and even masks to cover their faces and dull any reflection from exposed skin.

Alyssa checked their body cams so she could monitor their progress when they were inside the building. James located the electrical disconnect box and stood by, waiting for instructions to cut power. Marie said she would go to the security box and place the transmitter after the power was cut. James and Mickey would work their way through the building, looking for rooms where they might need video and audio. They were all in place, and Toni showed up outside the van. Veronica let her in and introduced her to Alyssa.

"Hello, Toni," said Alyssa.

"Hi," returned Toni. "I like all the computers lined against the wall. Are they all part of the surveillance?"

"Yes," answered Aly. "We agreed to let you be here if there is a problem and can advise. We'll have visuals from the body cams on this monitor," said Alyssa, pointing to one of the monitors. "The other monitors will show the areas the other team members will see as they work their way through the building. You sit down, be quiet, and don't disturb me. Understand?"

Toni nodded her head. "What'll Ronnie be doing?"

"Watching you," answered Alyssa.

Veronica was sitting silently in the corner. "If they need something, I'll be the runner from the van to deliver it," she said.

Toni blurted out, "Are you cutting the power?"

"Yes," said Alyssa.

"Good. That particular system has about a 45-second delay from any entry or power outage before it goes off and dials out distress to the monitoring company or police. You need to get in, disconnect the backup power, or you're caught. I suggest whoever is going in hit that first and fast," stated Toni.

"Why didn't you say that the other day when we first got the transmitter from you, Toni?" asked Veronica.

"Well, duh. We agreed that I'd be here. I didn't need to tell you then. If you backed out, it would have been your problem. Now, I'm here to tell you these things."

Alyssa turned and gave Toni an icy stare but didn't say anything. Already she didn't like this girl. She turned back to her screens.

"Is everyone in position and ready to go?" she asked over the comm unit.

"Copy that," came the answers.

"James cut power. Mickey Ray, unlock the door but hold off opening until the power is off," Alyssa ordered.

They heard the jingling and soft clanging of the bolt cutters taking the lock off the electrical cabinet, and they heard a clang as James pulled the cut-off lever down.

Meanwhile, Mickey was picking the door lock. Just as he unlocked it, they saw a car turn from a side street and start up the road toward them. Marie and Mickey stepped around the corner of the building, out of sight of the car until it passed. After the lights of the car disappeared from sight, Alyssa gave the order to go.

Marie and Mickey quickly entered the building. James scaled the fence at the loading dock area and placed a wireless microphone in the loading dock area. He placed another one on the wall near a personnel door and put the mic in an obscure location that would still pick up conversation.

Inside, Marie headed for the office where the large man had scolded her. Mickey headed in the direction of the outer door to let James inside.

Marie got to the room, and it was locked. She called for Mickey to help her unlock it. They didn't want to destroy anything that might alert someone that they had been there.

James ran off in another direction when Mickey let him inside and started running for the door back into the hallway, where Marie was trying to pick the office door lock. Mickey got there and used a lockpick gun to open the door. A lockpick gun was a small handheld device with a handle and small lockpicks used to snap lock cylinders open. Landlords used them to open locks on units when a tenant rekeyed or changed a lock without permission from the landlord or rental office.

The lock popped open, and Marie ran inside the door. As she was trying to open the door, they heard clicking inside. They knew the system was dialing a number to the security monitoring company, the police, or building owners.

"Open you, SOB," she cursed as she tugged at the edge of the door. Mickey moved up, grabbed the door, and yanked it open. Just as the ticking finished, the sticking door opened. Marie reached inside and pulled the battery out, pulling several wires loose in the process.

In the background, they could hear Toni saying, "You have to reconnect those wires. If you don't, when the power is restored, the system will default to a damage code."

"What does that mean?" whispered Marie.

"It will sound an alarm that the system base had been tampered with. Which means someone will know you're here," Toni said into the microphone inside the truck.

James cut in, "What's going on there?"

"Taking out the backup battery, I pulled some wires loose," Marie answered.

Toni spoke up again. "I can see it on the cam. You need to solder it back into place."

"We don't have a soldering gun here. Can't we just twist the wire together?" Marie asked.

Mickey told Marie to go out and help James place the mics and any extra cams they might need. He would stay and get this mess straightened out.

"Toni, what can I do?" Mickey asked.

"You need to solder the connection. I can see what happened. It pulled loose from the connection point. You don't have two wires to twist together."

Alyssa reached into a drawer and withdrew a tiny battery-powered soldering pencil. This should do it. We need to get it to Mickey," she said.

Before Veronica or Alyssa could move, Toni snatched the tool, opened the door, and bolted out of the van. She ran across the street to the entrance of the building. Mickey was waiting for her.

"You were told to wait in the van. Ronnie's the runner."

"What's your point? I'm here, and I know how that system works. Let me in to do it, or I'm outta here. I mean now. You don't have long before the default kicks in."

"What default?" Mickey said as they both took off for the office.

"That is a state-of-the-art system. It has backups and backups for the backup. As you already know, it has a backup battery, but if that's disabled, it defaults to damage mode, as I said back in the van. If that's disabled, it still sends a message out that it's been tampered with and still sends out an alarm call."

"Why didn't you tell us all this stuff in the first place?"

"Never mind that right now. Let's just get it fixed and get out of here. Sooner or later, someone will show up, and we'll be sitting ducks," Toni said, running behind Mickey.

She quickly soldered the wires back in place when they got to the office and then sighed. "While I'm here, let me take care of all the other stuff, like switching out the transmitter in the inline cable."

"If this system is so high tech, why is it still wired and not wireless, like all modern systems?" Mickey asked while she worked.

"It's the one area they skimped on. Wireless is more expensive and can be hacked. Another thing is, if you go wireless, you have people going around every few months to put in new batteries, and my guess is they didn't want anyone coming in here and seeing what's happening. You need to get into the secure area and physically tap into the cables when hard wired. There it is, we're done."

They heard sirens in the distance, and a voice came over their earbuds. Alyssa was saying, "Everyone out. The cops are on the way. Whatever happened, it wasn't in time to stop the call to the police. Are you done, Mickey?"

"Yes, Toni got the system hooked up. We're moving out. How's Marie and James doing?"

Marie's voice came over the earbuds, "We're almost done. And on the way out. James will restore power as soon as you're clear of the building."

James' voice came over the air. "Exiting the building now from the loading dock. Will go over the fence and stand by the power box, waiting on your sign."

Toni followed Mickey out of the building. She couldn't hear anyone's conversation because she had no earbud. Mickey stayed by Toni's side until James turned the power back on when they got out, and James and Marie were back in the van.

Outside the van, Mickey gave Toni a handful of cash. She looked down at it and back up at Mickey with disgust.

"I told you I didn't need money." She handed it back to him, walked away into the night, and disappeared.

In the dark area, they watched as a police car pulled up and parked at the loading area gate. A few minutes later, another car pull up. The man that had called Marie in the office got out and went to the gate. The man talked with the police officers for a couple of minutes, and they left. The man went inside the building, returned, and left in a few minutes. They let out a collective sigh and left.

CHAPTER 10

Conversation at the Factory

Mickey got up around five o'clock the following day and went to the command room. When he walked in, everyone was there drinking coffee.

"Hey, I didn't think the breakfast area was open until six each morning," he asked as he scanned the drab command center they set up in the old building.

"For everyone else, it isn't, but we're special," Aly answered. "Do you even know what was originally in this building?"

"Nope," Mickey answered. "Do we care?"

"I guess not, since it suits our needs."

Mickey poured himself a cup of coffee and went over to stare at the screens. "Did we get anything worthwhile last night? Is everything working okay?" he asked.

Alyssa turned to the screens. "He walked around and went through every room but didn't suspect anything. Since there wasn't anyone around, there was no sound. It was close, but I think we got away with it. Now, we'll be able to see everything they see and a few more places where they didn't have cameras, and we also have sound. Mickey, what happened to Toni after it was over?"

"I don't know, I turned around, and she was gone," he said, taking a bite from a donut.

"Do we need to worry about her?" Alyssa asked.

"I don't think so. She doesn't know any of us except for Ronnie and me. Ronnie says she's trustworthy."

"She's obnoxious, and I don't like her," Aly said.

"I don't either, but we don't need to like her as long as she doesn't rat us out," added Marie.

James said, "Now it's sit and wait. Wait and watch those infernal monitors to see what happens. What did Valerie see that scared her enough that she wrote in her journal in code?"

"That's why we're here, I guess," Marie said. "I have to get ready for school. Today, we are learning exotic spices," she said, rolling her eyes in mock disgust and laughing.

"Marie will be in school. Aly will be on the monitors. Aly, can you get in touch with Brian?" asked James.

Aly shook her head, "No. Brian is on the same mission that Bertrand is on. Bertrand is who I would have called if we didn't have Toni. They're both tied up for a while."

"Mickey, why don't you call Ronnie and ask if she can run some background checks on the staff at the school. Also, ask if they have someone that can hack into their computer system."

Mickey dialed Veronica, and when she answered, he realized it was still much earlier than her usual wake-up time.

"Hey Ronnie, sorry to get you up so early. We need some help here," he said.

"You what? Is this Mickey?" she said groggily.

"Yes. Good morning, sleepy head," he said cheerily.

"What time is it anyway?" she asked.

"It's about five-thirty."

"After what went down last night," she said, "I just got to bed. What do you want?"

"Can you run some checks on the staff at the school?"

"I guess, but I have to have a reason. I can't just ask our computer people to run backgrounds without reason."

"Can't you do it?"

"I can try, but I have other cases I need to work on also," she said, sitting up in her bed. "I must have some names and any information you have on them."

"Sorry, I don't have any names yet. I was hoping you could find out for us," Mickey said.

"I do have a few contacts at the police station. I can get someone to run deep background checks, but we can't hack into their bookkeeping system if that's what you're referring to."

"Okay, thanks, Ronnie. Yeah, I was hoping you had someone in the department to do that for us."

"No, we don't, but if we did, any evidence we found we couldn't use in court. At least not without a warrant to do that, and at this point, we don't have enough information to get a warrant."

"Sounds like a catch-22," Mickey said.

"That's exactly what it is. Sorry, Mickey, I've got to go to work now. I'll talk to you later."

"Okay. Thanks anyway. Have a good day," he said and disconnected.

"Sorry, Aly, Ronnie can't help us on this one. We are on our own to find out info," Mickey said.

James thought for a moment, then turned to Alyssa. "Can you get Brian or Bertrand to help us with the hacking?"

Alyssa shook her head. "I'll try, but they're both pretty busy and sometimes hard to get."

"Do what you can."

Marie left to get ready for classes. Mickey and James went to drive around the city.

James drove the rental car leaving the Humvee at the command building. He didn't want it to become too familiar around town.

"Who is Brian?" asked Mickey as James drove, making turns and measuring times and distances.

"He's our computer expert. His full name is Brian Duncan, but everyone calls him Digger because he can find anything and anyone on the internet. He's also an expert in searches on the dark web. I guess you could call him a 'black hatter.'"

"What's a 'black hatter?'" Mickey looked puzzled.

"By definition, a black hatter hacks computer systems, like government, banking, or even medical systems, for financial gain. Sometimes they do it purely for spite. Digger is a computer geek but never really did it for personal gain. He works as a freelancer."

"Hey, why don't we go by the school and take some time and distance measurements there? Who is Bertrand?"

"I'm headed that way as we speak," James said, turning a corner. "A freelancer in computer talk is just like a freelancer in any line of business. A freelance soldier is a soldier of fortune, more commonly known as a mercenary. I guess that's what I've been since I got out of the military. Although some of the missions I've been on, we were hired by the government. We provide them with plausible deniability."

"Okay, but back to Digger and Bertrand," Mickey prodded.

"Oh, yeah. Digger helps us by doing deep research, usually getting special equipment, munitions, and ammo from the deep web. Sometimes we need to get a person's financial records, maybe even medical records. You need a good hacker for that. Bertrand does very similar things. Digger and Bertrand can do internet searches, but Bertrand is a hardware computer specialist. Brian makes acquisitions and stuff on the dark web."

"But that's illegal," said Mickey sarcastically.

"And what we did last night wasn't? What we're doing now by bugging the place with cameras and audio. It could take months to get a judge to sign off on that, and whatever is going down would be gone. We go in, kick butt, and get out. Problem solved. Don't split hairs with me, Mickey. What we're doing now will land us in jail just as quickly as any black hatter hacking into a bank's records," James explained as he drove. "We don't steal money and only look at information to get justice for people."

They drove by the school, and James noted the odometer reading and time as he passed. He took a turn, pulled into a hidden driveway, and then backed out again. He returned to the school and took another road turning down the block. He did it repeatedly until he felt he had a good feel for the distances and was thoroughly familiar with the road layouts.

The phone rang, and it was Alyssa on the other end. "James, where are you?" she asked.

"A few blocks from the school," he answered.

"Get back here ASAP," she said. "You need to hear this."

"What is it?" he said as he picked up speed as fast as possible without attracting attention.

"Just get here. I have something you need to see," and she disconnected.

A few moments later, James pulled into the parking lot. Both men jumped out, ran into the lobby, and silently went to the command room.

"What's up, Aly?" they both asked.

Aly sat in front of one of the screens. She looked up at them and pointed to the monitor. "I ran it back to where it begins. This is in the room just inside the loading dock. Look at it."

They watched as men wrapped plastic around disassembled automatic rifles and placed them compactly inside boxes. After packing the various weapons components, they poured liquid wax over the entire package, sealing the weapons inside. Then they secured the tops of the containers. The lids were stamped and labeled with Florence City Flour Baking Company. "This container contains the finest ingredients in the world and is shipped to the most discriminating chefs worldwide."

Aly, James, and Mickey watched the recording.

"They're shipping weapons! Val was right. Now we need to find out where they're shipping them," said Mickey.

Aly backed against her chair and folded her arms. "They packed them, put the box on the back wall, and put other boxes on top. They're hiding it in plain sight.

"But that's not all. Take a look at this. I was going to wait and give it all to you at once when you got back, but it keeps getting better or maybe worse. Watch this," she said as she moved to another monitor and turned the volume up so they could hear the conversation.

It was inside the man's office that called Marie in a couple of days ago.

Another unidentified man walked into the room. The heavy-set man started talking.

"I told you earlier that something is off. I don't know what it is," Grant Littleton said.

"What's off?" the other man said.

Mr. Littleton kept talking. "I don't know. It's just a feeling. It's like someone has been here. I told you earlier that the power went off last night, and the cops showed up. I told them everything was fine, and they left. I came in and walked around. Nothing was missing or even moved that I could tell. I just had a creepy feeling that someone had been inside. Be on your guard. Walk around the building and check everything. See if anything is out of place, and keep an eye on that new girl. When the first girl leaves, I find it odd that this other girl shows up days later."

"She's okay," the man said.

"I don't know. I caught her on the monitors wandering around the building. She may have seen something."

"She didn't see anything. She's new. She was just looking around. Everyone does that when you get to a new place."

"Hey, the other girl that left. What was her name?" asked Littleton.

"Valerie Green."

"Yeah, Valerie leaves, and this girl shows up. That's strange."

"It's a coincidence, Grant. That's all!" he said.

"I don't believe in coincidence, Nick," Littleton said.

Mickey looked at James and asked, "Should we pull Marie out? What if they do a background check on her?"

"No, we don't pull her out now. Her credentials will stand up under anyone's check. They're solid. But we do need to warn her to be careful," James answered.

Aly was relaying instructions to Marie. "Listen, girl. They know someone was there last night. Be alert at all times. Do not, I repeat, do not misbehave. Stay under the radar."

"Got it," came the answer over the speaker.

They continued to watch the monitor, and Alyssa was switching from one camera to another so they could catch a glimpse of activities in all areas.

James asked Alyssa if she had contacted Brian and when could he be here.

"He can't. He can't be here, I mean. He'll do everything we ask from his present location. He's still out of the country and can't leave there until the mission's complete," she said.

"Ask him if he can hack into the CIOF's computer and pass control to us so we can see what's going on here."

"Sure, get me a satellite phone, and I'll make the call, but he might be busy now," Alyssa said.

"I understand. Make the call so we can get on his return call list," James said, handing her his satellite phone.

Aly spoke into the phone. "Brian, my friend. How's it hanging? No, not that! Pervert!" she said, laughing. "Okay, seriously, we need some help here. Can you hack into a computer from there for us? Yes, I know you can. I mean, will you do it for us? We need info."

She sat waiting for him to do something at the other end. "Yes, I'm still here. Sure. We'll try to get that to you. Okay. I'll call you back and give it to you. When can you get us in? That long?" she asked, shaking her head.

"Hey, if you can get back to me in an hour, I'll owe you big time. Yeah. No, I won't give you that. You heard me! Not on your life! Okay, Brian, Thanks tons, and yes, I'll still owe you, but not that much. Great. I'll be here waiting for your call. Out," she snapped the phone off and folded the antenna down.

James laughed and said to her, "Did he hit on you again?"

"Yep, he always does. He knows that I always say no, but it's a game we play. He'll get back to us in about an hour. We must run the plates on trucks coming and going at the factory. Once we get into their computer, we'll have a better shot at their staff."

Mickey's phone rang. When he answered, it was Ronnie.

"Hey Mickey, I've been trying to get some info for you about the CIOF. So far, all I can get is Grant Littleton, the owner, has an agreement with the local sheriff and the local court system that paroled inmates can get a job there to help them transition back into the workforce. He gives them monthly reports on their job performance. Sometimes they work their way up, others get good reports, and they can transfer to other states and work in similar programs. On paper, it sounds good," she said.

"On paper. Yeah, right. I thought one of the provisions of ex-cons is that you can't have contact with other ex-cons," said Mickey.

"Normally, that's the case, but not so with programs like this. It's like a work-release program. Theoretically, it's a good thing. The parolee has a job, learns some skills or training, so that he can support himself when he's permanently released. That's a real problem with parolees. When they can't get a job, they resort to crime to pay rent. It's a vicious circle for them."

"Why did the initial checks on him come back clean?" asked Mickey.

"Because he is clean. He has nothing illegal as far as the court is concerned."

The satellite phone rang, and James answered. "Hey there, Digger. Yeah. Things are going pretty good here. We have a dead girl, and we need to find out who and why she was killed. We need a complete staff list here and get into the company records. Can you do that for us? I'll turn you over to Alyssa. Can you guide her into the system for us?"

James moved over to where Alyssa was sitting in front of her computer. "Here she is, Digger. Thanks, Brian."

When James handed the phone to her, she took it and began typing on the keys. "Yeah. Hold on. Let it load. Sure I can. It's up now. Guide me through it."

She typed, then told him what was on the screen. Occasionally he asked what she was looking for, and then she would continue to type.

While Alyssa was working with Digger, James turned to Mickey, "We need to get into that warehouse area again before they ship that stuff out. We need to go tonight."

Finally, Alyssa got off the phone.

She suggested that she make a loop so they could go in undetected. James needed a loop for all areas they planned to go so Littleton or the security company wouldn't know they were there.

"Also, you need to disable the alarms while we're there," added James.

Alyssa nodded in response as she began recording a segment to be inserted into the system later.

Alyssa was printing out some background information on some of the staff members.

James picked up the sheets and started reading. Mickey took the ones that James passed over to him.

After a few minutes, Mickey looked at James and commented. "James, these are some terrible people. They aren't your ordinary B and E guys. A couple are cold-hearted killers. It looks like they got out on technicalities, inept representations, and maybe even some corrupt government officials."

"I saw that. We need more info on some of the guys. Some are lightweights, but a couple are true street thugs."

"Yeah," said James. "Aly and I will take a look and evaluate them.

"There isn't much you can do now," James said, "Why don't you give Ronnie a call and see if she can run some of these guys through her database and get a full report on them? All we have so far is basic information."

Mickey called, and Ronnie said she was wrapping it up for the day and would meet Mickey outside the police station.

Mickey pulled up at the station an hour later, gave her the list, and waited while she took it inside to pass it along to someone who ran searches for the detectives.

"I want a huge slab of cow," said Mickey.

Veronica laughed and said, "Why am I not surprised at that? But I agree. I'm tired of take-out pizza, Chinese, and bagged burgers from greasy spoons."

At the restaurant, Mickey looked at the menu and ordered his steak extra rare. Ronnie just shook her head. "Oh my gosh, Mickey. How can you stand it rare like that? I like it well done."

"Ronnie, well-done cooks all the taste out of it and makes a juicy steak dry and hard."

She shook her finger back and forth, "No. No. No. Silly boy! That seals in the flavor! And a nice robust red wine helps bring out the flavor."

Mickey smiled and picked up his glass, and when she lifted hers, they clinked them together in a toast. "On that point, we agree, dear lady!"

They talked and laughed and thoroughly enjoyed their time together at the restaurant. When they finished, they left and started back down the street. It had gotten dark while they were eating, all the street lights had come on, and the shops had turned on the lights in the shop windows showing off their goods. As they got closer to the coffee shop, they stopped, and she took his hand. They walked in and picked a seat at a small table. Henry walked over to their table, greeted them, and took their order. He was friendly but not as much as usual. Ronnie asked how he was doing and inquired about his son, Nicolas. He said that Nick was working at his other job tonight.

"Maybe when I retire," he said, "Nick will leave that other job and take over here. I don't know. We'll see. I'm very busy. Please forgive me." He turned and walked off behind the counter.

"Ronnie, do you know where Nick works at night?" Mickey asked.

"No. Why? I never thought to asked."

"Because, on one of the videos we got from CIOF, there was a Nick that Grant Littleton was talking to. Can you describe Nick?

"You said he was overweight. Was he balding with long, out-of-style sideburns?"

"Yes. That sounds like him. Are you sure it was Henry's Nick?"

"No, I'm not sure. I don't know what he looks like. I would be willing to bet it is Henry's Nick. We'll talk when we get out of here."

They sat, talked, ate the cinnamon roll Henry named after her, and had a cup of coffee. After leaving the coffee shop, they walked down the boardwalk. There was a slight salty breeze blowing as they walked hand in hand. They stopped and gazed at the stars.

He said to Ronnie, "Did you know there's a place you can send off, and they'll name a star after you? You can name it after a loved one or even your dog if you choose."

"I've heard that. I don't know who I would name one after, though. But it might be a fun thing to do sometimes, as a novelty thing."

He turned toward her and looked deeply into her eyes. The lights of the store reflected in her eyes. He gently took her chin and lifted her face to his. Pulling her close and embracing her, he kissed her passionately. He felt her quiver as he slowly released her.

Meeting his eyes, she smiled, pulled him close, and kissed him again. Breathing deeply, they continued walking down the boardwalk, hand in hand. After a while, they turned and headed back to the car.

Mickey called James at the command building and told him he would bring Ronnie back to the command center.

"Mickey, are you sure that is a good idea?" James asked.

"We aren't doing anything seriously illegal," he answered.

"Yet," James said. "We are shacked up in an abandoned building, stealing power and water, but other than that, we're just a bunch of armed squatters."

"I know. I think it'll be fine. If she doesn't feel comfortable, I'll take her home. Besides, she knows Nick in the video we watched earlier."

"Okay, but if we think she shouldn't be here, I'll take her home for you. You got it, bro?"

"Yeah, I got it," Mickey said and disconnected the call.

When they got to the abandoned building, and Mickey drove around the back to the roll-up door, Veronica didn't say a word. She just looked around at the facility.

"I've never been inside here," she said.

"Do you know this place," he asked.

"Sure, I know it. It was the Colonial Candle Factory. They made and shipped scented candles all over the world. Years ago, they even had a small candle shop in town, but eventually, it was bought out by a larger company, and they moved the operation out of this area. It was a shame. They employed about two hundred people in town," she said.

"We didn't know that," he said as he pulled the roll-up door back down and led her to the command room.

"Good evening, everyone," Veronica said as she followed Mickey into the room.

Alyssa and Marie looked at Veronica, then at Mickey with icy stares.

James took the lead and said, to Mickey and Veronica, "Okay, you're here. Ronnie, here are the rules. First, we don't usually let people in on our operations. We're only doing it as a courtesy to you. We are here to solve a crime, and don't follow your rules. If you understand that, we'll get along. If you feel that you can't keep our secret, we'll ask you to leave now. Can you agree to that?"

"I guess so, but I am a cop. I can't condone any illegal activity, even for moral reasons."

"We understand that, so we ask you to keep this location our secret. Will you do that?"

"For now. So far, all you have done is trespass, so I don't have to report it. That's a misdemeanor as far as the law is concerned," Veronica said flatly.

"Good. If you feel we are stepping too far out of your comfort zone, we'll ask you to give us the courtesy of leaving," James said.

"I can agree to that," she said.

Mickey said, "Okay, everyone, she knows Nick on the video. Alyssa, will you bring it up again, please?"

"Give me a minute," Alyssa answered. After a few minutes, she pulled it up and played it.

"I see what you mean," said Ronnie, "but all it proves is that Nicky knows or knew Valerie, and he knows she's no longer there. I'm sure he is in on the operation, but as far as a court or jury, that short scene or dialogue doesn't prove anything. I won't report anything I know here."

"We've decided we need to put trackers on the coming and going trucks. That way, we can keep up with them. Some will be legitimate shipments, and others will be carrying contraband. We need to figure out which ones are which. Marie has spent some time downloading files from the school computers since we finally accessed them. We can cross-reference them and get an idea of the network. Also, we need to run checks on the businesses at the destinations," James said.

"Mickey, you need to get some rest because you and I'll take a late-night run to the school to check out their inventory. Marie will go along to be a lookout," he added.

Veronica spoke up. "How can I help?"

"You can't. You may see something you feel compelled to report. Stay here and watch the monitors with Aly," answered Mickey.

"Look, guys, I may not be some super-soldier like you, but I'm a trained cop. I did go through the police academy, and I keep in shape. If all Marie is going to do is be a lookout, I can do that. I know it's not legal, but I don't have to say anything if you don't get caught. If we get caught, I'll say I was undercover," she said.

James and Mickey looked at each other. "I guess that's okay. Marie, you stay here, and Ronnie can go. Besides, it's a school night. We don't want you out too late," said James with a grin.

Marie flipped him a raised middle finger, then smiled back.

Ronnie sat down, still feeling a bit uncomfortable. Mickey offered to show her around the building.

CHAPTER 11

Late Night Run at the School

James, Ronnie, and Mickey dressed in black and were ready to check out the school again that night when Marie decided to help Alyssa watch the monitors.

They arrived at the school in the Humvee and checked in with Aly at the command room to ensure the alarm system cameras were on the loop, and all other areas were clear and turned off. They checked their earbuds to ensure they were all connected and entered the building.

They quietly walked in and headed for the back storage area. Mickey and James went straight for the box in the corner, where they saw the men pack crates with guns. Veronica stayed in the front, watching the street through a window.

Mickey and James methodically opened boxes and rummaged through the inventory, looking for anything that didn't belong. They found guns in some boxes, ammunition in others, and even several packages with a white powder they suspected were cocaine fillers. Those were mixed in with cooking ingredients. They snapped pictures of these and took samples in small baggies to analyze later. They walked around the bakery division, then to the packing areas, and saw several machines used to load food ingredients into boxes for shipment.

Veronica called over the comm units. "Hey guys, a car has gone pass the building several times. It's circling the block. It slows down every time it gets near us. I think someone knows we're here."

Aly's voice crackled over the earbuds. "Good work, Ronnie. We don't have cameras in those areas. Mickey, and James, you guys need to clear out NOW. We must have missed a camera or some warning system."

Mickey and James quickly restacked the boxes on their way out.

As they ran for the door, Ronnie called over the comm units, "Guys, get out NOW. Two SUVs are roaring down the road in this direction. I think the destination is here. Go! Go! Go! I'm right behind you! Go out the back, way over the fence. I'll follow. Don't wait for me. I'm good."

As Mickey and James scaled the fence, Ronnie came out the door. She jumped up and climbed to the top as they dropped to the ground. Veronica jumped over to the ground and slipped when she hit the ground. Spraining her ankle with the fall, she stumbled, got up, and favored her ankle as she ran.

Four men ran out as the back door opened, and shots rang out as they raised their guns and fired. Bullets whizzed around them, and James turned, pulled out a handgun, and returned fire, wounding one of the men. Mickey helped Veronica up from the ground just as a bullet caught her in the shoulder. She went back down with a thud and a loud cry. Mickey picked her up and slung her over his shoulder while James held the men back with return fire. They retreated amidst a crossfire of bullets, but the man James had hit no longer moved, while the other men crouched behind one of the transport trucks and kept firing.

When they returned to the Humvee, Mickey carefully placed Veronica in the back and put pressure on her bleeding wound. James had fired up the vehicle and roared into the street.

As James bounced around, turning corners, he asked Mickey, "Can you call Aly and have her call for a medivac pick-up?"

Aly's voice came over the comm units. "I hear it, but it might take thirty minutes or longer for a copter to get here, even if I do. Can't you pull over and secure the bleeding until they get here?"

"No!" yelled Mickey, "If she doesn't get care immediately, she'll bleed out. James, take us to the ER NOW."

James took another hard turn slamming Mickey against the door. Mickey tried to keep his hands tightly against Veronica's wound, but the blood was seeping through his fingers.

"Faster, James. I can't stop the bleeding."

James slammed the gas pedal to the floor, and the Humvee picked up speed, and he yelled back at Mickey, "Hold on. We've got one more hard turn, and we'll be there."

Mickey braced himself and tried to hold Veronica still as James drove. Finally, the last turn and the vehicle's tires screeched, and the Humvee slid sideways as it stopped in front of the emergency room's automatic door, which slid open. James jumped and grabbed a gurney at the entrance as Mickey slid Veronica out and onto it, still holding her shoulder to slow down the bleeding. Two men and a woman came running, followed by two more women. Mickey stepped aside and called out to them.

"GSW in the shoulder, no vital organs but severe blood loss. She's in shock. Stop the bleeding. Type O Negative blood, severe allergies to sulfa-based drugs. Into surgery now."

"Who is the department head? I want to talk to that person now," called James as he followed them inside the building.

Mickey hung back and then ran toward the entrance to the Emergency Room. When the SUV that had been following them slowed down, Mickey shot a few rounds into the side of the vehicle. When he fired the shots, the two men looking out of the windows dove down into the vehicle out of sight. Instead of slowing down further, they sped up and disappeared in the distance. He had to tell James so they could get out of there before the SUV came back with help.

Mickey stood in the shadows as he watched. He then noticed that he was covered in Veronica's blood. Mickey took a mental note of the license plate and called Aly while it was fresh in his mind, then returned to the ER and told James what he'd done.

"Good. We don't want to have a battle right here in the hospital. Let me talk to this guy and get out of here before they get back," James said.

James talked to a person who looked like he might be a doctor and was showing him a wallet with a gold badge inside. James flashed the wallet, then shut it and put it back in his pocket.

As he approached James and the man in the scrubs, he heard James say, "This is a case of national security. This incident did not happen. You will not call the police to report this."

The man protested, "It's state law, and I'm required to report all gunshot wounds. It's beyond my control, and I could lose my license if I don't."

James got right up in the man's face and said, "My badge trumps your hospital ID, and I'm telling you, you will not report it!"

"Can I see it to get your badge number so I can call in and verify you?"

"No, you can't. Even if you did call it in, they'd deny my existence, and you would have to give them your ID. When they get your information, you'll be fired for NOT cooperating with a federal officer with a valid ID. Do you understand?"

"But if I can't verify your ID, how do I know it's real?"

The man could see that James was getting madder by the second. "Because I said it's real, and I do have your ID," James said, and he yanked the man's badge and lanyard from around his neck. "Do you want to test me? If you do, and I'm real, I'll have you fired and all your certifications revoked for interfering with a national security detail."

"But what if you're not official?" he asked hesitantly.

"I'm tired of talking to you. You may call. AS YOU SAY, if I'm official, you'll be fired and lose all your creds. What do you think I'll need to do if you call and I'm an imposter?"

The man looked terrified by that possibility. "Umm, okay. I'll believe you. You won't hurt us, will you?"

"Correct. This never happened. Tonight was a regular slow night. Nothing happened. Someone will be here by morning if it's reported, and all hell will break loose. Either you let some criminals go or violate national security laws, and you'll probably get jail time. Your choice," James said and walked toward the doors leading to the emergency surgery area.

Mickey saw the man shaking with fear. He walked up to the man and opened his arms showing him all the blood covering his hands and clothing.

"Can you help me with this?" Mickey asked.

The man jumped back, "Are you shot also?"

"No, this is her blood. Can you lead me to a place so I can clean up?"

He regained his composure. "Sure, follow me, sir."

"Hey, don't be afraid. We aren't here to hurt you. We just want your first aid, and we'll be gone as soon as a chopper gets here to pick her up," Mickey assured the man.

"A chopper? Here? It'll be landing here?" he said in amazement.

"Yes, that's why we need your cooperation. Nothing in the records. You must talk to all the staff working tonight or involved with her care. Got it?"

"Yes, sir. I'll tell everyone not to say a word," he said insistently. "I've never heard of national security doing things like this."

"Of course, you haven't because we insist that word doesn't get out. We can count on you for that, right?"

"That was my boss," said Mickey, "and he can be a real stickler for total information blackouts like this. Now, lead me to an area where I can clean up."

Mickey washed his hands, and shortly after that, they heard a helicopter landing in the parking lot. Mickey and James took Veronica out and loaded her onto the helo.

As Mickey started to climb in, James grabbed him and pulled him back out. "You can't go with her, Bro. We need you here."

"But I need to...."

"You need to be here, Mickey Ray. She'll be fine. She's in the best of hands right now. We'll have news first thing in the morning. I promise," said James as he walked off.

When they got in the Humvee, they heard the sound of sirens blaring in the distance, getting louder as they got closer.

"Crap, Mickey, that doctor called the police. If he knows Ronnie, she'll be in serious trouble."

Mickey turned to James," And you don't think she's in trouble now? She's shot, for heaven's sake, and she might die. She didn't sign up for this. We did."

"Yes, she did, Bro. She signed up when she volunteered to go in the building and promised not to report us. Now, someone will have to do some serious explaining to her bosses."

Mickey sat back in his seat and kept looking to ensure they weren't being followed.

Alyssa was frantically on the phone and watching the monitors. The CIOF was swarming, men looking in every corner, opening boxes, and checking shipments.

"I want to know what they were looking for. What did they want? Were they feds or competitors looking to steal from us? I want answers, and I want them now! Look and look again," said Grant.

"I want a staff meeting first thing in the morning. I also want a list of everyone employed here less than six months," he said to one of the men.

"What happened, Alyssa? What did we miss?" James asked when he walked into the room.

"I don't know. They must have had a backup silent alarm system we didn't know about," she said.

"No one has a backup system!"

"Apparently, they did. That's the only thing I know. Maybe Ronnie ratted us out?"

"No," said Mickey. "She's the one that warned us that someone was on the way so we could get out. And she took a bullet while we were getting away."

"I have to take Mickey's side on this one, Aly. We screwed up big time on this one. Where's Marie?" asked James.

Aly answered, "I told her to get some shut-eye because she must show up for class no matter what happened. We need inside information that she might be able to get if she's onsite."

"Good. She'll need to be at the top of her game," James said, picking up a pile of papers on the table. "Did you have a chance to look over these background checks on the people at the school?"

"Only a couple. I checked out Grant Littleton, the owner, and that Nicolas guy. I also checked out his father, who owns the coffee shop that Ronnie and Mickey have stopped at for dessert. He's squeaky clean. We got him all the way back to childhood. He's clean as a baby's butt."

James shook his head at that analogy. "Sometimes a baby's butt is smeared in crap."

"Alright, smart aleck, you know what I mean," Aly said sarcastically.

"And you know what I mean."

"The old man's a good guy. The son, Nicolas, not so much. He's worked for Littleton for five years, much against his father's wishes. Daddy wants to retire and have Nick take over the family business. There is nothing big on Nick's record, but lots of small stuff since he was a juvenile. Minor shoplifting, vandalism, lots of traffic violations, and even some minor fender benders that he was mysteriously cleared of. As I said, nothing serious, but a lot of minor things," Aly summed up.

"What about Grant Littleton? What's his story?"

"He's a different story. Years ago, he was caught stealing from a restaurant he was working in and spent two years in jail. While there, he worked in the kitchen and studied cooking. He took online cooking classes and excelled at them. He began giving people cooking lessons and finally opened a restaurant when he got out. After a couple of years, he closed the restaurant, started a cooking school, and began selling the ingredients for his restaurant dishes. And the rest, they say, is history. The town paper wrote about him and his business a few years ago. He worked out a deal with the local and state officials to give parolees a job on a work-release program. After two years, if they pass his courses and work without problems, he gives them certification as a trained chef."

"How about the guy that approached Marie the other day? Was he included in the lineup as a parolee?"

"Yes, he is. His name is Rollo Cross, assault and robbery. Surprise, surprise. He gets the trophy! Did Littleton report him and send him back?" James asked Alyssa.

"What do you think? Littleton let it slide. He did call him in the office and reamed him out for his contact with Marie, but that was all."

Mickey listened to all of this, saying nothing. Finally, he asked Alyssa, "When will we know something about Ronnie?"

"I'll give them a call right now," she said, punching buttons on the sat phone.

James turned to Mickey, "How did you know what to tell the ER personnel when they came out to get Ronnie?"

"I read her file. Remember Dee checked her out, and her blood type was there and the note about her allergy to sulfa drugs."

"Now, you're beginning to impress me, Mickey," said James as he gave him a knuckle bump. "I didn't even think of that!"

Mickey shrugged his shoulders. Alyssa talked into the phone, disconnected, and placed the phone back on the table.

"She's out of surgery. Mickey, you saved her life by slowing down her blood loss. And the med unit did call the hospital back to get some information about Ronnie that Mickey gave when she came in. Whoever it was that both of you talked to at the hospital, you scared the crap out of him."

"Sure we did. The guy called the cops before we even left. We could have been caught if they hadn't had the sirens going."

"What are we going to do about it?" asked Mickey.

"We can immediately remove him from the area until this is over," James said.

"What do you mean, removed from this area?" Mickey asked.

"Someone will discreetly pick the doctor up and hold him until we solve this case. We don't know if he or someone in the hospital recognized Ronnie. We don't want anything to reflect on her when this is over. After this is over, he will be returned unharmed," James explained.

"And what will happen to Ronnie?"

"They'll keep Ronnie for another twenty-four hours and bring her back here," continued Alyssa.

Mickey sat down and let out a sigh of relief.

James and Alyssa looked at Mickey. Finally, Alyssa said, "Hey, Mickey. I admit I didn't like her at first, but she proved herself last night. She's now one of us. She's part of the team."

"Thanks, but I don't want her part of the team. I like her. I really like her a lot," he said.

"Are you saying you love her?" said Alyssa.

"No. I don't love Ronnie, but I like her a lot."

"Okay. If you say so, Mickey Ray," she said.

"Hey, don't make fun of me. I like all of you a lot. At this point, I'd take a bullet for anyone of you, but I don't love you. At least not like you're talking about," defended Mickey.

Aly stood up, walked over to Mickey, pulled him out of the chair, and gave him a big hug. "Yeah, I got it. We're brothers and sisters in arms. I understand."

"I'm wiped out. I'm going to try to get some sleep. Call me if anything happens that I need to know about." He walked out of the command room, went to his sleeping area, and lay fully clothed on the bedding.

CHAPTER 12

Morning Meeting at CIOF

Mickey tossed and turned restlessly across his bedding. Finally, he gave up and went back to the command room.

"You look terrible," said Aly when Mickey walked into the room.

"I feel terrible," he answered. "Don't you ever sleep?"

"I don't need much sleep," she answered.

"Everyone needs sleep," he said.

James walked in and joined in the conversation. "She's telling the truth. Some people need less sleep than others. Thomas Edison had a polyphasic sleep habit. He would lie down on a tabletop for a few minutes, nap, get up and go again. Aly does that." He looked at Aly, "Sitrep, please?"

Mickey knew James was asking for a *situation report* from Alyssa.

"They cleared out of the building about an hour later but left one person behind to watch out and make sure you didn't go back. I did take a nap after that, but I came and did a quick speed watch on the video. Nothing happened, but Grant was furious that someone got inside, even more so that you got away. You did get one guy. He's dead, and we don't have an ID on him yet. I made several calls to see if we could get a facial rec on him. No luck so far."

"Okay," sighed Mickey. "What do we do now? They'll be on high alert from here out."

James spoked. "We send out the samples and pics that we got last night. I got some pics of the serial numbers on a couple of the guns and samples of the powders. We should get results on those within a few hours after we get them out."

"How do we get samples out, and where did that helo come from last night."

"Need to know," Alyssa said, turning back to her monitors.

"Wait. What do you mean, need to know?"

"After what I have been through with you guys, you don't trust me enough to give me that info?"

"It's not just you, Mickey. None of us know that stuff. They don't tell us where things come from or where it goes. We're all on a need-to-know," she said.

"Sounds crazy to me," Mickey said.

"It keeps all of us safe that way. We can't tell the enemy what we don't know," James said.

"When will they bring Ronnie back?" Mickey asked.

"They'll drop her in later this afternoon, assuming she's doing well enough," she said as she continued punching keys on the keyboard. "Grant just came into his office. Quiet guys, let's listen to his meeting."

They saw Grant sitting at his desk with four men standing in front of him. Alyssa took a screenshot of each man. With a few keystrokes, she sent it off to some undisclosed location so someone at that location could run a facial recognition program to find out who they were. While Alyssa did this, Grant was talking.

"As you know, someone came in last night and went through the building. No matter what, it wasn't good. We wounded one of them last night. Go back to the hospital and find out who it was. If they admitted him, get him out alive and bring him here.

"Roger, you see to that. Hospitals are supposed to report gunshot wounds to the police. Go, and talk to hospital personnel. Ray, you and Sarge go through the plant and find out what they looked at. I want to know what they were looking for."

Roger asked Grant, "Do you think it was the police, FBI, or the CIA?"

"No. They would come with a warrant if they wanted anything more than a casual look. And to get a warrant, they would need probable cause. Same with the FBI, and the CIA isn't supposed to work inside the country. They don't break-in in the middle of the night. Anything they found would be illegal and not admissible in court if they did. No, this is some private group. Competitors maybe, but who?"

"Maybe someone is checking in to see what they're up against if they want to take us over," Roger said.

"Take us over? Whoever they are, they aren't invading another country. You don't do things like that if you want to take someone over. It's also not 1930s Chicago and the Saint Valentine's Day massacre."

Grant thought for a moment, then looked down at a pencil and rolled it in his fingers. Finally, he looked up at Roger. "You may be right, but I think we would have heard something through the grapevine. Or some inquiries from a customer."

Grant continued, "I think whoever it was, was looking for something specific. I want to know what! Grayson, go around and check out the backup system to see if it was tampered with. It worked last night, but now they know we have a workable system. We don't want them shutting it down in the future and coming back here a second time."

Grayson nodded and walked out of the room.

"What did Amir do with Nick's body?" asked Grant.

Roger answered Grant's question. "Amir took Nick's body down to the shoreline and dumped it off the rocks. It shouldn't be found. It'll only take a few days, and sea life will pick the bones clean, and if any remains wash up on the shore, he won't be recognizable."

"Okay, all of you, get out. Clean up any messes you see. Classes will be starting in a while. I don't want anyone at the school to know anything happened. Got it? Roger, tell Amir to come in here. I want to talk to him."

Roger said, "Got it, boss. I don't think he's back yet, but I'll tell him you want to see him. I'll get someone to go to the hospital and talk with them."

They all shook their heads as they filed out of the room.

Grant punched in numbers on the desk phone.

"Jason, have you completed a background check on that new girl in the class?" Grant asked.

The bug they placed on the phone lines came through loud and clear. "I'm still working on it," said the voice at the other end of the line. "There isn't a lot online about her."

"Well, that in itself is suspicious. Everyone has stuff about them online. How about checking accounts, social media, and educational background? Anything?"

"Nope, so far, she's squeaky clean," the voice said.

"Keep looking," Grant said and hung up the phone.

Alyssa turned to James. "He's right. When it comes to checking someone out, nothing is almost as bad as finding something bad. No one is spotless, and everyone has some kind of background. I'll get someone to fill in some blanks about Marie."

"One more thing, Aly. Why didn't the backup alarm go off the first time we were there?"

"Oh, that one's simple. We cut the power the first time. Apparently, the backup system didn't have a battery backup. I've never had a case where someone had a backup system. But if you remember, someone showed up even with the power out, so maybe it did go off. I'll keep an eye on the monitors. Maybe we can see if they had a second set of cameras and where the sensors are located. Grant told that guy to check the backup system. He didn't tell him to check the main one. Even if he does check the main system, he won't find anything unless he checks the incoming cable above the drop ceiling. That's where we put the inline transmitter. It's well hidden."

"All we can do is sit and wait until we get more answers," James said.

"I'll watch," she said, turning back around. "I'll keep a watch on Marie, too. They might be getting close. We need to check her background and ensure we didn't overlook something that might raise a red flag."

Aly watched as Grant walked through the plant. He walked over to various boxes and stopped and talked to employees. Some he greeted with a friendly smile. Others he pulled aside and spoke to them in low tones so others couldn't hear. Sometimes he would gesture by pointing around the room or at a box or crate in a corner. One employee left the room after Grant spoke to him. Room by room, he proceeded through the plant. After Grant left, the employees seemed a bit more on edge. Grant returned to his office, locked the door then left the building.

Aly could tell by how everyone moved that Grant had alerted everyone. She knew that the risk had escalated exponentially. They had to be more careful.

Mickey was sitting silently during all of this. He turned to Aly and asked, "Do we have a tracker on Grant?"

"Not on his car, but if he powers up his phone, we can track him that way," she answered.

"Do it," he said.

"Already done," Alyssa answered. Aly pulled up a screen showing a map with a small red dot moving down a road.

Mickey picked up the printed pages when the printer began buzzing and dropping paper into the paper tray. He shuffled through them and handed them to James.

James read the sheets, and as he finished, he handed them to Aly.

They're seasoned criminals with transition jobs or work release programs from the city and state penal systems. Sarge was the one exception. He was an ex-military gunnery sergeant who had served a five-year sentence for stealing government equipment and was given a dishonorable discharge. He went to work for Grant directly out of incarceration. Roger served eight years of ten years for smuggling guns over state lines. Grayson and Ray were sentenced for car theft and running an illegal chop shop. Amir had no background. It looked like he was here illegally, so he had no rap sheet yet.

"Quite a motley crew," Aly said. "Hey, Grant's stopped in town. He'll have his phone, so we'll know exactly where he's going. If we had a car tracker, we could only track that."

Alyssa called Mickey back to the monitors in a couple of minutes, saying, "It looks like he went into that address. It shows up as a clothing store."

"Maybe he's going to pick out a new suit," said Mickey sarcastically.

"Do you really believe that?" Aly answered.

"Didn't you note the sarcasm in my voice?" he said.

"Yes, I did, and I'm trying to get into their computer system as we speak. It'll take me a while, but I think I can do it. I shouldn't need Digger on this level. Small businesses are easy to hack."

Mickey knew she was referring to Brian Duncan, nicknamed Digger, that did a lot of computer hacking for them.

Meanwhile, Mickey went back to reading the computer reports on the employees.

Finally, Aly called to Mickey, "Hey, Mickey. I'm in the computer system at the men's clothing store. You wouldn't believe what I found out!"

"Try me," he said, looking over her shoulder at the screens. "Oh, yes. I see it. The owner is one of Grant's graduates from his prison release program. Instead of going into some type of restaurant, it looks like he opened a clothing store. Can you dive deeper into their system?" Mickey asked.

"Yep, I'm working on it," she answered. His system isn't nearly as secure as Grant's system. Okay, I'm in the bookkeeping part of the system. Whoa......Look at this, Mickey!"

He leaned over Alyssa's shoulder to look at the screen. He could see numbers in the millions of dollars. He also saw addresses of pick-ups and drop-offs.

"This is a copy of the entire network that Grant's servicing. His suppliers and customers, and transfer points," said Mickey.

James said, "Mickey, we're here to do one thing. That is to get justice for Valerie. We can't take down an entire network of gun runners and drug dealers. We need to keep on point, bro."

"As usual, you're correct. Maybe we can look into that later," Mickey stated.

"Maybe, but not today. Let's see what we can do right now," added James.

Grant returned to his office at the school, and Aly listened as he picked up the phone on his desk. "Roger, get Marie Alverez out of class and bring her in here," he said and hung up the phone without another word.

Aly pulled up the picture on the monitor and opened it to full-screen view.

Roger escorted Marie into Grant's room, backed out, and closed the door. Grant motioned for Marie to sit down. He sat silently, looking at her.

Marie wasn't easily intimidated, but she tried to look scared and began smoothing her dress. She moved around in the chair and rearranged her hair to look uncomfortable and nervous.

As they watched, they knew it was an act. Marie had stared down men much more threatening than Grant. If it were a fight between them alone, he would surely end up on a coroner's table.

"Miss Sanchez. Who are you?" he said slowly and deliberately.

"What do you mean," Marie answered with her fake accent, looking confused and repositioning herself in the chair. She was moving so they could get a clear look at Grant's face.

"I mean, Miss Marie Sanchez, who are you, and why are you here?"

"I'm sorry. I don't know what you mean," she answered, reaching up to her hair to ensure the earbud was not visible to him.

He picked up the phone. "Roger. Come back in here and bring someone else with you," he said and put the phone back on the receiver.

He sat still, staring at Marie until the door opened, and Roger and another man entered the room. It was the same man that had accosted her the other day in the parking lot.

She turned so they could get a good picture of both men. Grant began talking again.

"Miss Alverez, or maybe I should address you by your real name. Marie Sanchez. We know who you really are. We also know that you've never been to Mexico, so you may drop that act. What we don't know is why you're here. Tell me. Who do you work for?" He sat in silence. "We know that you were part of an elite military team, and now you are part of a mercenary group. We… no, I want to know who you're working for and the names of your group members."

She sat silent, looking at him in blatant defiance.

"If you must play it this way, Miss Sanchez, you'll see we aren't a group of idiots here. We also have people. We have people who know how to use the internet and dive into the dark web to get information. We know you are here for a reason, and I want to know what that is. We found out who you are and will find out who you are working with. If you are wondering how we found out, everyone has fingerprints.

"Now, if you decide not to talk, they'll make you glad to answer all my questions," he said, motioning to the two men standing behind her chair on each side.

He looked up at the men, "Take her away and tell me when she's ready to talk. And make it hurt. She will beg you to stop. You may bring her to me when she pleads to answer my questions, and I warn you, she's very dangerous. Watch yourself when you take her away."

Marie leaned forward and spat in his face.

He reached up and calmly wiped the spittle off his face, then got up, walked around the desk, and slapped her. He said, "You're a very beautiful little lady, but I will not stand here and let anyone spit in my face. Do you understand me?"

She spit at him again and stared at him with fire in her eyes.

He raised his hand to slap her again, just as the goon did that tried to slap her in the parking lot.

She launched out of the chair like a rocket and drove her body into Grant's chest, knocking him against the wall. Both men grabbed her arms from behind as she did this in a futile attempt to subdue her. She reversed her movement and pushed herself away. Grant was now gasping for breath against the wall. As the two men also stumbled back, Marie pulled herself free, spun around, and punched Roger in the gut. She then turned toward Rollo Cross and caught him with an uppercut to the chin, and he dropped to the floor unconscious as his head cracked on the concrete. Roger tried to keep himself from falling, and she kicked him in the groin, then turned back to Grant. He was looking at her, surprised and afraid for his life. She stepped over to him and drove her foot with all her weight into his face. She felt the cartilage in his nose crunch, and his jaw cracked under her kick's power. He let out a loud cry of pain.

She bent down toward the bleeding pulp of his face. "I am Marie Sanchez. No one, I mean, no one, lays a hand on me without my permission. Do you understand me?"

He just stared at her with one clear eye. His other eye, covered in blood, was streaming down his face from her footprint on his forehead.

She raised her hand to slap him.

He nodded his head. Yes, then mumbled something, but she couldn't understand him with his broken jaw.

She got up and walked over to the door. As she grabbed the doorknob, she saw a cardboard door hanger like they have hanging on hotel doors. On the card was printed the words, "Do not disturb." She took it off and hung it on the outside of the door as she walked down the hall out to the parking lot. She put up her middle finger to the camera as she walked to her car.

Aly, James, and Mickey heard and saw the whole incident. They all smiled as James calmly said, "That's my girl, Marie." And they all "high-fived" each other.

CHAPTER 13

Veronica Comes Home

When Marie got back, they talked about the repercussions of what happened. They decided to keep the recordings going, but when Marie returned, they closed the doors and headed for a restaurant outside the city limits of Florence. It would be less chance of being recognized as a group.

Mickey didn't have any experience the others had in actual combat situations, so he sat and listened.

Marie was the heroine of the party. She took long drinks out of her bottle of beer. "I think we underestimated them," she said to no one in particular.

"I agree. We never thought that he would take fingerprints and have a way to run them," answered Alyssa. "Grant visited a clothing store in town today. I hacked into the security system and his computer. They have a pretty state-of-the-art computer set up. The guy who works it is a gadget freak but not so sophisticated. Some people think that a great system is more secure, but you have to know computers and the ins and outs to use it to its fullest. I can only guess the operator knows someone that knows someone and is able to run your prints.

"Whoever it is, knows his stuff because we had a good cover for you that would pass any average background check. Also, whoever did the background check may have had facial recognition. That can overcome a lot of fake information we put out there. Sometimes, it just happens. It's the other side of the coin when we check someone out. Facial recognition software and DNA samples are run through private labs. Who knows. I can handle most stuff, but I call Digger if I need serious help. Maybe they have access to a person like Brian."

"I'm just glad it was a small office. It may not have gone down that easy for me if they could have backed off and regrouped. Or even had time to draw a weapon," Marie said.

"I think you did great. You're fast as a snake," said Mickey.

"Yes, she is," agreed James. "She's faster than lightning. I've never seen anyone that could move faster than her. Her speed is her superpower."

Aly just sat and grinned. Each person on the team had a "superpower." Everyone, that is, except Mickey. The closest thing he had to a superpower was his passion for good and justice and his desire to help people in trouble. His biggest weakness was his reluctance to kill. They looked after Mickey because he was a good person.

While the others ate and drank their beers, Mickey sat in a corner. He had nothing against an occasional glass of wine and sometimes a glass or bottle of beer, but today he wasn't in the mood. He no longer loved Valerie. He knew that, and she was gone. But she didn't deserve to die and not be murdered. He cared for her like he would any other person. He wanted justice for her and her memory. The team would continue investigating and doing whatever was necessary to get justice for Valerie. Veronica was injured because of him, and he wondered if he had become a curse to those around him, to anyone he cared for.

"Hey, Mickey," called James. "What's wrong? You're not saying much tonight. One of our own took down the enemy and came home. It's worth celebrating. Come on, join us, Bro!"

"Yeah, sure. You're right. A toast to Marie," Mickey said, raising his glass containing a soft drink.

His cell phone rang. It was Veronica. She told him she was waiting for him at the command building. When he passed the word to the others, they all took the last drink and returned to celebrate the return of their newest team member.

When they got back, they immediately went to the command room, where Ronnie waited with a medical escort. They saw men meeting in Grant's office on the monitors. Aly went to Ronnie, hugged her, told her she was proud of her, and then went to the monitors. Marie hugged Ronnie while Mickey and James talked to her escorts.

"How's she doing?" James asked.

"She's doing great. She lost a lot of blood, but we topped her off. She's drugged up now, so she's in no pain. Nothing vital was hit, and she'll need a lot of rest, but she'll be fine. She's a trooper. I gave her a bottle of antibiotics to take until they're gone. If she starts running a fever or you see anything that doesn't seem right, give us a call, and we'll give you more instructions. She needs rest and a few days off," said one of the men. The other stood almost at attention, looking around the room.

"We appreciate what you did for her," said Mickey.

"Just doing our jobs, Mickey. Good luck, and we hope you don't need our services again."

They all shook hands, and the men left the room and boarded the helicopter parked outside in the back of the parking lot.

"Oh, my God, Ronnie," said Mickey. "I was so worried about you. They wouldn't let me go with you on the helo and wouldn't let me call. They said it wasn't allowed."

"They told me the same thing. I couldn't call you either," she said.

Mickey could tell she was drugged. She talked slowly and with a bit of a lisp in her voice. "Let me take you to an area you can rest," he said as he helped her to her feet.

James looked over at them and said to Mickey, "Hey, Bro, why don't you stay with her for the rest of the night. Nothing is going on here that we can't handle. Grant and the rest of his crew are having fits over Marie. They're on the warpath and claiming they'll hunt her down and kill her. We need to stay and monitor their actions. We'll call you if we need you. Get some rest also if you can."

"Thanks, James. Ronnie needs some rest," said Mickey. He helped Ronnie to her feet, and they walked slowly to the room where he and James bedded down.

When Mickey got Veronica to the bedding area, she almost collapsed. Mickey sat down beside her. In a few short minutes, he laid down at her side.

James shook Mickey awake. "Come here. We've been going over the recordings made while we were at dinner celebrating Marie. You need to hear this," said James.

Mickey went down to the command room and sat at one of the monitors to watch the recording. Grant had bandages almost all over his face. He had blood-soaked gauze on his forehead, and his nose was stuffed full of cotton with a bandage over the bridge of the nose. His jaw was wired almost shut, making it hard to understand what he was saying.

Aly explained to James and Mickey what had happened at the factory, "We fast-forwarded past the foul language as they left for the hospital. This is where it picks up when they got back. There was a flurry of activity after he left other plant areas. We checked and noted the places where they had contraband, such as weapons and different food ingredients. When we can, we'll check those out. They could be simple, innocuous spices for legitimate shipments or concoctions like drugs. We don't know, but we'll check them out when we can. This is what we thought you would want to hear," said Aly as she checked the views and turned up the volume on the speakers.

Grant, Roger, and the man they deduced was Amir was in the room. Amir was the one person Aly had trouble finding background information about. Aly suspected that Amir was smuggled in from a middle eastern country.

"I don't know who she was, but I'll kill her if I ever see her again. I mean it, Grant," said Roger.

"Yeah," came the muffled sound from Grant's puffed-up and bloated mouth. "I'll be glad to do that one myself. I'll stuff her head in a box and personally drop her body in the ocean."

Amir said, "Do you think she has any connection to that Valerie girl?"

Grant shrugged his shoulders. "I don't know. Maybe."

"The Marie girl showed up here right after getting rid of that Valerie girl. Valerie did a lot of poking around when she was here. I'm not sure, but I think she even took pictures of stuff."

"What stuff?" asked Grant.

"I don't know exactly what, but she always took pictures of everything. She took pictures of the classroom and the food she prepared. She took pictures of other people in the class and their dishes."

"So? What's wrong with that? Everybody takes pictures today. It's what people do. They take pictures," Grant said.

"I know, but she took more pictures than everyone else put together," Roger said.

"Okay, go back and check her out and see if there's any connection to Marie Sanchez," said Grant.

"Sanchez must be staying around here, somewhere. Check hotels, then check out the car she was driving. Check all the rental car companies and car dealers to see if she bought the car locally. **FIND THAT GIRL**." Grant mumbled. "I want her head on a platter!"

Roger said, "We can get pictures of her from the videos of the security system. The same with the car. We can get license plates and run them."

"How long ago was this recorded," asked Mickey.

"About an hour ago," James answered.

James turned to Mickey and said, "We got all the cars at the same car rental. When they find the cars, they can trace them by the factory-installed GPS to this building. We need to clear out NOW. I'll get Ronnie up and start gathering up equipment."

"Where can we go?" asked Mickey.

"I don't know, but we can't stay here," said James getting up and heading for the door.

James went to get Ronnie. He got her up and helped her into the van. While doing that, Aly and Marie disconnected the computer equipment and began putting it all in the back of the van. After taking a load of equipment, James lifted the hood.

"What're you doing?" asked Mickey.

"He's disabling the GPS," said Aly. "That's how they'll find us if they haven't found us already."

"Yep," said James as he clipped some wires. "We just figured that out."

Aly and Marie began almost running with the equipment. Mickey picked up one of the weapons and went to a window in front of the building. He took out his phone and dialed James, who was in the back loading area where all the vehicles were parked inside the building.

James slammed the hood on the van just as a car pulled into the front of the building lot.

They had ensured that nothing outside would give away their presence to outsiders. Grant's men knew they were inside and weren't hasty in getting out of the vehicle.

Very slowly, the driver's door began to open. Mickey broke a window, placed the rifle on the steel base of the frame, and put a bullet in the side of the front window to warn the driver not to exit the vehicle. The door slammed shut.

James said over the phone, "Was that you that fired?"

"Yep. I also have some extra clips with me. Get the others out in the van."

"You may need more clips. I've got plenty in the back of the Vee. Hold them off while I help them get the rest of the equipment into the van. Then we can drive out of here. I'll come up there, and we'll cover their getaway. We'll leave your rental car here and report it stolen later."

"Got it. I'll hold them off until you get here."

Mickey fired two warning shots in front of the car. Two men had exited the car on the side, away from the building. When Mickey fired again, they jumped and crouched behind the car and returned fire also with automatic weapons. He thought they would stay inside, or get out, hit the ground, and remain immobile. One started firing while the other moved behind the car to fire simultaneously. Soon an SUV pulled behind the first car. It pulled up, almost touching the bumper. Men got out on the car's opposite side and formed a firing line.

Mickey quickly aimed a few rounds into the hood, hoping to disable the car's engine. He repeated the action in the SUV in the rear, and then he shot out all the tires.

At least Ronnie and the girls were safe. He felt that he could hold them off himself.

"Where was James?" he thought. His phone rang.

"I'm coming around the far end outside on your right. When I get there, I'll start firing. When I start, the van will come out from the left side of the building. We will each start shooting to draw their attention to us and from the van driving away. When they get away, you keep firing, and I'll move back to the Vee and pull it around to the side. There's a door on the side of the building. I'll let you know when I'm there. Remember, the Vee is fully armored and will repel their small arms rounds. Just don't stop running until you get inside."

Mickey kept firing bursts of bullets to keep their heads down, and when they tried to look up, he would discharge another blast. He listened between the gunshots for the Humvee moving to the building's side. Finally, he heard it slide to a stop. And his phone rang. He didn't answer because he knew it was James.

He fired another round of bullets into the side of both vehicles, then took off through the room and into the hallway heading for the side of the building and the exit door where the Humvee was waiting for him. When he saw the door, he opened it just far enough to look around. He looked to his left and saw the men starting to raise their heads to get a look his way. He sprayed the area around the cars, and they all dropped back down. He heard James yell for him to run to the Humvee and get in, and when he saw the back passenger's door open, he began running.

As he ran, he held the gun outward in his left hand and sprayed more bullets toward the cars. He also saw James with his arm out the window, shooting to cover him as he ran for the Vee. As he got near, he dove into the Vee, and James stepped on the gas, causing the door to slam shut. He reached for another ammo clip in the back of the Vee and pressed it home in the gun. As James pulled out of the building parking lot, they heard and felt the pinging of bullets bouncing off of their escape vehicle.

James looked over at Mickey, dry heaving in the back seat. "Are you okay, Bro?"

"No," he shouted. He turned toward the door and looked out the thick bulletproof glass.

"Where to now, boss," James said calmly.

"I don't know," Mickey answered.

CHAPTER 14

Moving to a Campsite

When Mickey answered his ringing phone, it was Marie, no longer using her Mexican accent.

"Mickey, we're outside of town in the parking lot of a park. I think it is a picnic and public camping area."

"Yes. I know the one you're talking about. How's Ronnie doing?" he asked.

"She fine. Sort of. She's still in and out of it. We keep pumping her full of drugs to manage her pain. She did wake up enough to know we were pulling out and insisted that we go to her house. Do you think it'll be safe to go there?"

"Only as a layover," said Mickey. "We don't have any indication that they know it was her who was shot in the facility last night. We don't want to take any chances. Stay where you are. We'll be there soon, and I'll lead you to her house."

Mickey disconnected the call and instructed James where to go. As they drove, Mickey took stock of the munitions in the Humvee. When they got to the public campground, they moved to the back of the camping area.

"Hello, Mickey," Veronica said in a drug-induced state. "Are we home yet? I need a nap."

"No, we aren't there yet. Are you sure you want us to bring the war to your house?" Mickey said cautiously.

"I don't care. I think I'm hurt. Am I bleeding, Mickey?" Ronnie asked with a slur in her voice.

"No. You're not bleeding. You'll be fine, but we need to get you back into a bed to rest. Can we go to your house to regroup?"

"I don't care. Let's go to my house. I want to take a nap," she said and drifted off.

Alyssa and Marie were talking nearby. Mickey joined them.

"How's she doing, Mickey?" James asked.

"She's drugged up right now. She said we could go to her house for a while."

Aly said, "She may have said it, but she's on some powerful painkillers. She doesn't know what she's saying. She may not even remember telling us to go there when she comes out of it."

"I agree with Aly," said Marie.

Mickey thought for a moment. "You're both right, but we need somewhere to go for at least a couple of hours. The police will soon be at the scene, and the goons will be staking the roads."

"No, they won't. The building we were in was out of town. Unless someone heard the gunshots, those guys wouldn't report it. It may be hours or days before anyone knows about it," Alyssa said.

"We can stay at Ronnie's house until the heat dies, then move out again. You follow me. I know a back way to her house that won't have much traffic."

Mickey and James got back into the Humvee, and Mickey gave him directions to Ronnie's house. They went into the house, and Mickey took Ronnie to her bedroom and put her to bed. James stood lookout outside the house. Aly and Marie set up some essential equipment to have eyes and ears in the school facility.

As soon as they came online, they saw Grant throwing things at the wall and screaming at some of the men at the plant. His bandages hadn't been changed and were dirty and blood-stained. He ranted and screamed that the men were idiots.

"Tell Amir to get back in here and get on that computer and find out who these people are!" he screamed. "Right now, I don't know who we're fighting or why. All we know is that Alverez or Sanchez girl is part of them. And this is some professional group of mercenaries. Why are they doing this? What did I do to them?" he screamed at no one in particular.

"Get out of here, and find those people. I want answers. Do you understand?" he called out.

Several men nodded and promised to find Marie and the men hiding her.

Amir came back into the room and stood while Grant calmed down.

"How did you find out about Marie? What's her name?" Grant asked.

"I told you already," Amir answered. "The Dark Web."

"Yeah, I know that, but have you found out who she's working for?"

"She moves around. Kind of freelances."

"What do you mean she freelances?"

"She doesn't work for any one team. She's semi-retired. She specializes in undercover work."

"Like what she did here?"

"Yeah."

"Why? What's she looking for? I bet it had something to do with that Valerie girl," said Grant.

"We found out she's worked for several teams over the past couple of years. The latest is the team led by Alyssa Hendricks."

"Who's that?" Grant asked.

"The military trained her. She was a lookout and spotter for black ops teams. Now she runs her own company of mercenaries out of Virginia Beach, Virginia. Sanchez helps her on some missions."

"A woman running a black ops mercenary team?"

"Yeah, and she's good at it too. She has a full complement of men and puts up drones and surveillance equipment. She used to go in on the ground, but now she sits in an oversight position and directs the action."

"Do you think she is surveilling us now?" asked Grant.

"Hard to tell. And we still don't know why, if she is. It could be that Valerie girl. We've had to eliminate several people in the last year or so. Maybe we just eliminated the wrong person. That's all," Amir said, shrugging his shoulders.

"You say that like it's stamping out a bug or something."

"Yeah, well, it kind of is like that. They're something that gets in our way. It hurts business."

"You are one cold Mother, Amir," Grant said, shaking his head.

"Isn't that why you brought me here, to handle unpleasant things like, umm…Let's see. Like pest control?"

"How many people have you gotten rid of for me in the past twelve months."

"Not that many. Let's see. There was that Valerie girl. Then, the guy in packing that was stealing products from us, and that's it. No, wait, there was that cop last year."

"I shot him because he was snooping around and getting close. He didn't know what we were doing, but he would have found out if he had stayed with it, and we couldn't take the chance."

"What was that guy's name? He was a detective, I think," Grant asked. "It was some whiskey's name, I think. I think Daniels, no, it was Walker."

"No, it was Morgan, like the Rum," said Amir. "I shot him in a drive-by. It was easier that way."

When they heard that, they all looked at each other. Mickey knew he would have to tell Ronnie. She needed to know. But he decided to wait a few more days to give her some healing time.

So far, they were safe, but they knew they wouldn't be safe long. James began downloading maps from the internet and started looking for public lands that had open space. He found a piece of public land with remote areas that they could use as a command center.

Looking at one of the downloaded maps, he showed Mickey where they planned to set up the new command center.

"How will we get internet service out there?"

"Satellite dish," James replied. "We go into the next town, buy a generator, get a satellite dish, and Aly can set it up. She knows this stuff."

"Can we even do that?" Mickey asked.

"Sure, they do it for campers all the time. Haven't you seen those sat dishes mounted on the top of campers?"

"I guess so. I never paid a lot of attention to them. But where do they sell them?"

"At camping stores. If we leave now, we can be back by dark and be set up by morning right here on the map," he said, pointing to a grassy area.

"We also need more camping gear if we hide in the woods. The factory had bathrooms, and our sleeping bags were fine, but out in the weather, we need more."

"Yep, we can get it all at a camping store. Everything we need, even civilian-made MREs," James said.

Mickey knew that an MRE was a "meal ready to eat." They were tasteless but generally high in protein. And they required no refrigeration.

"Okay. The others can meet us there. I don't know if Ronnie should be left here, and it certainly isn't good for her to be bouncing around in a vehicle."

"Right, but we can't leave her here. She isn't safe. We should take her with us," said James.

When James went to Aly and told her what he and Mickey had decided to do, she agreed that it was a good move, and they would meet at a place in the forest. They each had SAT phones and could hook up there.

James and Mickey left the others and started for the next town closest to the area they planned to camp. Mickey went to the store to get sleeping gear and food supplies, and James went for a generator and gas cans. They met at the front of the camping supply store and loaded the gear.

They talked on the way back to the park.

"What do you think about Amir killing Ronnie's father?" James asked.

"Right now, I don't know what to think. Amir also admitted to killing Valerie."

"It's dark. I'd hoped we could get back before dark," James said.

"Yeah, I know, but things just don't always work out the way we plan, does it, James?" Mickey said sarcastically, still looking out the window.

James could tell Mickey was still upset, so he didn't respond.

Mickey called Marie on the satellite phone when they got to the forest turn-off.

"Hey, Mickey. We are about two miles inside the forest beside a small stream. Keep your lights on so we can see you coming down the road. It gets narrower and rugged as it goes deeper into the woods. The van almost didn't make it here. When we leave, we may have to leave it."

Mickey answered, "It's already getting rough. Can you shine a light or something so we can see you also?"

Mickey and Marie talked as James drove on. After about ten minutes, Mickey saw a small light swaying back and forth.

"I see your headlights. I'm waving a flashlight," she said.

"I see it," he said, and James continued for about a hundred yards, pulled beside the van, and parked.

James took a battery-powered lamp and set it on the ground to unpack the supplies when they got out. They left the interior lights on in the van and the Humvee and unloaded the generator first, then James poured some gas and started it up. Mickey pulled out a string of electric lights onto the ground. After about an hour, they had set up camp.

Mickey checked on Veronica. She was awake but still in pain, but she refused to take any more painkillers because she wanted to be alert when Mickey returned. Aly and Marie helped James and Mickey set up camp as best they could. They would rearrange it better in the morning when the sun came up.

James collected some firewood and built a fire, and they sat around the firelight and talked about the day.

James, Alyssa, and Marie slept on the ground. Mickey slept in the van beside Veronica. When he awoke, he sat up and stared down at Veronica. She was looking up at him but said nothing. Her eyes were bright and clear. He smiled, and she smiled back at him, still silent.

"Good morning, beautiful," he said to her.

She reached up and touched his face but remained quiet.

"How are you this morning?" he asked.

"Sore," she answered. "Where are we?"

"Somewhere in the woods outside of Florence."

"Are we alone?"

"Only in here. The rest are outside. Do you smell the coffee brewing?" he asked softly.

"Yes. It smells good," she said.

"Would you like me to bring you a cup?"

She nodded her head yes.

He opened the van door and climbed out, and the others greeted him.

"Good morning, sleepy head. How's Ronnie doing?" asked Aly.

"If she feels up to it, why don't you bring her out here? It is going to be a beautiful day," added Marie.

"Sure, I'll ask her if she feels like coming out."

They heard Ronnie call from inside the van. "Yes, I want to come out, but I need some help getting up."

Mickey turned and went back to help her. James had set up a folding lounge chair for Ronnie to sit in when they got back out.

"How're you doing, Ronnie?" asked James as he helped Mickey get her to the chair.

She sat down, laid back in the chair, and took a few deep breaths as they waited for her to talk. "I'm doing fine. I'm a bit sore, but a couple of days rest, and I'll be okay."

James handed her a cup of coffee and a plate of eggs and bacon.

She looked down at it, then back at James. "Do you always come prepared to go camping when you go into a 'mission' or whatever you call this? Where did all this come from?" she asked, waving her hand around the site.

"No, we don't come prepared for this. After we left Florence yesterday, Mickey and I went to the next town to get supplies. We only got one lounge chair. We thought you might need it. We got some basic food supplies. We don't have refrigeration, so we must eat it today, or it'll spoil."

Veronica sipped her coffee and looked around the campground. It was near a small river with a clearing among the trees. In the distance, she could see mountains. She thought to herself, it was a beautiful view.

"How did you find this place?" she asked.

Aly answered, "James found it. He always finds the best or the worst location to hide out when we need it. In this case, he found the best."

"I just pointed out the general location. The ladies picked the site," James spoke up as he poured himself another cup of coffee.

Alyssa laughed. "I remember once when we needed a place to lay low for a few days, James picked out a small cave on a mountainside. We had to clear out a nest of snakes before going inside."

"Yeah, but they weren't venomous snakes, Aly!" he said.

"It doesn't make any difference. It still had snakes, and I hate snakes, my dear friend," she retorted.

Veronica said, "You mentioned laying low for a few days. What did you mean by that?"

"We left Florence in a total uproar. There'll be cops all over. They may even call in state or federal authorities. We don't want to be around that until it cools down," answered James.

"You're right about that. My chief will be there working the case himself. I hope we didn't leave anything behind. If we did, he'd find it," Veronica said.

"I'm sure we didn't. We're pretty good about cleaning up after ourselves. But sometimes, things slip through the cracks. We'll know what they know in a day or so. In the meantime, we hunker down and keep quiet."

"I see the dish and generator over there," Veronica said, pointing toward a satellite dish twenty feet from the campsite out in the open. "I guess we have communication here?"

"Yes, we do. We can keep in touch with what's going on in Florence. We also tapped into the police station's internet and phone lines to monitor what was going on through them. It's surprisingly quiet."

"You said that you tapped into their phones and the internet. Why can't you listen on the scanner?" Veronica continued.

Alyssa said, "Because everything is not broadcast over the air. There are a lot of private phone conversations, and the instructions are given by phone, etc. so we need to hear everything we can. Even the private stuff, and because they're still on site."

"They'll upload the reports with their findings in a day or two," said Veronica. "Then we'll be able to read the reports."

"Good," said Aly. "I guess we'll take a few days and enjoy this beautiful country then. Do you fish, Ronnie?"

"Not since my father passed away. He was an outdoorsman, but not me."

Mickey had been sitting quietly eating and finally got up. "James, why don't we scout out the area?"

"Sure, let's go," James said, getting up and moving toward Mickey.

They walked to the edge of the woods to talk.

As they walked out of sight, Mickey asked James. "What's your take on this situation?"

"Mickey, I don't like it. We're on the run here. Usually, the enemy's on the run. We're on the defensive, not offensive. We have a man down or woman. That's not acceptable. We need to re-organize and attack."

"We didn't expect Marie's cover to be blown so quickly. I'm sure that kind of crap happens."

"Yes," said James, "but I don't have to like it. We could have had a casualty, not just a setback with Ronnie being wounded," James reflected.

"But it did happen. Crap happens. You know that better than I do. As you said, regroup and attack. It'll take us a few more days to get more intel. Since we still have eyes and ears inside, we can let them show their hand. Then we go back in and kick butt!"

James took a look around. "Yes. Good pep talk, Mickey. At least we do have a beautiful hideout. We've been going almost around the clock, and we need to sit tight and rest. Then we'll give 'em all we got!"

"Okay. Hey, I got some fishing line at the camping store and a package of hooks. We can cut some branches for poles and teach the girls to fish," suggested Mickey.

"Maybe your girl doesn't know how to fish, but Aly and Marie can fish this stream clean. We could stay here in this wilderness and gain weight from what they can catch with a fishing line and snares for land animals."

Mickey shook his head, "I should have known." And he walked away farther into the woods.

They searched for animal trails to set traps and get some bearings on their surroundings. After about an hour, they arrived back at the camp.

When they walked into the opening, Marie held a gun at them. When she saw only James and Mickey, she lowered it and called to them. "Next time, announce your entrance. I could have shot both of you."

"Next time, we will," responded Mickey.

James and Aly set up the equipment inside the van to be secured from casual intruders like wildlife and to keep it out of a potential rainstorm. They took turns watching the school and baking facility monitors the rest of the day.

Grant was still on the rampage. He constantly gave orders and demanded information on the intruders' identity and Marie's whereabouts. Nothing new until he gave out a name to contact.

"James, come here!" called out Alyssa. "Grant just gave us a name. It's bad news."

James came running to the van, "What name?" he puffed, catching his breath.

"Clayton Reece. He's the Sultan of mercenary information."

"Yeah. I know exactly who Clayton is. This could be bad for us," James acknowledged. "We need to get to him first!"

Mickey heard Alyssa call James, and he, too, came running. "What's happening?"

James turned to Mickey, "Grant is trying to get in touch with Clayton Reece."

"Who's he?"

"His nickname is the *Sultan*. He has a database of almost everyone globally that has or trains mercenaries. And, yes, we are in that database. He is for sale to the highest bidder. The one thing he does have is criminal integrity."

"Criminal integrity? What the heck is that?"

"He sells to whoever gets to him with the highest bid, and if one team hires him, he is loyal to that team until the contract is fulfilled. In other words, if Grant gets to him and hires him, Reece will go on a worldwide search for us. Since he doesn't know who we are, Reece will run an algorithm to see who matches our methods of operation. Then he'll narrow it down to a few teams. Then narrow it even farther by elimination until the guilty team is left. For example, if he narrows the situation down to five teams, he'll track each one down until the one left is the only one in the general vicinity of the crime. Let's say we're in a group of five teams, and all the others are deployed out of the country, the only one left is us. Reece will identify us, and Grant will come after us."

"Can't you just pay Reece a higher price to keep his mouth shut or give Grant false information?"

"No. That's why it can be bad. Once the Sultan's hired, he's loyal to his current employers. He won't take us as a client until Grant releases him. His base fee is a million dollars a contract. Aly's going to try to hire him first. She has to go to the dark web to find him. Let's leave her alone. She's got work to do."

"Even if Grant find's out who we are, he still has to find us. I mean, we're out in the middle of the woods. Reece can't help him find us here, can he?" asked Mickey.

"Know thy enemy. Once he knows who we are, he will know our strengths and weaknesses. He'll know how we act and react. We'll literally head for the wood's which is exactly what we did."

They both walked away deep in concentration.

As they walked away, Mickey asked. "Is there anything we can do to stop Clayton?"

"No one knows his true identity. He's located somewhere in Europe. No one knows where. He uses a ghost protocol program. That means no one can initiate a connection with him. You put out the word, and he gets back to you. In this case, Aly will have to go into the dark web. It could take minutes, hours, days, or months to reach him. We'll find out if he contacts us."

"I see," said Mickey. "I've heard of the dark web. Does it really exist?"

James said, "Yes. It does, and it's very dangerous," James said. They walked to the little stream's bank and sat down. "First, there are three levels of the World Wide Web. The *clear net* is the highest level. It is the one people see when they log on to the internet. When you google something, it's done on the clear net, and it's only about four percent of the internet.

"The next level is the *deep web*. That's where about ninety percent of the web is used. You can access it if you have a need and have a password. It's used for confidential things like medical records, financial records, government tax records, military communique, and even PayPal subscriptions are located there.

"The last and evil part of the internet is the *dark web*. It accounts for about six percent of the internet. It's truly a cesspool of humanity. It's used by drug dealers, human traffickers, and the infamous black hat hackers."

"I've heard of black hat hackers. What are they, exactly?" asked Mickey.

"They are just mean people. They hack into systems, usually to wreak havoc. Sometimes they do it to hold a system ransom, like going into financial institutions to drain money out of accounts or places like hospitals and forcing them to pay ransoms to release the system. They are evil in their own way, which is usually financially motivated."

"How do you access the *dark web*?" Mickey asked

"I don't know the details, and even Aly doesn't like to get into that aspect. She gets in touch with Digger. All we can do is wait. Digger gets in touch with the Sultan, and the Sultan gets in touch with us. Let's do a little fishing with the ladies," he said, getting up and dusting off his pants.

Aly stayed in the van trying to reach Digger, while Marie, Veronica, James, and Mickey tried their luck at fishing with poles made from tree limbs tied with fishing line. Veronica sat in the recliner that Mickey moved to the edge of the stream so she could fish while sitting.

"Mickey, I don't understand you. You come out here and kill people but talk about how you hate killing," commented Veronica.

"I came out here to claim Valerie's body, take her home and give her a proper burial. But things changed. She deserves justice, and for your information, I have nightmares about the people I've killed. I don't like it. I kill in self-defense."

"But you go looking for trouble, Mickey. Let the police handle these things," she added.

"Hey, listen, pretty lady, you are one of us now!" Mickey said.

"No. I'm not. I just went in that night at the CIOF to help you set up surveillance, and I got shot. I'm not part of your group. If we had gotten caught, I might have gotten a reprimand and desk duty for a few months, but that's all."

"What would happen since you got shot?" Mickey asked.

"I'm sure Grant would say that we were burglars, and they were protecting their property. Yes, I would have pressed charges, but I or we were in there illegally, so he wins. Case closed, and you would go home," she said.

"How many cases did you have on your desk when you took leave to help us?" he asked.

"Thirteen," she answered.

"How many are you working on now, including this one?" he asked.

"One."

"Who's handling the other cases now that you're working with us."

"My partner."

"I think I made my point," Mickey said. "Two people worked on thirteen cases, and now only one is working on that same number. Even with the two of you, you only worked on them a bit over 3 hours a week. That isn't a lot of time per case. Also, your father was killed how long ago? We solved it in a few days."

"What do you mean you solved it in a few days? Are you saying that you know who killed Daddy?" she said, sitting up, wincing in pain, laying back in the chair, and taking a few breaths.

"Calm down, Ronnie,"

"What do you mean that you know who killed Daddy? Tell me NOW!" she said with clenched teeth.

"While you were drugged up the last couple of days, we listened to the recordings we got from the equipment we placed."

"Why didn't you tell me this sooner?" she asked, glaring at Mickey.

"I told you, you were drugged up, and we weren't sure how you would take it."

"So, you wait days later when we're sitting beside a stream in the woods fishing like we're on vacation?"

"No, I couldn't. Things were happening too fast, and I wanted you to be strong enough to deal with it."

"That's a lousy excuse, and you know it. You should have told me as soon as you found out. It wasn't up to you to decide when was the proper time to tell me. Now, who was it? Who killed Daddy?"

"Amir."

"You mean that Mideastern guy that's Grant's right-hand man? I would have guessed Grant himself or that guy Roger."

"Nope. It was Amir. He admitted to it."

"Can I see the video?"

"Not now, Veronica."

"I want to see it!" she demanded.

"Okay, I'll get Aly to set it up for you to watch."

"Today?" she asked.

"Yes, today, and another thing, when we went into CIOF the other night, it was Nick that James killed. Nick was one of the men that was shooting at us."

"Okay, you, I'm in with you guys. I denied it, but as of this minute, I'm in all the way," she said matter of factly. "I want to kill him myself."

"No. You can't do that. We will try to capture Amir and turn him over to the authorities," said Mickey.

She looked down at her lap in sadness. "You're right, Mickey. But if we resorted to the same tactics you and your team use, it wouldn't work. We need rules, not unbridled ruthlessness."

"Criminals don't follow the rules, and we fight crime the way they commit crime. Fire with fire. I agree you can't do that. And the people we kill deserve it."

"You're vigilantes. We, the law that is, can't have wild west vigilante justice. Your team's going on a vigilante run tonight, and there's a good chance someone will get killed. Just because someone deserves to die doesn't give you or me the authority to be judge, jury, and executioners."

"If they don't try to kill us, we won't kill them. We get information that proves they're criminals. They try to stop us by trying to kill us. We are defending ourselves," Mickey said.

"You're justifying your actions, Mickey. In the eyes of the law, you're also criminals, and since I'm now part of the team, I am also one."

"Do you want to leave? You can, you know. We will take it from here, and get justice for you, your father, and Marie."

"No, I don't want to leave, but I want it according to the law of the land, not your law."

"Whatever, Ronnie. Let's see how you feel when you look into the eyes of the man that killed your father!"

Mickey went over and asked Aly to let Veronica see the video where Amir admitted to killing her father.

Aly called Veronica over and let her watch the recording. When it was over, Veronica got out of the van and silently walked into the woods to grieve alone. Mickey saw her as she walked away but let her have her privacy.

Occasionally James would go back to the van to check on Aly. Finally, he informed everyone that she had gotten hold of Digger. He would get back to her as soon as he contacted Clayton Reece.

After a couple of hours, they had enough fish for a nice dinner. Veronica was up and moving slowly around the camp, but everyone knew she had watched the video and left her alone. James and Mickey gathered more wood for the fire. Another day came and went, and they did regular camping duties waiting for the furor over the shootout to calm down. No one heard from Digger nor the *Sultan*, and Grant still ranted daily.

Aly reported to them that Grant had hired two more professionals to replace the men he had lost. This was a great concern to the team because they were no longer against street thugs. There were going against their professional equals.

James sat and looked at the maps they had downloaded. "Mickey, this has turned from a simple mission of justice to Val's and to Ronnie's father's killer to a real war. We are playing a deadly game of chess. Only one of us will come out alive."

Mickey sat and looked at James. "Can't you call a truce or something?"

"No, Mickey. There are no truces with mercenaries. There are no surrenders. We fight to the death, or one of us runs. I don't run. At this point, you may leave. Heck, any of you can leave, but I will stay and fight. My honor and Marie's life is at stake now. What do you want to do?"

"I am here for justice for Valerie, and since I am part of this team, I will stay."

James got up and walked over to the rest of the team. When he returned, he said they were also here for justice. None chose to leave. Even Veronica was now adamant about staying with the team.

With all of this waiting, the shipments continued to go in and out of the CIOF facility. Whoever was watching the monitors made notes of the license plates of the trucks. When possible, and the trucks were new enough to have GPSs, they also took notes of their destinations. Most were to legitimate distribution centers that delivered the food mixes to be sold and delivered to restaurants. Two were not. They went to undisclosed locations, and the drivers dropped off their loads.

That night as they sat around a fire, eating a wild rabbit they snared earlier that day, James said, "We have two trucks that didn't unload at distribution centers. We need to keep tabs on them. When they return, we should meet them down the line after they leave the facility and stop them," James said at dinner.

They all agreed.

Marie asked, "What do we do with the shipment if we find something illegal?"

Mickey spoke up, "We destroy it."

"Okay. Then what? Let the men go?" she asked.

"We let the authorities take over," he answered.

"If we destroy the shipment, there'll be no evidence," Aly said.

"We can destroy them by making them unusable," James suggested.

"No good. If they're unusable, then a good attorney will get them off. It's not illegal to own a non-fireable weapon. If the firing mechanism is removed, it's no longer a threat. That is unless the carcass has a serial number of a stolen weapon."

Mickey said, "Okay, we secure the prisoners and call in the authorities."

"We know they're all thieves and murderers," Marie said, "Why can't we just kill them all? We'd be doing the world a favor."

"No unnecessary killing," Mickey said vehemently.

"Okay. I suggest we watch and check any truck entering the loading dock. As soon as each truck arrives, we get information on the truck and the driver if we can. We get ready for them to pull out if it looks suspicious. If we stop it down the road and it's legit, we let it go. We secure it and leave before the authorities arrive if it's not. We must stay below the radar. Since what happened earlier this week, we're wanted criminals, even though we only defended ourselves. The good thing is, they, being the authorities, don't know who we are. We want to keep it that way."

"What about me? What can I do?" Veronica asked.

"You sit tight and heal."

"I can do something. I can monitor the situation here while you go out," Veronica protested.

"Sure. If you think you can do that. It would free me to go out with them to stop the truck," said Aly.

"I can do that."

Aly turned back to James and stared at him with a knowing stare.

"Fine, Ronnie, you stay here and be our overwatch," he said.

James walked away from the ladies toward Mickey, who was sulking at the edge of the woods. "Hey, bro, don't look so sad. It'll work out. I know it will."

"Sure. I've become a killer," Mickey said.

"You help people. You won't hurt anyone if it can be avoided. You help people, and you hurt in their place. You're a good person, Mickey. I'm the rotten killer. I kill people, and most of the time, I feel no remorse. I try to kill only bad, evil people, but innocents sometimes get in my way. I did a job. It has to be done. You only did what had to be done. You're a hero. Not a villain. Now, go back out there, and be the hero you are. You are a hero to Ronnie. The girls look at you as their equal now."

Mickey looked at James with a strange expression.

"Okay. You know what I mean. An equal in battle. A warrior like them. Don't look at me like that!"

Slowly, Mickey got a sardonic smile on his face.

"Thanks for the pep talk. I don't feel any better, but I know you meant well. Let's finish eating. That was some tough rabbit you snared earlier," he said and walked back toward the evening fire.

When they finished, they got ready to bed down for the night. Veronica now slept outside on the ground, so someone could sit in the van to keep monitoring the video of the Bakery. She did have an air mattress Mickey bought for her because of her injury, but the others slept on the hard ground. She was almost weaned off her pain medication but was still sore and could only walk short distances.

Mickey took his turn watching the monitors and took the first watch. As everyone fell asleep, all he could hear was the steady hum of the generator placed at the edge of the camping area to minimize the noise. At about two in the morning, James took over from Mickey.

Mickey was sound asleep when he was awakened by James shaking him. "Hey, Mickey. Wake up. We gotta go! Wake up, Ronnie. I'll get Aly up. Move out, Bro!"

Mickey heard James waking the girls, and they got up, and within minutes they were ready and standing by the Humvee. James jumped into the driver's seat, and they all piled inside while Ronnie did an audio and video check of the equipment.

When everyone got in, Aly looked around the interior. "This is a real military Humvee, isn't it, James?"

James pulled onto the road. "Yes, and no. It's a real Humvee, but with heavy modifications. Since it is a civilian model, it's street-legal. It has heavy armor and real bulletproof windows. And the back glass isn't in the military model. That's custom and can be removed to fire weapons from the back."

"Where're we going, James?" asked Mickey, sitting in the back seat.

James said, "I estimate it'll take them about half an hour to load up and pull out. I guess they're running something illegal because of the early hour of the morning. Legal shipments would go out at regular operating hours. We'll pick them up on the way out of town if I guessed correctly which way they're going."

They continued bouncing around in the Vee while James drove at the top speed that it would go. It wasn't fast but durable and rugged, which was more important.

Finally, they slowed down, pulled to the roadside, and backed into a side road out of sight. James called Ronnie on the communication unit.

She answered immediately. "Guys, I was able to connect to the truck's GPS. I had to run the plates to do that, but we're good to go. It should be closing in on your location in about ten minutes. You have time to set up whatever you need to stop it."

James answered Ronnie, "Copy that, command." He turned around to Mickey in the back. "Get out the rocket launcher from the box and load it."

"Wait, we don't need that do we? We don't need to blow it up!"

"We aren't going to do that. They'll stop when they see you standing in the middle of the road with it on your shoulder. You won't need to do anything but look like a tough guy with a huge killer weapon. They'll mess their pants at that."

"I hope you're right. You'll shoot out their tires if they don't stop, right?" Mickey asked.

"We'll do that anyway, even if they do stop. We don't want them going anywhere," he said as they got out of the Humvee.

Marie took her weapon and headed for an embankment on the other side of the road. Aly stood beside James as they went toward one on the same side where they were parked. They all sat and waited for the truck.

In a few minutes, they saw headlights in the distance. James called over the comm units. "Heads up, everyone. They're almost here."

"Copy that," they all said.

James said, "Marie and Aly, take out all the tires. I'll move out on the road beside Mickey. When the truck comes to a stop, move out on both sides. Show them you mean business if they try to exit the truck."

"Copy that," came from all.

The men in the truck saw Mickey and James standing in the middle of the road and slammed on the brakes. As the truck began to skid, Marie and Aly took out every tire on the truck, and it dropped down to the rims and skidded to a stop. The door on both sides opened, but the driver and the passenger stopped when they saw Aly and Marie with automatic rifles pointed at them.

James walked over to the driver and said, "Get out of the truck and open the back door."

"We can't. It's locked, and we don't have the key," he answered as he got out of the truck.

James couldn't help but look at the front of the man's pants. It was wet around the crotch area. James knew what had happened and felt a bit sorry for him. "We don't want to hurt you. All we want is to look at your cargo," he said, raising the rifle to the man's head. The wet area got larger.

"I swear on my mother's grave, we don't have keys to it. Don't shoot. If we could open it, we would. Honest, man. Don't shoot. Please," he pleaded.

James stood and continued. "Okay. Tell us where you're going."

"I don't know. We won't get additional instructions until we get to the next stop."

"Okay, where is your next stop?" James asked.

"They give us instructions as we go from one leg to another. We have no idea where the final destination is. I swear, man, I don't know," he continued to plead.

"Hey, rocket man, hold him while I open the back door," James said, looking at Mickey. James walked back to Aly, and together they went around to the back of the truck.

Mickey knew James had shot off the lock when a gunshot rang out. He heard the sound of the roll-up door opening, and after a few moments, James came back around to Mickey. Waving off Marie and Alyssa, he told both men to lie on the road and not get up.

He said quietly to Mickey, "Come around to the back of the truck."

Mickey followed him to about one hundred feet behind the truck. "Want to blow it up?"

"Sure," Mickey answered with a grin.

"Okay, back up about fifty feet more and put a rocket right into the back of the truck. You want to get back far enough that you don't get caught in the force of the explosion or get hit with shrapnel from the blast. I'll wait over here by the embankment," he said, walking away.

James went to the embankment just over the edge so Mickey could see his torso. He gave Mickey a thumbs up. Mickey aimed and pulled the trigger. A blast came out of the front of the weapon's tube, and a flame shot out of it along with a flaming object. It soared across to the truck, went inside it, and lit up the back with a loud explosion. Mickey had a huge grin on his face as pieces of the truck flew outward.

When the sound subsided, James popped his head back up and waved for everyone to converge at the front of the flaming truck.

As they returned to the road and over to the men still lying on the ground, James looked down at them and said, "I said we wouldn't hurt you. We keep our promises."

Both men were visibly shaking. "Who are you?" The driver asked.

James bent down over the frightened men, "We are mongooses, and we kill snakes. You may get up and find your way back to your boss when you hear us leave. The kind of person he is, he'll kill you for not delivering your cargo. That's not our problem. Go back to him or run away. That's your choice."

James stood back up and gestured for the team to follow him to the Humvee. When they got in, they drove off into the night back to the campsite.

"Wow. That was a rush," said Mickey. "I've never shot a rocket launcher before."

Aly said, "We usually call them RPGs. That stands for rocket-propelled grenade. What made you think of getting an RPG, James."

"When I went to buy the Humvee and get the weapons, the dealer said he was having a BOGO sale on rocket launchers."

"A BOGO sale?" said Marie.

"Yeah, you know, buy one get one sale," James said with a grin.

"I know what it means," Marie said sarcastically. "I thought only women got caught up in that kind of sale. You surprise me, James."

James laughed, "I admit, I'm a sucker when it comes to a good sale on weaponry, ladies."

They all laughed at James' humor as they drove down the road.

"Let's go, pick up Ronnie, change clothes, and find an all-night diner," suggested Marie.

Mickey and Alyssa chimed in, "Yeah, we're hungry!"

CHAPTER 15

Fall Out at the Factory

After eating, they all went back to the campsite and took a short nap. They wanted to hear Grant when he found out the news about the truck. They weren't disappointed.

Grant still had bandages on his face, but that didn't keep him from throwing foul language that could be heard over many areas of the plant.

"Did they find the bodies?" he screamed.

The two men, Amir and Roger, shook their heads. "No."

"What happened to them?" he said with continued rage.

"We don't know. Even the police don't know what happened to the men."

"How do you know that the police don't know? Have you been talking to the police? I want answers, and I want them now!"

"We saw it on the news, Grant. It's on the local and network news channels. They're investigating it, but they don't know who's responsible so far. They didn't mention anything about bodies. They think that the truck was abandoned, then exploded."

"Abandoned? No one abandons my shipments. Do they know it was one of our trucks?"

"I don't know anything more than that right now," Roger said.

"I lost over fifty thousand dollars' worth of weapons in that truck. I want answers. Have you tried to get in touch with Clayton Reece again?"

"Yes, but he hasn't returned our request yet."

"Call him again."

"We don't need to call him again. He'll call us when he's ready, Grant."

"I said to call him. Do it!"

"Okay," Roger said and left the office.

"And you," he waved his hand at Amir, "Get out and go back to work. Do something. Just get out of my sight. My mouth hurts. Get me some painkillers."

There was nothing the team could do until dark. They napped and took turns watching the screen in the van. James filled up the generator with gas, while Marie went to a neighboring town away from Florence to get more supplies. Aly watched the monitors. Mickey and Veronica took a stroll through the woods and worked their way upstream. The weather was sunny and warm, and it was a relaxing day for everyone.

James called to get the lab reports about the white substances they collected at the bakery plant a few days ago. Nothing illegal came back. It was a collection of legal spices and flour in the prepared cooking mixes.

At dinner that evening around the fire, Mickey took the lead after most of the food was eaten. "Okay, ladies, James said that the lab reports nothing illegal with the substances we found the last time we were inside. That may be, but a gut feeling tells me more is going out of that facility."

"Sorry, Mickey, but just a gut feeling isn't good enough to risk going back in. I say we just burn it down and move on," Marie said.

Mickey took the defensive, "No. Grant will make a fire insurance claim and rebuild if we burn it down. In a few months, he'll be right back in business. We need the information to get Grant and Amir, the man who killed Valerie. I want both of them in jail. That's what'll get justice for Valerie."

Marie took a breath, "Okay, we'll do this for you, Mickey. When you mess with one, you mess with all of us."

They all nodded their heads in agreement. Even Ronnie agreed to continue.

"When do we go back in?" asked Ronnie.

"You don't. You're still recovering from the last time. James and I will go in with Marie as the lookout this time."

"I want to help," Ronnie said.

Aly spoke. "You already helped. But we need you to continue healing. Anyone wounded in the field doesn't go back until they're cleared. You aren't healed yet. There are other ways you can help around here. Nothing personal. Any one of us in your condition would also be grounded."

"Okay," Ronnie said.

"Have you called in to work?" asked James.

Veronica said, "Yes, I called in to the captain and told him I was going to take some personal time off."

"And?" said James.

"He said okay. I haven't taken any time off since I joined the force, so he didn't question it. But he did ream me out for not calling in sooner, and they had a situation at an abandoned factory where he wanted me to work when I got back."

"What excuse did you give him about not calling in sooner?" questioned James.

"I lied. I told him I did call in and talked to Janet, his secretary. I don't think he totally believed me, but I've never called in before, so he'll let it go."

"What if he asks his secretary?" asked James.

"I don't know that either. Again, I'll deal with it when I get back."

"Do you think he will let it go? Especially if he puts two and two together about the female that had a gunshot wound at the local Emergency room a couple of days ago."

"I don't know what I'll do. I don't have a choice right now," she said, grabbing her shoulder. "I'll deal with it when the time comes."

"You know that if and when he connects the dots, you may not have a job to return to, don't you?"

"I know. I've never been in a situation like this. As I said, I'll deal with it then."

"You seem to have a lot of I don't knows in this conversation. But we'll do what we can to help you," said James.

"You can fix things like that?"

"Not always. Most of the time, no. I said we'll try. I make no promises understand?"

"I understand," she said.

Mickey continued, "I think we should go in again tonight. We can get there around two in the morning. Can you shut off the alarms, Alyssa? Including the secondary ones?"

"I don't know. Of course, I can shut off the main system, but we aren't totally familiar with the backup one yet. I can check and see how long the response time was on the last event. That way, we'll know how long you could spend there this time, so even if the backup system is in working order, you can get in and back out before they arrive."

"Okay, find that out, and we'll go in tonight with an approximate time limit," Mickey stated.

Aly looked at James, "Is that acceptable with you, James?"

"Sure, I'm willing to go. Marie, are you with us?"

"Yep, I want that SOB that tried to attack me. I'll be all for whatever it takes to take them down. Let's do this!"

Mickey looked at James, "That girl's got a mean streak, doesn't she?"

"Yep, as long as the Nile River and as wide as an eight-lane highway, Mickey," he answered. "Okay, boys and girls, class dismissed."

They slowly got up and walked away from the fire. Mickey got up and went over to Ronnie.

"Hey, there. How are you feeling today?" he asked.

"I'm getting better. It's still a bit sore."

"Good. Let's take a moonlight stroll."

"Sure," she said.

Mickey reached out to take her hand as they made their way to the stream. "You know, you literally took a bullet for James and me. We don't take that lightly. I want you to know that, Ronnie."

"Thank you, Mickey. There is one thing that's beginning to bother me."

"What's that?"

"You said that you no longer loved Valerie. I believe that, but you must still have some powerful feeling for her to put your life in danger and all of this to get justice for her."

Mickey picked up a small stone and threw it out over the stream. At a distance, they heard it plop into the water. He picked up another and did the same. After it plopped, he turned to Veronica.

"Yes. That's true. I did. No, I still have feelings for her. I guess I always will have feelings for her. But I don't love her as I did long ago. I can't explain it. She was my first girlfriend. It took me a long time to admit to myself that I loved her. Then she called off our marriage and left Bridgton. That doesn't mean there isn't room for someone else."

"Mickey, I've come to care for you in just these couple of weeks. I'm not saying that I'm in love with you. I don't know how I feel, but I wanted to go the other night because I wanted to be with you. I was afraid when the shooting started. I was scared that you might be shot. Then, instead of you, it was me. I, too, can't explain it, but I was glad it was me and not you. I wanted with all my heart for you not to be hurt. That's all I can say. I care for you. I care for you a lot."

He put his arms around her, and they kissed. A long and slow kiss. They pulled apart and stared into each other's eyes in the moonlight.

Finally, Mickey said, "We better get some sleep. Two a.m. will come early."

They held hands and walked over to their sleeping area. Veronica laid down on her air mattress, and Mickey lay beside her in his sleeping bag. Soon the camp was quiet, with only the sound of crickets and the quiet hum of the generator keeping the monitors up and running. Aly was sitting inside the van on an air pillow, watching those monitors.

Promptly at two a.m. the alarm on Mickey's watch began to ring as he turned it off, reached over, and woke up Veronica. James was waking Aly, who had relinquished the task of watching the monitors to Marie a couple of hours earlier. While Aly checked the communication units, James and Mickey checked the guns and ammunition. They also carried small flashlights, zip ties, and small rolls of duct tape. Each had a small pouch of tools containing wire cutters, flat and Phillips screwdrivers, and electrical tape. They had gloves, so they didn't leave fingerprints that could be traced. Marie put her hair inside a tight cap to avoid getting in the way. James drove.

They arrived in about three-quarters of an hour and parked around the back of the loading dock area since it would be the fastest exit when they needed to get out. Aly shut off the alarm system remotely back at the campsite. James, Mickey, and Marie climbed over the fence where they had come in that last time. They didn't cut the power since the alarm was off, but most lights were turned out because of the late hour. Mickey silently picked the lock as he did before. They stealthily went through the building heading for the stock room. Marie worked her way to the front of the building to be the lookout like Veronica had done before. Mickey and James saw three men sitting at a small table talking. The men were supposed to watch the building since they were the night security team. Mickey and James put on hoods to disguise their faces, and James worked his way to the other side of the room behind boxes stacked six feet high. When James got to the other side, Mickey stepped out into the open area.

"Hello!" he thundered.

The men jumped up and started to grab their weapons lying on the table.

"What the…" one of the men started to say.

Mickey said, "Don't even think about touching one of those guns."

"If we all reach simultaneously, you can't shoot all of us before one of us gets you," he said.

"That may be true, but which one will I shoot first?" Mickey answered. "Are you willing to take the chance that it won't be you I kill first?"

James called out from behind the men, "I'm trained on you, and I'm a very fast and dangerous man. I can shoot all three of you before you can reach your gun."

Mickey smiled. "Is he just pulling your leg, or is he telling the truth? Who wants to call his bluff?"

No one moved.

Mickey moved forward with zip ties and duct tape in his hands. He had a handgun, but it was still in its holster. "Good choice, guys. Now, if you don't mind, where's the good stuff?"

"What do you mean, good stuff," one man said.

Mickey had decided that the one that spoke up was the night boss. "You know what I mean. Now, where is it?"

He told them to each put their hands behind their backs. When they all complied, Mickey pulled the ties around their hands and cinched them down until they cut into the men's wrists.

"We don't know what you're talking about," the boss said.

James walked over to them when Mickey tied the last one. He put his gun against the man's temple.

"I might get trigger-happy if you don't answer my friend's question."

"I don't know what you're talking about," he repeated.

James calmly pointed the gun at the floor and shot the man in the foot. The man screamed and fell off the chair onto the floor.

"I'll tell you. Just don't shoot us," one of the other men called out.

James turned to him. "You should be the boss, not the stupid man lying on the floor with his foot bleeding like that. All he had to do was cooperate like you're going to do. Right?"

"Yes, I'll cooperate with you. What you want's in that box back there. The one that's third from the bottom with the red printing on it."

Mickey and James turned to where the man said. There was a stack of printed cases with blue printing except for the one the man had named. That printing was red.

Mickey went back to the man and clipped his zip tie. "Get it out and open it for us."

The man walked over to the stack of boxes and began taking them down to the red box. It was cardboard, and he could tear open the top. Then he backed away from it and looked back at Mickey and James.

James walked over and looked into the box. It had smaller boxes with printed labels saying "Oregon's Premier Seafood Seasoning." James looked back at the man. The man looked at the floor, not meeting James' glare.

"What kind of drugs are in those boxes," Mickey asked.

"I don't know. It's cocaine or heroin. They don't tell us which ones are going out. Honest. Are you going to kill us now?" he asked.

"No," said Mickey. "We're going to let you go. But only after you show us the rest of the stuff."

"Hey, man. That's the most valuable stuff in here. Do you have any idea of the street value of that one shipment?" the same man asked.

The man on the floor was lying in a puddle of blood. Mickey looked at him and then at the last man standing at the table. "Where do you keep your first aid kits?" he asked.

"There's a first aid station in the next room near the packaging machinery," he answered.

"Why don't we take a stroll over to it?" said Mickey. "You lead the way."

They returned with a handful of bandages, gauze, and ointments a few minutes later. Mickey ordered the man to put a compress on the moaning man's foot. After dressing the wound, both men got up, and Mickey told them to sit down again around the table.

Walking back over to the man next to the open box, Mickey asked him. "What's your name?"

He mumbled something that Mickey couldn't understand and told the man to speak up.

"Say it louder."

"Grady Steele," he said.

"And your address. And don't you lie to me, or there'll be hell to pay." Mickey said.

Over the comm unit, Mickey heard Aly say, "Got him. His address is 409 East Ocean Drive."

"It's 409 Farm Lane," he said.

Mickey took his gun out of the holster and pointed it at the man's head. "Is that your final answer?"

"Yeah. That's it. I swear," he said.

Mickey shot, barely touching the tip of the man's ear. He fell to the floor and fainted.

Mickey shook the man awake and said, "You lied to me. Your address is 409 East Ocean Drive. Isn't it?"

"Yes," the man said, holding his wounded ear. "I didn't mean to lie!"

"Yes, you did, and I don't like liars," scolded Mickey.

He moved over to the man with the wounded foot. "And what's your name?"

The man said, "Earl Raymond and I live at…"

"Stop. I didn't ask you where you live," Mickey said, giving Aly enough time to run a background on Earl.

Finally, her voice came over the comm unit. "Earl Raymond lives at 2813 Cliff Face Drive."

"You know I'm a mind reader, don't you, Earl?" Mickey said.

He nodded his head. Yes.

"You live at 2813 Cliff Face Drive. Don't you?"

Earl nodded again.

Mickey looked over at the last man. "Now, why don't you tell us your name and address and the names of your wife and kids?"

The man's eyes grew wide with fear. "Don't hurt my family. Please. My name is Charles White."

"Okay, we've wasted enough time here. You know that we know about all of you. So, Grady, why don't you lead the way to the other stuff? If you all be good prisoners and cooperate with us, we'll let you live. Heck, we'll even call an ambulance for Earl here. How about it, guys?"

They all nodded their heads.

Mickey pushed Grady to get him moving. They went around the plant, opening boxes. There was a variety of guns, from simple handguns to automatic weapons. There was a pharmacy of illegal drugs, from prescription pills to heroin. The school/factory was a department store of unlawful contraband. James and Mickey had them bring everything out and place it in the middle of the pavement in front of the loading dock.

A man silently walked up behind Marie in the front room of the plant's office area. When he put a gun to her head, he spoke quietly. "Miss Sanchez, why don't you slowly put down your gun so I don't have to blow off your pretty little head?"

She started to move, and he pressed the gun more firmly against her head. "If you move another millimeter, I swear you'll be dead before you hit the floor."

"Do I put the gun down or stand here? Your choice," she said defiantly.

"Stand still until I tell you to move," he said as he stepped back. When he had backed away about five feet, he told her to put down the gun slowly. "Now, lay on the floor face down, and put your hands behind your back. Slowly. I have permission to shoot you if you don't comply. I would love to do that, Miss Sanchez."

She slowly got down on her knees, lay on the floor as ordered, and put her hands behind her back. She then heard someone else come into the room. Again, she felt the gun barrel against her head as the man ordered someone else to tie her arms behind her back, then tie her feet and legs together so she couldn't kick out with her feet. They gagged and blindfolded her. One of the men reached to her ear, took out her earbud, and smashed it on the floor.

"Now, we wait," the man said. "We wait until your people leave our building. Then we will have a little talk. You'll tell us everything."

"Hey, guys," Alyssa said over the comm units. "Marie is in trouble. I heard strange voices talking to her, then they ordered her to the floor, and her comm unit went dead. You need to look into that now."

"Yes, we heard it," said Mickey.

Alyssa said into the comm unit, "I'll go check on her. James and Mickey can keep getting things into the loading area." She took off for the front office area.

Mickey and James made the three men sit about 50 feet away from the pile of guns and drugs in the middle of the lot. They zip-tied their hands and feet and tied them all together.

As they were doing this, they heard gunfire from inside the building. Aly's voice came over the comm unit.

"They have Marie, and they're taking her out of a side emergency exit. I can't follow. Can you do something if they head your way? If so, be careful. Marie is in the back seat, so watch your gunfire. They have automatic weapons."

As she said this, a car whizzed by the front of the building and sprayed gunfire as it passed. Mickey and James ducked behind some crates. The men they had tied up all hit the ground to avoid being hit by the passing bullets. The car disappeared at the end of the road. Mickey and James went out of the fenced area and called the fire department, an ambulance, and the police. As they left, they lit a fire under the contraband.

Alyssa recommended getting out because the first responders were on the way to the site. They needed to get out and leave.

Reluctantly, after circling the block to the point they felt someone might recognize them for their presence, they left and went back to the campsite. Like the last time, they were all hungry, but no one felt like eating. No one got any sleep that night. One of their own was MIA. Missing in action. This was bad.

Mickey tossed and turned the rest of the night, and he heard the others in the camp rustling and doing the same thing. Finally, around daybreak, he got up. James was already making a pot of coffee on the camp stove. Mickey went down to the stream, and washed his face. James poured both of them a cup of coffee.

"What do we do now? Mickey asked James.

"We get her."

"What if they killed her like Grant said he would do?"

"Then we get her body, and God help anyone that gets in our way!" said James looking down at his coffee cup. "If someone so much as bruises her little finger, I'll personally chop the hand off the person that does it! I swear I will."

"I get the feeling that blood will be spilled over this," Mickey said.

"You can bet your bottom dollar it will."

"Bet your bottom dollar on what, James?" said Veronica as she walked up to them, grabbed the coffee pot, and filled her cup.

"If they hurt Marie, James will get revenge," said Mickey.

"Yeah, I got that feeling last night," she answered.

They heard splashing water and knew Alyssa was up and washing in the stream. They had a cup of coffee waiting for her when she walked up.

"What's the plan, James? You're our tactician?" Alyssa said.

"First, we need to find out where Marie is being held, in the factory, or if they move her somewhere else. Then we go in and extract her."

Veronica took a deep breath. "You make it sound easy."

"It all depends on his men. If they're all street thugs, it'll be a cakewalk. If he brings in experienced help, it'll be a bit more dangerous. Actually, a lot more dangerous," said James. "We don't want to overreact. We wait for more intel, then make a plan and go."

"Okay, how do we do that?" asked Veronica.

"Grant should be in the factory anytime now. I'm sure he had already been updated about the assault on the school facility and Marie's capture or death."

"She's missing. We don't know if she was captured or killed," said Veronica.

"If they weren't holding her, she'd have found a way to check-in. We haven't heard anything from her, so the only two things left are whether they have her or killed her," said James.

They went to the van and looked at the recordings of what had taken place while they were gone. It showed the authorities swarming over the pavement areas of the facility last night. Grant was acting like a deranged man running all over the place. He refused to let the authorities inside since the fire was restricted to the outside. The audio wasn't clear, but they could tell the officers were questioning Grant about the charred weapons in a pile. Grant insisted he didn't know how they got there. When the fire marshals arrived, they found some debris containing burned drugs. He gave them the same story about drugs. He didn't know anything. Maybe some disgruntled employee was trying to frame him. After all, he did hire ex-cons. Everyone in town knew that. He had a pretty good story for himself. Eventually, the FBI showed up, followed by the DEA and ATF.

Aly began running a complete background check on the three men. She asked Mickey how he knew Charles was married and had a family.

Mickey laughed, "He had on a wedding band, and on his key chain that was lying on the table had a fob of a little troll doll. That would have most likely been given to him by a child, probably a girl."

"Good guess. Charles has three daughters," said Aly. "I'll get a complete printout of the others soon."

"Let's take stock of what we got in the raid last night," said Mickey.

Veronica spoke up first. "At this time, we've only hurt him financially. It doesn't put him in jail or get justice for Valerie. We need to decide what we want. Justice or financial ruin."

Mickey said, "I want it all. He ordered Amir to kill Valerie."

"True," Veronica answered, "but if he goes to jail, he will lose it anyway. So why don't we get him and put him in jail?"

"Amir killed your father. Maybe Grant didn't order him killed, but it was done to protect Grant and this whole stinking operation. Do you just want him to go to jail, Ronnie?" said Mickey.

Veronica seethed at Mickey. "Don't go there, Mickey! I may have joined this team, but I am still a sworn cop. I have a duty to uphold the law!"

"If you feel that way, then why don't you just leave," he answered.

James stood up, "Hey, you two, stop it! You both have reasons to want this whole thing to go away. You're both right, but we all know if we left right now, Grant would go free. Ronnie, Grant is connected to the killing of your father. Mickey, he's connected to Valerie's death. Let's just get what we all want and go home."

James turned and waved his hand at everyone and continued. "We're all here to support both of you. Now bury your differences, and let's do what we came here to do!"

James said, "Ronnie's right, Mickey. Jail is kind of justice for him."

"No, it's not," seethed Mickey.

"Yes, it is, Mickey," said Aly. "You don't want justice. You want revenge!"

"Fine, if that's how you feel, go home! I'll do it myself. I don't need any of you. Just go back to where you came from. I don't care. I'll get justice for Valerie."

James said, "Calm down, Mickey. We're here for you. We aren't going anywhere. We just want you to be focused on the goal here. You want revenge, but the right thing is to get justice, which also goes for Marie and Veronica's father. We'll support you all the way. You know that."

They could all see the hurt in Mickey's demeanor. They got up, and as they passed him, each one put their hand on his shoulder, pledged their support, and promised to get justice and maybe even some revenge for Marie. They left him alone with his thoughts and grief.

Mickey sat alone on the stream's edge for hours as the time ticked away. Finally, Veronica came to him, sat down, and put her arms around him. "I know how you feel, and on a certain level, I want revenge also.

"You need to get some rest. You haven't slept in almost twenty-four hours. You must be at the top of your game when we go out again. Go. Get some sleep. We'll all work together to get what we want," she said softly. "I think James is putting together another run tonight. Just before dark, around the fire, I think he'll spell it out to us."

Wordlessly, Mickey got up, walked to the sleeping area, laid down, and soon dropped off.

CHAPTER 16

Following a Truck

Around the fire that night, James told the team that Grant had gotten desperate since his inventory had been destroyed.

"Isn't that the idea?" said Veronica.

"Yes, it is. Grant's ordered another one delivered tonight. When the first truck arrives with new inventory, they'll offload it, reload it onto another, and ship it out immediately. He hopes to do this before we can get to it and destroy it. He still hasn't figured out how we're getting our intel. He thinks he's got a leak in his staff. He has orders he needs to fill."

"What do you suggest we do about it, and what are we doing to extract Marie?" asked Veronica.

"We want to find out who his customers are and take them down also. As for Marie, we can't do anything until we have some intel on her location. We have to be right, or they might kill her before we can get her out, if they haven't already done it."

Alyssa said, "We're all in. Tell us your plan."

"Aly, you keep monitoring the loading dock. Ronnie can check the license plate when the truck comes in. That might give us its home location and a lead."

"How does that give us any useable information?" asked Mickey.

"Maybe it will, perhaps it won't, but while the first truck is being unloaded, we'll be sitting down the road waiting for it to come to us. We follow the truck to the end of the line. When it gets to the end, we destroy it. We'll have enough information to pass on to the authorities and let them take it from there. Our job is done," said James and looked around at the others.

"We'll need to concentrate on rescuing Marie," he added.

"What if the truck is new enough to have a GPS? Do you still want to follow it?" asked Mickey.

"Yes, a GPS will give you the location, but I want to see the site to decide what to do with it later. We'll be there to follow it if it doesn't have a GPS."

"Got it," nodded Mickey.

They bedded down at dark to be ready to go when Aly told them a truck had pulled in. Around midnight, a truck pulled into the loading area, and Aly awakened James and Mickey. They freshened up in the stream and got ready to leave and meet the truck.

"Hey, guys, this truck doesn't have a GPS. I hope your gas tank is full. We don't have a clue how long the haul will be," Aly said.

"This baby's got extra fuel tanks for a long-range," James said, referring to the Humvee. "We should be able to keep up. Also, when he makes a potty stop or snack and rest break, we'll attach our own GPS if necessary."

Alyssa gave him a thumbs-up sign.

They drove out of the campsite fully prepared. When they got to Florence, they parked down the street and out of sight, so Alyssa would have to inform them when the truck left and which direction it went.

"James, do you ever regret getting out of the military?" Mickey said while they sat waiting for the truck to pull out.

"Yes, I do, but I'm doing the same kind of work privately now instead of for the government. Before, the government told me what to do and gave me it's blessing. Now, they'll put me in prison if I get caught doing the same thing."

"That's scary, James."

"No. Not really. The same thing would happen if I got caught by a foreign government. Our government would disavow me. They wouldn't even admit that I'm alive. I accepted that possibility long ago."

Their comm units cracked. Alyssa called to them. "You guys on deck?"

"Yep, ready," answered James.

"Truck is headed your way," she informed.

James cranked up the Humvee and waited for the truck to pass. When it did, he pulled behind it, barely visible to the men in the truck. He didn't want to get too close, or the driver might make them as a tail.

Finally, they turned onto the highway, and James pulled up, went around the truck, and pulled ahead.

"Why'd you pass him?"

"Because this part of the road has no turn-offs, we can't lose him. When we get to a section where there's traffic or turn-offs, I'll drop back behind him again. I'll keep several vehicles in front or behind him to separate us when I can."

In silence, James drove on, weaving in and out of traffic, trying to stay within sight of the truck. Sometimes he was in front of the truck. Other times, he was behind him, but it was always in sight. Just before dawn, the truck pulled over at a rest stop. The driver got out and was followed by the relief driver. Mickey placed a magnetic GPS under the chassis. When he got back to the Humvee, he traded places with James. In a short time, they were driving into the town of Eugene, Oregon. They went to a large warehouse on the outskirts of Eugene.

Mickey passed the warehouse and continued down the road, and pulled over. They walked along the road back to the warehouse, staying out of sight of traffic and anyone working security at the building. James and Mickey circled the building to the loading area. When the truck was loaded, the two truck drivers switched vehicles and started to pull back out.

Mickey and James returned to the Humvee and called Aly at the campsite. "Aly, we have a GPS on the first truck, but we'll stay with it to get to the final destination. We assume that the other truck will return to the school plant with the same drivers that left with this truck. We'll send you a picture of the return truck to verify its return."

"Copy that, James. I'll keep track of you and your truck. Out," said Aly.

They continued forward, fueling up and switching the driving until they arrived at Caldwell, Idaho. The truck stopped, the cargo was taken off, and another load was put in it. And new drivers started the route back to Florence.

Mickey suggested to James that they stop the truck as they got near Florence.

"Okay, I was thinking the same thing. What's your reason," asked James.

"First, to see what the cargo is. Second, if we wait until it's closer to home, they won't know that we know the final destination."

"Bingo," said James. "If they know what we know, they might change it. Then we're at square one."

They drove on toward home behind the truck, keeping their distance.

"James, did you rent this Humvee or buy it?" Mickey asked.

"I rented it with the option to buy. Why?"

"I just wondered. What happens if it gets damaged?"

"We pay the rental, plus a hefty repair bill. If it's beyond repair, we bought it"

"Last question, I know you didn't sign any papers. You went through some private person. What if you don't go back to return or pay the bill?"

"Hefty cash deposit upfront. I mean greenbacks cash. No credit of any kind. It's not that we don't trust each other, but in some cases, the person's killed, so there's no one to pay the bill."

"What if you take it back and the person tries to stiff you on the damage deposit?" asked Mickey.

"He won't," stated James.

"Got it."

They rode on in silence as Mickey tried to comprehend the mentality of this strange group of people that call themselves mercenaries.

It was midnight of the following night when they got back to camp. Ronnie was sitting at the computer monitor console. Aly was asleep. Mickey and James also bedded down for the remainder of the night. They slept until almost noon the next day.

Mickey and James woke up to the smell of fish frying and coffee brewed over an open fire. They washed their faces in the cool stream, came back, and ate breakfast, sitting on the ground around the late morning fire. As they talked, Aly and Veronica took turns filling them in on Grant.

"What did you see at the final destination in Caldwell? Is it legit or a front for the drugs and weapons you found at the plant the other night?" asked Veronica.

"Because they were running the stuff at night, we can assume it's a distribution center like the one here, but we know that many drugs are brought here, disguised, and sent out mixed in with real food mixes. As for the weapons, it's just a stopover. We need to have more info on Grant's operation. Maybe he's just a terminal, or perhaps he's the wholesaler. We don't know."

"Actually, we do know. While you were gone, we switched watching the monitors and running background checks, and we got into the computers and their bookkeeping system. We didn't just sit around for two days while you were joyriding around the country," Aly laughed.

"We thought you ladies were just playing house while us men went out and brought home the bacon," James laughed.

Mickey quickly added. "I don't have enough guts to say something like that, even in jest. I've seen all of you in action, and you can be some mean ladies. You'd kill me if I said that!" he joked.

"Good deduction, Mickey. And James is one of the few people in the world that could say that and get by with it," added Alyssa.

Alyssa continued, "Seriously. We got a lot of background on those guys while you were 'bringing home the bacon,' as you said. Some employees are just simple-minded people who are doing a job and going home. Grant has brought some into his organization that went from a work release to full-time criminal employees. That guy you shot in the foot the other night is one of them. At least he's out of commission until his foot heals. He got a nice bonus for keeping his mouth shut. Nice touch, by the way. I wish I could have been there to do that for you."

"My gosh, you are one cold lady, Alyssa," said Mickey.

She looked at him with a fake smile and continued talking. "The other guy that started talking after you shot, Earl. He was Grady Steele."

"Yeah. We remember," said Mickey.

"Well, he won't be reporting for work anymore," Aly said.

Mickey and James shook their head in understanding.

Aly continued, "Grant, as we know, is the head of the operation here. Roger is his lieutenant. Most of the others are just drones that need constant attention. A few more are hired guns with zero brains."

"Did the drivers of the truck we blew up ever come back to the plant?" asked Mickey.

"Nope, they haven't been heard of since that night. I don't blame them. Grant isn't very tolerant," Aly said.

"We should go out tonight, just like we did the other night. Keep then on full alert," suggested Mickey.

"I agree," said James.

"Great," said James. "We roll at midnight! Aly can go again. Ronnie, you're not fully healed yet, so you can stay here and be overwatch."

Mickey could tell Veronica was disappointed, but she knew James was right. She was getting better each day but still had a long healing period ahead. She could watch the monitors and direct things from a chair in the van.

"Now, what happened with Grant while we were gone? What's he done with Marie?" asked Mickey.

"We don't know what he's done with her yet. As soon as we get a lead, we'll move to get her free. First things first," Alyssa said and continued talking. "He heard from the Sultan, Clayton Reece, which is a bad sign. Because of that, we assume Grant has some information about us.

"He knows who we are."

"How did he find out?" asked Mickey.

"He doesn't know about you, Mickey. You aren't in any database like we are," Aly said.

"But we were careful NOT to leave anything around that could trace back to us," he said.

"Okay, here's how it went down. After the Sultan got his retainer from Grant, he...."

"How did he get a retainer?" interrupted Mickey.

"Bitcoin. That's how most transactions are handled now over the dark web. Now, as I was saying, Grant got Marie's cover blown with her fingerprints in her classes at the school. Then it was a matter of deduction. Marie works for several teams but isn't working for anyone else at this time. The Sultan narrowed it down to three teams. Taylor, but he is in Europe right now, and Steinheim's team. He's taking a sabbatical in Israel, so he's out of action. That left me. He somehow tracked my flight plan here, and bam...we're blown."

"Wait a minute, Alyssa, you filed a flight plan to come here?" asked James surprised at this bit of information.

"Yes. I didn't think it was a dire situation, and besides, I had to refuel, so I had to file one, or I would have been reported to the FAA. They do have regs on certain aircraft, and my plane is one of them. I counted on it being a quick in-and-out situation. Not a full-blown op, James."

"Yeah, well, you thought wrong."

"Hey, don't blame this on me. You said it was a simple track a person down and go home."

"Okay, okay. You're right. I underestimated the whole thing. Go on, Aly."

"Fine, but the two things here are good and bad."

"Tell us the good first," said Mickey.

Alyssa smiled and said, "Mickey, you're invisible. You're the unknown. All of us are ex-military, but you aren't in the system. Now for the bad. James is, but when he goes on an op and wears a mask because of his previous injuries, they don't have any definitive information on him. They don't know who he is. He's known only as the Mongoose. The Sultan had determined, by simple deduction, that the Mongoose was in on this operation. The Mongoose has a reputation as being a cold-blooded killer, a psychopath with no heart or soul. He's the baddest of the bad. We know it isn't true, but that's the reputation he cultivated for his persona."

James smiled, "Yeah, it's a blessing and a curse."

"Yeah, the blessing is, it makes the enemy scared. The curse is that they prepare with the best they can find to pit against him. So, with that, Grant has called in some big guns of his own."

James asked, "Do you know who he has called in?"

"No, but we think he has assembled his team from the asset of others."

"What's that mean, Aly?"

"It means he gets individual men instead of calling an entire team. For example, Marie doesn't work exclusively for me. She'll work for anyone that pays her a salary. Or who will pay the most at the time. Grant's doing that. So, he's putting together his own elite team out of freelancers."

"How many? Do you know?" asked James

"Not exactly, but probably four to six to make up the team. The first one he'll get is a tactician. Someone like Steinheim himself."

"Whew, Steinheim's good. Who else?"

"I don't know yet. But we need to get some more men here. I'm going to call in Stretch and Shorty," Alyssa said.

"I agree. That'll give us five. Six if we count Ronnie."

"No. Ronnie isn't up to it. She may be a good detective, but she's injured. We can handle it with just five," insisted Mickey. "Aly is the best in her field, and as you said, James is the giant here, so if you get Stretch and Shorty, that's all we need."

James thought for a moment. "Yeah, I guess we can do with that many. Call them Aly."

"We don't know if he has gotten anything out of Marie, but she's tough and knows how to run an interrogation even from a prisoner's position. Grant's determined to punish her.

"We need to do something about Marie. We need to get her out of there before he makes up his mind. He hasn't said much about her yet, so I believe he's holding her somewhere onsite at the school facility. The problem with that is some innocents work there in the legitimate part of the bakery production company, so we can't just 'storm the Bastille' and get her out. And another problem has developed, we're down two people. Veronica's still recovering from her injury, and Marie's in danger of being killed. We need more experienced help. I've got in a call for Stretch and Shorty."

James knew who she was talking about. Stretch and Shorty, his working partner, went by the nickname because he is as tall as Stretch is short. They worked on a prior rescue mission with James and Mickey. They are good men that are sharp and efficient mercenaries.

"I'm sorry to have to bring in more people, but I concur. We need to fill in the gaps," James said.

"I'm having them bring in more equipment, like my drones. If they move Marie, we'll no longer have eyes and ears wherever they move her. My drones have infrared capabilities. We can't use that in the facilities here because all the machinery creates heat and makes it hard to see. Stretch and Shorty have their own weapons, but we need additional ammunition, so they'll also bring more ammo on the plane. We can't ship that commercially. They'll be boarding a chartered flight tonight and will be here first thing in the morning."

They spent the rest of the day getting ready for another midnight run. Mickey and Ronnie walked in the woods and waded in the cool stream. James did some fishing. Alyssa kept watch on the monitors and continued to run background checks on the employees.

They had fish again that night that James had caught in the stream. Mickey told James about the cars in Veronica's garage. Everyone noticed that Ronnie and Mickey seemed to click so well together. The others stayed back, giving them space. James was married to Mickey's sister Darcy, so he kept his distance from Alyssa and Marie. They were comrades in arms. That's all, but they made a good team. Mickey didn't have the unique skills that James, Alyssa, and Marie had, but he had learned to wield a gun as well as the others. Veronica was a marksman with a pistol, and Mickey suspected she could also fire a rifle.

The time went by quickly, and they were already talking about tactics and what they planned to do when they stopped the truck.

"I think we should do it exactly like last time," James said.

"Sounds good to me, but they might be armed and semi-prepared this time," said Ronnie.

"That's a distinct possibility," said Alyssa, "but we still have firepower and skills they don't have. They're a bunch of street thugs."

"I think it'll go smoothly. Grant somehow found out about Marie, so he might know about the rest of us. He doesn't know about me," added Mickey.

"Yeah, about that. I think when this is all over, you should get more training. If I remember correctly, your only training is some target practice shooting. There's a lot more to what we do than shoot a gun. You need tactical and strategic training and more," said Alyssa.

"I don't need that as long as you're here!" Mickey countered. "Besides, this's not a military unit. We don't go by any rules here. We make the rules."

"That's enough, boys and girls. We're here to help get justice for Valerie and Marie back safely. Mickey is our brother. We'll talk about training later. We all have special skills and training in different areas," James said.

"You're right, James. Sorry, Mickey, I didn't mean anything. I guess I'm just tired of sleeping on the ground and eating food cooked over an open fire."

"I know. No offense taken. Some people pay a lot of money to live like this," Mickey laughed. "They call it getting away from the world by camping."

Aly laughed, "We're all getting tired of this. Sleeping at odd hours, working at night. It's what we do when we actually get paid!"

"What do you do when you aren't on some job like this?" asked Veronica.

Alyssa said, "Work on developing a good case of skin cancer by sitting on the beach when we aren't training to hone our skills. With this kind of work, we won't live long enough to collect social security or even spend the money we're putting away for a rainy day."

"Aren't you a morbid bunch of people," said Veronica. "I'm a cop and expect to live well into retirement."

"It's different for us, Ronnie," said Alyssa.

"I guess it is."

"Okay, team," announced James. "Let's rest so we'll be ready when the truck leaves the loading dock."

"Since I can't go with you, I'll stand by the monitors," said Veronica.

They each got up and walked away from the fire to different corners of the site to be alone, rest, or just relax with their own thoughts. A while later, Veronica told James they had started loading the truck. They all got ready to move out.

"Let us know when they're about ready to pull out," said James.

"I will. They have the truck pulled in at a weird angle right now, and I can't see exactly what they are loading in it, but it should be easy enough to tell when they're wrapping it up. I'll let you know."

They all sat around the fire, drinking one more cup of coffee before getting into the Humvee. Finally, they got in and pulled out to meet the truck at Veronica's signal.

After Veronica confirmed the truck was on the same road as it was the last time, the team parked on the side of the road about a mile farther down, just around a bend from where they had stopped the first truck. They waited for the truck to come around the corner where they were stationed.

When they saw the lights on the road, they knew the truck was seconds away and would soon be in sight. As they expected, the truck turned into the bend, and Mickey stepped into the middle of the road. Mickey had the rocket launcher. James had an automatic rifle and moved to the side of the roadway to flank the truck when it stopped.

The truck sped up, and Mickey dove off to the side of the road. The truck passed them and skidded sideways to a stop just ahead, even with the Humvee. The truck's rear door raised, and men lined up at the door and began a continuous spray of gunfire back and forth across the road. None of the team members were hit, but they kept their heads down just in case. Mickey and Alyssa were on one side of the road, and James was on the other. They all kept hidden behind the embankments until the firing stopped.

Mickey whispered into the comm unit. "How did they know we were waiting for them?"

"The heck if I know. This shouldn't be happening," said James. "Cover me while I take a look. Rake the area with gunfire."

As Mickey began firing in the direction of the truck, James carefully raised his head to look. Inside the back of the truck were two giant searchlights shining back and forth across the road. He couldn't see any details because it meant looking directly into the lights, and he put his head back down.

"Take out the lights?" he called to the others.

"Copy," came an answer from Alyssa.

"Okay. Wait until the light passes away from your position, and take them out. I'll take the one on the left side. Aly, take the right side. We need to hurry before they start firing again."

The light once again began scanning across the road and on the embankment. When the light swept over and back to the pavement, Alyssa rose and put out the light with a hail of gunfire. She was followed by James, continuing the hail of bullets.

When the lights went out, all was quiet. Everyone held their positions. Everyone waited for a sound.

James and Alyssa raised their heads to look at the back of the truck. Sitting in the middle between the two men was Marie. She was tied to a chair with a bomb strapped to her chest. From the bomb to one man's hand was a wire connected to a switch. He called out.

"I have a dead man switch in my hand to the bomb strapped to your lady friend. I will drop it if you shoot us, and we all die. Got it?" he said.

James spoke up, "We won't shoot. What do you want?"

"We want you and your team to come out with your hands up, and we'll let her go!" the man called back.

Marie called out, "No. Don't do it. He has orders to kill all of us. He'll shoot you, then me! Shoot them. Shoot them all and blow the truck up. I'm a dead person walking."

James called back to the man, "Why don't we do it this way? I believe Marie. If we come out, you'll shoot us. We'll let you go if you put down your guns and come out. We all go home. I call that a win-win."

"No can do. How do we know that you won't kill us if we walk out?"

"Remember the truck we torched the other night?" James asked.

"Yeah, and the men are gone."

"Because we let them go. You didn't find any bodies, did you?"

"Maybe you took them away to dispose of them," the man answered.

"We don't take dead bodies. We want the bodies to be found if we kill someone," said James. "Also, when we came into the plant the other night, we didn't kill anyone. We could have. We zip-tied their hands and left them for the authorities. We'll do that with you if you come out unarmed."

The man thought for a second. "Then we'll be dead men walking. Our boss will have us killed."

"Not if we let you go. You can leave and not go back to the facility. Go somewhere where Grant can't find you," suggested James.

"We have families. We can't get them and get out of town before he sends someone after us. No. We go back," he said and opened up with a hail of bullets.

Finally, they all heard the side door of the truck slam. The truck started up, spun around in the direction it came from, and drove off as the gunfire started from the back of the truck as it disappeared.

When it had disappeared from sight, they all got up from their positions and converged in the middle of the road.

"What the heck just happened?" asked Mickey.

"I don't know, but they were prepared for us," said James.

"We didn't expect that," said Alyssa.

"We returned to the same road we took the truck last time," said Mickey.

"Yeah, and smart planning says never hit the same place twice," said Alyssa.

"That's why I thought it would be good because no one would expect us to do it. It's against all rationale in warfare," said James.

"We need to go back and regroup. We can't let something like this happen a second time," added Alyssa.

They drove back to the camp in complete silence. Each one was in shock that they had been outmaneuvered. No one was hurt, but it was a blow to their egos and a setback to the overall plan.

They got out when they returned to the camp, and James stoked the fire. They all sat down around the fire.

James started. "We need to assess what happened back there, so it doesn't happen again. We got complacent and paid the price for it. No one was hurt, but it was a potential disaster."

"No, kidding, Sherlock!" said Alyssa.

"First, let's get a good look at the video. Ronnie, can you pull up the truck's time period in the loading dock?"

"Sure, give me a minute," she said, leaving to go back to the van.

She called out for the team in a few minutes to see what she had found. She moved the monitor around so they could stand outside and watch the screen. They could see the truck back up to the loading dock in a few minutes at a slight angle.

James said, "Stop there." He looked at the picture, then said, "Move it forward a few frames."

As they continued to watch, they saw the forklift move forward with a large box about six feet high and park close to the back of the truck. They could see shadows clicking by upon close inspection, but they were obscured by the box and lift. The truck bounced slightly. Then the driver got back on the forklift, moved it out of the way, and closed the truck's rear door.

"There it is," pointed out Alyssa. "See the truck bouncing? That's the men entering the truck and moving around. We totally missed it."

"I missed it. I was the one watching the monitors at that time," said Veronica.

"Yes," said Aly. "That wasn't what you were looking for. Anyone could have missed it. They parked the truck at an angle and moved the forklift with the tall box to block the view of the men loading."

"Yes, but still, it was on my watch, so it was my fault," said Ronnie.

"It was your fault. We are trained to look for the tiny details, and so are you, but it happened, and you get a pass on this one. As

James pointed out, we've all been a bit slack. We underestimated them," said Alyssa.

"And that won't happen again," said James.

Just as he said that, the lights went out as the generator died. James called out, "Grab your weapons if you can reach them and take cover. Ronnie, get away from the van."

The weapons were stacked against the side of the van, where they put them when they got back to camp. James went to the right, and Mickey to the left. Ronnie followed Mickey, and Aly disappeared into the edge of the woods.

Shots rang out, and the side of the van was being peppered with bullets from automatic weapons fire. All went quiet as the team settled into defensive positions. They still had in their earbuds, so they were still communicating.

Mickey heard James whisper over the comm units, "Does anyone see who's out there?"

Aly answered back, "I see one. He's hiding about fifty feet from the van's right rear."

"I see him too," said Mickey.

"There has to be more," said James. "Find them before we move. Stay down."

Ronnie had been at the console, so she didn't have an earbud, but she was with Mickey in some low brush near the front of the van.

She tapped Mickey on the shoulder and pointed about sixty feet away near the Humvee. Mickey nodded. He saw him also, and everyone remained quiet.

Finally, a voice rang out. "You can come out. We have you surrounded," said a man with a thick Mexican accent.

"Over my dead body," answered Mickey.

"That can be arranged," answered the voice.

"Don't answer him," James said over the earbud. "They'll use the sound of your voice to get a fix on your position."

"We can't lay here all night," whispered Mickey softly in response to James.

"We can if we have to. Let them make the first move so that we can get a fix on them."

Aly said nothing because she knew James was right. So, they lay there unmoving, waiting for the other side to move. Mickey and Ronnie kept an eye on the man they had spotted, while Aly kept an eye on the man she had spotted.

After several minutes, James called over the earbuds, "Can anyone get a stick or rock to throw to create a noise diversion?"

"I can," said Aly.

"Good. Do it," said James.

"Use that noise as a diversion to move closer. Can you do that?"

"I'll move," said Mickey. "I've got him in my sight."

"Why don't you just shoot him?" said Alyssa over the earbud.

"If we take him alive, we can make him talk," said Mickey.

"Did everyone get their weapon as they went for cover?"

Mickey said, "Ronnie didn't, and she doesn't have an earbud. She's with me."

"Copy that, Mickey. On my count, everyone shoots a round in the air, and Aly, you throw the diversion near the man. The noise and the diversion may give Mickey enough time to get to him. Got it?"

They all reported back, "Copy that!"

Mickey said, "If I can't get to him, fine, but if it's him or me, trust me, I'll shoot him. If I have to."

James said, "Do what you can. On my mark. Three, two, one!" he called into the night. Three shots sounded off simultaneously, and there was a loud thump near the man between Alyssa and Mickey. There was a rustle. A body could be seen flying in the shadow of the campfire light. Mickey emitted a bloody scream as he landed on top of the man, and there was a hail of gunfire for a few moments. Aly and James tried to target the light from the gun barrels of the automatic weapons. There was a thud, a male grunt, and silence. They each sprayed the areas where they saw the guns fire. For the third time, silence. The team lay in the tall grass, waiting for noise from the enemy. Nothing. They waited. Silence.

Softly, quietly they heard the sound of heavy breathing. A man's voice called out. "Help. I'm hit. Help me, please."

Mickey started to rise, but James called out, "Get back down fool! Don't move, Mickey Ray."

There was another spray of gunfire right over his head as he dropped back down and lay hugging the ground. Ronnie was beside him, motionless a few feet away. He instinctively rolled over and pulled Ronnie with him. The soil in that spot erupted with bullets pelleting the ground as he did.

Mickey heard the sound of a rifle. One shot and another grunt. He knew James had pinpointed the shot source and shot the man.

There was a slight movement of grass on the other side of the campfire. Aly fired a volley of shots, and the movement stopped. They all lay there until dawn. When they finally left their positions, they moved around the campsite to assess the situation.

Four men, all dressed in black, were dead. They had automatic weapons. Mickey and Ronnie had laid all night long next to the man he had killed. He had driven a KA-BAR knife almost through the man to his spine, and he had bled out as Mickey had moved to get to Ronnie. Mickey was covered in the dead man's blood.

James said to Mickey. "Don't ever assume a man is wounded and calling for help. He may have been wounded, but as you saw, another was waiting to take you out if you moved to help him. They would have shot you if you had not dropped as I told you to."

"Thanks for the warning," Mickey answered.

One was shot in the head, another in the gut, and had laid there and bled out on the ground. They dragged the bodies into the clearing and laid them side by side.

Mickey stood and looked at the dead men. "How in the world did they find us?"

"Another detail we overlooked. GPS trackers," answered Alyssa.

"What do you mean?" he asked.

"Remember earlier when the truck stopped last night?"

"They continued running toward you and slid to a stop almost beside the Humvee."

"Yeah, they opened the back and started firing on us."

"They skidded at an angle and stopped. The angle hid the passenger's door. While we were pinned down behind the embankment, they blinded us with the searchlights and kept our attention with gunfire. A man got out of the cab on the passenger's side, went to the

Humvee, and put a tracker under it. Don't you remember hearing a door slam just before they started back up?"

"I heard it."

"That was the sound of the man closing the door after he got back inside, and they drove back the way they came. They didn't try to kill us. When we didn't surrender to them, they wanted our hide-out or staging area, which is here. Base camp. Now go look under the Humvee and find that tracker, and we need to move out again."

James said, "Aly's right, everyone. We've got to move and do it NOW before they send reinforcements."

Mickey slid under the Humvee and immediately saw the tracker. And pulled it off and crawled back out.

"What do we want to do with it?" asked James.

"Turn it off now. We get ready as soon as we can. We'll turn it back on when we leave so they can find the bodies."

They grabbed things and threw them in the van and Humvee, put out the fire, and drove away from the area. They saw the truck they had stopped last night on the way out. Marie had been taken away before their team came to the campsite. Mickey drove it back to the camp, parked it beside the dead men, and set fire to it. They left the area in search of another site to pitch camp.

As James drove the Humvee with Mickey, Aly and Ronnie fol-lowed them. Mickey sat in the front as James drove. He was still wearing the blood-soaked clothes he had spent the entire night in when the man he killed bled to death.

James looked at Mickey and said, "You smell like death, Mickey!"

"I know it," said Mickey. "I wouldn't have killed him as you asked, but he turned around and tried to shoot me when I dove at him. It really was him or me."

"I know," said James. "You did what you had to do. Sometimes it has to be done."

"I know," said Mickey.

James drove and went down several dirt roads looking for ade-quate campsites. They looked for something close to the water but away from the road with a small clearing.

After two hours of driving, they found a secure and secluded place, got out, and set up camp. After setting up camp, they checked the generator and fired it up. It started running, but not all electronics were working in the van. One of the computers had bullet holes, two monitors were riddled, and a keyboard was destroyed. The dish was ok since it was away from the action.

James and Aly headed to the nearest town to an electronics store to replace the destroyed equipment. Mickey got undressed and washed his bloody clothes in the stream. In minutes, Ronnie and Mickey sat down and were asleep, leaning on each other in the grass.

No one had slept for over 24 hours. They were running on adrenalin, but they had to continue until things were set up for business. In about four hours, James and Alyssa were back. They bought brought new monitors, a keyboard and a new computer. At the same time Alyssa was setting up the electronics, the rest of the team cleaned up themselves and got something to eat over the fire. James and Aly had gone to a grocery store and bought a few nonperishable types of canned meat, other meal necessities, and several steaks to grill.

Aly had also bought some motion-activated alarms they put in the brush around the camp to warn them of intruders. They also placed one at the road entrance to their site. When the site was secure, dinner was served.

Aly suggested they get another truck since the van was now pelleted with bullet holes. And they would be getting more equipment when Shorty and Stretch got here. They needed room for the drones, the necessary operating equipment, and the additional supplies for the extra men.

James and Alyssa went to get a large box truck and get rid of the van because they couldn't turn it back into the original truck rental full of bullet holes. They knew they would have to explain it. So, they called in that it was stolen, and they abandoned it in a public parking lot.

They stopped by the airport, picked up Stretch and Shorty and all the extra equipment, and stopped by a grocery store to get more fresh food and a gas station to get gas for the generator. Then they headed back to the campsite.

Stretch stepped out of the van and looked around the campsite. "Hey, you guys got it looking pretty good here. Just like home," he added.

He was a little person with dark hair around his shoulders, which he pulled back into a ponytail. His complexion was dark and swarthy, and his deep voice defied his small features. He wore camo pants and heavy boots.

His combat partner was Shorty. He was six foot five with a crew cut which helped disguise the fact that he was going bald and had a slight ring of hair around his balding head. He was also dressed in combat camouflage clothes and boots.

"How ya'll doin?" he said in a slow southern drawl as he got out of the van.

They both had extensive combat experience and had worked for Alyssa since they all got out of the military. Stretch was a master of hand-to-hand combat and was strong as a bull. Shorty's expertise was with various weapons, including automatic and sniper rifles. He was wiry and fast as a snake. They worked as a pair, and when you hired one, you got them both.

The evening was uneventful, and they all got a much-needed night's sleep. When they got up, Ronnie was sitting at the monitors in the new truck and taking in the foul-mouthed Grant as he fussed and cussed out anything and anyone around him that morning.

"Where is my truck, and where are my men? Somebody's got to tell me something. They left here the night before last, and we haven't heard a word. Where are they?" he screamed. His bandages were off, but his face was still bloated and bruised.

Roger sat across the desk from Grant and waited for him to calm down. When he did, Roger said, "We have someone on the way to check on them. The tracker they put on their vehicle is still active and hasn't moved. We should know something any minute. They're about 15 minutes out from the current location."

"We did exactly what Steinheim told us to do," said Grant.

"Yes, and we'll find out how it turned out when we find our men and the truck," answered Roger.

Alyssa turned from the monitors and looked at James. "He hired Steinheim! That's bad for us," she said.

"Not really. Now we know why they caught us off guard. That's all. We know who we are dealing with," said James.

"All we know is what we found out from that girl Marie. She's not working alone. That much we know. She and whoever she's working with has cost me millions of dollars in the past few days.

"Rudolf Steinheim is now running this show. See what he wants us to do next. Also, see when the men he recommended will be here. We need them now!" Grant said.

Grant sat silent for a minute, then spoke to Roger. "How did they know when our shipments were leaving? We have a mole. Bring everyone in and question them one at a time. Offer a reward for anyone that gives us information on a snitch. Give them a thousand dollars for a tip. A good tip. Five thousand for names and dates. Ten thousand if they give us some kind of proof of giving or selling information.

"Okay, now get out of here. I need some privacy to think," he said, waving his hand for Roger to leave.

James turned and left the two alone. Everyone spent the day getting ready for the next assault on the factory. Alyssa checked her drones and electronic equipment. The men, James, Mickey, Stretch, and Shorty, cleaned their weapons. Everyone exercised to limber up and keep mentally sharp. They ate sparingly and only high-protein superfoods to keep their energy and metabolism elevated for the evening.

Veronica still wasn't able to do a lot of moving around because of her injury. When she wasn't taking part in their field training, she monitored the situation at the school/factory.

About midday, Veronica called out, "Hey guys, you need to listen to this!"

Mickey, James, and Alyssa came to the truck to look at the monitors. Since Shorty and Stretch were not usually part of the mission planning, they continued with their training.

"Listen to this," Veronica said when they got to the monitors and looked over her shoulder.

Grant said, "Roger, we need to get Miss Sanchez out of here. Having her here is too much of a liability for us. The cops want to search the plant, and the FBI is keeping a closer watch on the place since the fire with those weapons."

"I agree. Where do you want us to take her?"

"Get a couple of the guys you trust, and move her to my hill house. This move is a need to know. Don't spread the word to anyone else. We still haven't found our mole."

After watching this exchange, they all sat in the back of the truck with their own thoughts.

"I don't know if that's good news or bad news," Mickey said to no one in particular. "If we had known she was still at CIOF, we could have gotten her out earlier."

James thought for a moment. "True, Mickey, but we didn't know, and it'll make it more difficult if Grant brings in some experienced people."

Alyssa spoke up, "Ronnie, can you do a search on Grant and find out where his hill house is located?"

"I'll start on that right now," Veronica answered. She moved to the computer in the forward section of the truck and started punching keys.

"That changes things," said Mickey as they all got out of the back of the truck.

"It does, but that's why we brought in Shorty and Stretch. We can do it. We'll wait and try to find out who he brings in. We'll know their weaknesses if we can get a background on them," said Alyssa.

"You really look at that stuff?" asked Mickey.

"When we can. It's like sports teams. You look at the players. The outfielders moved back whenever Babe Ruth came up to bat because everyone knew he aimed for the fences. Soldiers are the same. Some are sharpshooters. Some are snipers. Some are good at hand-to-hand combat, some are…." Alyssa was saying this when Mickey interrupted.

"Okay, I get it," said Mickey. "What do we do until then?"

James said, "I think we should concentrate on getting Marie free. As soon as we find the location they're taking her, we need to move. Night or day. We get her out!"

Mickey and Alyssa agreed. While Veronica started searching for Grant's house, they went back to training. She called them back to the truck command center in about an hour.

"Alright, I found out that Grant has several houses in the area. It seems he moves from one to the other, depending on his mood. During the summer, he stays at his home in a resort-style development that overlooks the eight-hole of the golf course at the country club. During fall and spring, he has a house that overlooks highway 126 for the view. During the winter months, he has an apartment downtown. He also uses that when he needs a place to keep a girlfriend. By the way, he's divorced. His ex and two kids live in San Diego, California.

"I have the address and downloaded some overhead satellite views of the one he calls hill house," said Veronica.

James looked at the maps and smiled. "This is great. I'll look at this and have a plan for us to take it. Ronnie, does the city have a floor plan for the house? Many cities have floor plans of a building that's submitted when a request is made for a building permit."

"They should. Florence requires floor plans, and they put them online along with other pertinent information about the property. I'll pull them up and print them out also."

While she was doing this, James and Alyssa looked at the satellite maps.

James pointed at the map. "I think we should come at it from behind. The owners rarely go into the front area. They enter from the back, away from view. We'll enter that way also."

Veronica came over and placed a set of floor plans on the makeshift table for them to see.

"The house is three floors," she said. "The first floor has a living room, kitchen, great room, formal dining room, and a bathroom. The kitchen area is on the side that faces the highway. That is backward from most homes, but you must understand they built this house for show on the outside, but you enter it from the rear directly into the living room. The main staircase goes up to bedrooms and bathrooms on the second floor. The top floor is a master suite area with a giant bathroom, bedroom, kitchen, and sitting area. That will probably be the area that Marie will be kept in. You can live in it. There is room for her and her security guards. She can't jump out of a window that's that high off the ground," described Veronica.

Mickey spoke up, "We only shoot when we are fired at!"

Shorty looked directly at Mickey and said, "If someone is near a gun, I'll shoot him. He has it there to shoot me, and I'll not give him that chance. Got it, Mickey?"

"Me too," said Stretch.

Mickey shook his head, "Whatever."

"If we run into non-combatants, do not shoot, understand?" said James. "Same as past rules, secure them with zip ties and duct tape."

"If we have to," said Shorty.

"You have to," said Mickey.

Aly then said, "I'll be flying an overhead drone with infrared signatures. I'll report and direct you whenever possible. As in other missions, I'll run a drone overhead back and forth to give you a description of the house and possible entrances we can't see from sat photos. I'll give you all the info to direct you when it comes to me. We get in and get out. We'll be using masks as in the past to prevent recognition. Secure everyone with ties and tape. If you can wound instead of kill, do it. And when you do, dress the wound to prevent bleed out, if possible."

That brought a sigh from Stretch and Shorty. They just wanted to shoot and move forward.

"When do we go?" asked Shorty.

"Be ready to move out at sunset. We can't take this truck. It's too big, and the Humvee will stick out like a sore thumb. Mickey and I will go into town and get another van."

CHAPTER 17

The Rescue at Hill House

Mickey and James left for town to rent another vehicle. They immediately went to a truck rental and got an extended-length van large enough to carry all of them and their equipment but not so large as to attract attention parked on the roadside down from the house.

They put the drones, weapons, and accessories in the van and piled in about an hour after dark. They discussed going late at night but decided against it because they might not expect an early rescue attempt. Either way, Marie would be guarded around the clock. Time of night wasn't an issue. Darkness was.

When they got about a mile from the house on a deserted stretch of road, they parked and helped Alyssa with the drones. She got them in the air and started them toward the house as the men started through the woods. In a matter of minutes, they heard the crackle of the comm units in their ears.

Alyssa spoke softly but clearly, "I'm over the house on the entrance side. The entire area is lit up, and a large open yard around the house. There's no way to make a hidden approach. There are two guards at the back door. That's the door entrance, driveway side.

Floodlights under the eaves are mounted on the corners on all sides. I'll move around to the front, facing the highway below."

Alyssa moved the drone overhead to the highway side of the house and continued her report. "There are two guards on the front porch. They're laughing and talking. Not very alert or attentive to their surroundings. Amateurs, for sure."

"Each side or end of the house seems clear. There are no guards, but if either guard from the front or back yard moves away from the house, they can cover the sides. Be careful if you decide to approach from the sides. I'll get higher so I can see everything directly overhead. Lights are on all over the inside of the house. So far, infrared shows three people in the back room of the third floor. There are three people on the first floor in the backroom, possibly a great room or kitchen dining area," Alyssa.

"All four guards on the outside are armed with automatic guns. I can't give you a make or model. They suspect something is overhead. I may have gotten close enough that they could hear the drone. I moved to a higher altitude to reduce noise, but they kept looking up. We still have the cover of darkness."

Mickey worked his way around to the highway side of the house. At the same time, Shorty went to the garage side if someone tried to escape from that area. Stretch went to the driveway that entered the house and began setting explosives around some of the trees if someone tried to get out in a vehicle.

James set his sights on the men stationed at the back door. Alyssa created a diversion by lowering the drone right in front of the men on the porch on the driveway side. When they looked directly at the camera, she began raising it to divert their attention from James, who was running at them.

By the time they saw James, he had thrown a punch at one man, knocking him over the railing of the porch. He grabbed the other man and drove the butt of his gun into the man's gut knocking the breath out of him. James took a zip tie and tied him to the railing. The other man got up from the side of the porch and reached for the gun lying in the grass beside him. James raised his gun and pointed it at the man.

"Do you really want to reach for that gun?" James asked.

While this was going on from the entrance side of the house, Mickey stood up and called to the men on his side of the house. "You're surrounded. Put your hands up!"

Each man reached for the gun, sitting against the railing next to where they were standing. As they grabbed and raised their weapons, two shots rang out. Each man fell where he stood.

Mickey looked around. At the corner of the house stood Shorty with his gun on his shoulder, pointing at the dead men. "You're welcome, Mickey!" he called out.

Mickey ran to the porch and threw a flash-bang grenade through the window at the three men inside. It went off, and Shorty opened the door and went inside with a gun raised, followed by Mickey and his weapon to his shoulder. Three men were on the floor with their hands over their ears, in obvious pain from the explosion.

James entered from the other side of the house, joined Mickey and Shorty, and zip-tied the men's hands behind their backs. Mickey and James went up the stairs with guns raised while Shorty stayed downstairs guarding the others.

Alyssa's voice came through their comm units. "Two of the three figures are moving toward the door where you're located."

James moved left and backed down the hall away from the walls on each side of the door, while Mickey did the same on the other side.

As they waited, soon the door to the room slowly opened. An extended arm came out holding a handgun. James stepped forward, reached out and grabbed it, and pulled the man out. He stumbled out the door, fell down the stairs, and landed at the bottom with his head at an odd angle. James quickly stepped back down the hallway to the side against the wall.

Someone inside the room call out, "Don't shoot!"

"Are you armed?" called James.

"No. The gun's on the floor. I don't have it in my hand," the person said.

"Slide it out the door," James called back to him.

"I can't reach it."

"You better reach it, or we open fire," said Mickey.

The sound of gunfire rang out, and holes appeared through the wall going from one side of the door to the other. James and Mickey hit the floor as the bullets whizzed over their heads.

James and Mickey rolled onto their sides, returned fire through the walls, and then heard a thump hit the floor.

"Is there anyone else in there," James asked.

A muffled, distorted voice came through the bullet-riddled walls. "Just me," which they both recognized as Marie's voice.

James and Mickey got up and stepped into the room, and Marie was in the corner. They stepped over the dead man and went to Marie. Her face was bruised with several cuts on her face and lips. One of her eyes was swollen shut, and her hair was matted with blood. One of her hands was bandaged, and her arm was in a makeshift sling.

James said through gritted teeth, "Someone will pay and pay dearly. Let's get her out of here. Be easy with her."

They looked at the dead man as they helped Marie out the door. "I recognize him. That's Hemingway. I'm glad we didn't get into hand-to-hand combat with him. He would have taken us both out. He was a good soldier," said James.

When they got outside, he called Alyssa to come to pick them up at the house. It was clear. As they waited, he told Stretch to take one of the explosives and set it inside the house, and when they left, to blow the trees in the driveway so that fire trucks couldn't get to the burning house.

Alyssa came, and they loaded Marie into the back of the truck as gently as possible. They got everyone out of the house, zip-tied them together, and tied them to trees beyond the house. As they drove off, stretch set off the explosives in the house, and finally, when they got to the end of the driveway, he set off the ones to make the trees fall across, cutting off access to the house.

On the way back to the base command camp, they stopped at a drug store in town and bought first aid supplies and bandages for Marie. They saw the smoke and light from the fire far away in the hills. They knew exactly what it was and how it started. And it made them feel a bit better, for Marie's sake.

CHAPTER 18

Marie Back at Base Camp

They got Marie back at camp and laid her on Veronica's air mattress upon Veronica's insistence. Veronica and Alyssa cleaned her up and dressed her wounds. She had bruises all over her body where she'd been beaten. She passed in and out of consciousness throughout the night but was awake and clear-headed by the following day.

They gave her fresh coffee and warm food, making it easier for her to eat with her swollen jaw. Although they could not check for internal injuries, they closely watched her for any signs of distress. Other than her superficial bruises, and soreness, she seemed medically okay.

After lunch, she got up and walked around, slowly adjusting to the aches resulting from her beatings. By evening, Marie insisted that she was ready to go back into the field. She said she would be prepared for combat with a few over-the-counter drugs. With respect to her ordeal and mental torture, everyone agreed to let her go with them for a bit of personal satisfaction of revenge. James swore he would help her get it.

Mickey took James aside and spoke privately to him. "Do you think it's wise to let her go out so soon?"

"That, little soldier, is the toughest woman I've ever met, and I wouldn't try to stop her from getting her pound of flesh. I think it would be unwise not to let her go. Trust me on this, Mickey," James answered.

Alyssa came to James and said, "Mickey said you recognized one of the men guarding Marie."

"Yeah, one of the men was Lawrence Hemingway."

"He is or was one tough cookie. You're lucky you shot him because he could take out a bull elephant single-handedly if you had gone in one-on-one."

"I know. I seriously doubt if he was one of Marie's interrogators. He wasn't that kind of guy. But he was one of the best to place to guard her," James added.

Marie walked up to them. "Hemingway never touched me, but the other guys did beat the crap out of me. Hemingway was the only reason no one raped me. He had his decent side, but if you had come through that door, he would have put you both down. He was hired to guard me, and he wouldn't have let his mother come in there. He was a professional," she said with a slight muffle due to her facial bruises.

"He must have been one of the pros that Grant brought in. We need to be extra careful. We were lucky on this one. Keep our eyes and ears open in the future," said James.

They watched the monitors when Grant got the news about his hill house. He was furious.

"What in the world happened? I had armed guards watching that little Latin tart! How did she get away?" he screamed. "I had some of the best men money could buy guarding her."

Marie flared up at that description of her. "I am NOT a tart, and if he were within my reach right now, I'd rip his face off!" she screamed at the monitor. "So help me God, if I ever lay eyes on him again, I will kill him! I swear to God, I'll do it."

She reached up to her face to her jaw and gently touched a large purple bruise.

Mickey laid his hand on her shoulder and said, "Calm down, Marie. Don't get so upset."

James and Alyssa looked at Mickey with a warning glance and shook their heads at him.

Marie turned around, slapped Mickey across the face, and screamed at him, "Don't you tell me what and who I can and cannot kill, Mickey Ray! You don't have a clue what I went through the last couple of days. You can walk away right now if you can't deal with it. I came here to help you get justice for Valerie. Now, it's my turn. I want justice for her, but for myself, I want revenge, and I will get it. Do you hear me?"

Mickey was shocked at her outburst. He didn't even raise his hand to the spot where she had slapped him. He just stood at attention before her.

"I said, do you hear me, Mickey Ray Christianson?" she repeated.

He nodded.

"Don't ever tell me to calm down again. Now get out of my face! I'll not follow you to that evil man when we go out. I will lead the pack, and I will kill him. I said get away from me!"

Mickey turned and walked down to the stream. All that could be heard was the sound of the running water in the stream and the gentle rustle of leaves as a gentle breeze blew them off the trees.

James came over a few minutes later and sat with Mickey beside the flowing water. He said quietly, "Sorry she blew up at you that way, bro."

"She was right. I should have never said that to her. I don't know what she went through."

"A bit of advice, Mickey. Every one of us has seen the worst of humanity. Don't ever tell us to calm down, especially a female soldier who spent time as a prisoner."

"I know that now. Maybe I should go and apologize to her," Mickey said.

"No. Just give her space for a while. She knows that you didn't mean anything by what you said. She's mad and wants revenge right now. Let her come to you when she's ready. Then you can apologize. She'll accept it, and she'll apologize in return. Just don't do it ever again," James said.

"Got it. Thanks for the advice."

"Come on, let's eat some of those delicious MREs we bought at the camping store," James said as he patted Mickey on the back. When they got back to the fire, everyone was eating.

"We need to run to the grocery store in town. I understand that we gotta eat these things when we're in a jungle, desert, or God's wasteland, but not when we're just a few miles from civilization," said Stretch.

"I agree," said Shorty as he wolfed down a small tin of what was described on the label as "roast beef."

James said, "Okay. Mickey and Ronnie will make the next run in the morning. Meanwhile, Ronnie will take the shift at the computers tonight, and since we had visitors in our camp earlier, Shorty, you take the first watch. Is that acceptable to everyone?"

They all mumbled, "Yes."

Mickey went back down to the stream and sat down with his bare feet in the water.

A few minutes later, Marie came and sat down beside him. They sat side by side for almost five minutes before she spoke to him.

"I'm sorry I slapped you. I was out of line. I was upset and just lost it," she said.

"You don't need to apologize. I understand. You were right. I don't understand what you went through. You have every right to be furious with me," Mickey said.

"I didn't have any right to be furious with you. And I wasn't. I just took it out on you, that's all. It won't happen again."

"Right now, you need to heal, physically and mentally. I respect that. I hope that slapping me made you feel a bit better."

"No, it didn't. I'm still sorry it was you and not Grant. You're a good man, Mickey Ray," she said, gently placing her hand on his arm and leaning against his shoulder.

After a few minutes, they each got up and went to their sleeping areas on opposite sides of the camp. They had moved Veronica's mattress to give Marie a bit of comfort for her bruises to heal. Veronica now slept in a sleeping bag next to Mickey.

The following morning, Marie was sitting in front of the monitors taking her turn, and Veronica was stoking the fire in the middle of the camp.

"What's the plan today, Mickey?" asked Stretch.

"I don't know. That's James' area of expertise. James, what do you suggest?"

Marie spoke up, "I want to go back and kill the SOB."

"No, Marie. Let's have some fun first," James answered her. "Ronnie said he has a house at the golf course."

"Yep. It isn't as nice as hill house, but it's assessed at over a million by the city," added Veronica.

Mickey spoke up, "Aren't all these homes insured? He doesn't really lose anything when they pay off. It just gives him an opportunity to get a new house."

"Not if we make it look like arson and frame Grant for it," said Veronica. "I know the city fire marshal. I'll call him and tell him a few things to pay special attention to. First, you took down a couple of trees in the entrance driveway at the hill house so fire trucks couldn't get in to put out the fire. Investigators know they didn't do it themselves when you left the guards secured with the zip ties. It'll be listed as a suspicious fire. That alone will hold up an insurance payout until the investigation is complete. If you do it again to his house at the marina, that's no coincidence. That's another reason to hold up the insurance payout."

"I still want him dead," Marie said.

"Didn't you say he had an apartment downtown? What can we do about that one? We can't burn down the building. Other people live there, and we can't put them at risk," said Mickey.

James fielded this question, "You're correct, but we can destroy everything inside and trash the unit. I mean destroy cabinets, carpets, and as the saying goes, everything nailed down!"

"Okay. What do we hit first?" asked Stretch.

"Caldwell, Idaho," said James.

"Do what in Idaho?" asked Stretch.

"We hit the drop point in Caldwell, Idaho," said James.

"Why so far away?" asked Veronica.

"Grant won't expect us to hit there," said James.

"Yeah, and it won't hurt him either," said Marie.

"Marie, please be patient. We'll let you have your pound of flesh from Grant. I promise," answered James. "You're correct. It won't hurt him directly, but when it gets out that he is at war with someone, and he doesn't even know who it is, other buyers and terminals will cut him off."

"I'll tell you what I'd like to cut off," Marie interjected.

James ignored that comment and continued, "We fly in to a small airport located about fifty miles away from Caldwell. It's the Weiser Municipal Airport. We hit the drop point and get back out the same night. We send out word that we'll take out his contacts one by one, and they'll drop Grant like a hot potato. Also, Steinheim won't expect us to hit so far away. He will beef up the guard at the other houses."

"What do we do after all his contacts stop shipments to the factory here?" asked Marie.

"We shut him down. We still have video and audio. We record it and turn it over to the authorities. He'll spend the rest of his life in jail. Everyone gets justice. Mickey gets justice for Valerie, Ronnie for her father, and Marie for what was done to her while they had her," said James.

Marie stood up, "Jail isn't good enough for him, and the guy he ordered to take me and, when it was over, to kill me. I want to see Grant dead."

Veronica sat quietly, wiping away a tear.

Mickey looked at her and asked, "What do you want, Ronnie?"

"He ordered my father killed, so as a daughter, I want him dead," she said, looking around at the group.

"But…," added James.

"But as a cop, it's my duty to bring him in alive to stand trial."

"What are you right now, Ronnie?" asked Mickey.

"A daughter!" she said with finality.

James said, "We'll let it play itself out. It goes how it goes. Okay, guys, I've got a plane to charter. Aly, you're the only pilot we've got, so I guess you have to go with me to rent the plane. We'll fly out tonight."

"Why don't we use my plane?" Alyssa asked.

"No. We don't want to use your plane. That can be traced and it might create a link to us. We want to keep us as separate as possible. It's a bit like robbing a bank and using your own car as the getaway vehicle."

"I see, but they can still connect us with the rental records," Alyssa answered.

"Possibly but it's just one more step between them and us. Let's go," James said, getting up.

Shorty and Stretch agreed to stay and guard the camp. Marie needed more rest for her bruises, so Veronica and Mickey decided to go to town and get fresh supplies.

As they drove to town, Mickey and Veronica talked.

"Hey, I'm sorry about your dad being involved with this case."

"Why?"

"I don't know. I'm just sorry this is all connected."

"I'm not. I wanted to find Daddy's killer ever since that day. A drive-by shooting is rarely solved. Two other people were also killed, so that family will get closure when this is over."

"That family, you say?" asked Mickey.

"Yeah, it was a little girl and her father. He had taken her out for a day at the park, and they were killed when Daddy was shot."

"Again, I'm sorry."

"I don't want to talk about this anymore. You are ruining a potentially fun evening."

Mickey saw the opportunity to lighten the mood, "Ha! You think this was supposed to be a fun evening. We're going to town to get supplies. Lady, you have a warped sense of fun."

"At this point, I'll use any necessary means to get my mind off what we're doing."

Mickey got serious. "I understand. You're right. Let's get a sandwich and maybe a dessert at the little bakery."

Veronica gave him a sarcastic smile. "Ha, ha. You think you're funny, don't you?"

They parked the vehicle and walked down the street hand in hand. She walked slowly and still favored the area she was shot, but it was getting better. They got a sandwich and soft drink at a delicatessen, then walked down to the Bake Shop that Henry Oswald owned. When Henry saw Veronica, he came to the little table to take their order.

"Hello, Henry," said Veronica. "How've you been?"

"Not so good," he answered. "I haven't seen you around town much the past couple of weeks. Hope everything is okay with you."

"Oh, yes. I've just been relaxing at home. Doing nothing special. You know how it goes. Sometimes a person just needs a little downtime. Why are you not doing so well, may I ask?" she said casually.

He looked sadly at the floor. "My son Nickolas was killed in the attack on the CIOF. Since you work for the police department, you already knew it."

"Oh, no. I didn't hear. As I said, I've taken a few days off, but I saw a clip on the news on television. I didn't know that Nick was the man that was killed. I'm so sorry, Henry."

"Thank you, Veronica," he said. "Is your shoulder okay? I see you kind of moving it like it's sore."

"Oh, yes. I'm okay. I pulled a muscle a few days ago, working in the yard."

"I see. The way you favor it, it looks like it's a bit more serious. Maybe you should see a doctor. I can recommend one if you like," he said.

"No. Really. It's just a sprain. I'm okay. We've changed our minds. Could we get the dessert and coffee to go, Henry?" she said urgently. "We need to go to a meeting."

"A meeting? What kind of meeting do you need to go to if you take personal or vacation days?"

"Nothing you would be interested in, Henry. Trust me. It's nothing. Please hurry, or we'll be late."

Henry put the desserts in a box, brought the coffees in a Styrofoam cup, and took their money. As they left, he walked over to take another order from customers at another table.

Mickey urged Veronica to move quickly down the street so they could do the needed shopping and leave town before someone showed up and put a tail on them.

As they rushed out of town, Veronica said to Mickey, "Do you think we have someone tailing us?"

"No, but we need to stay away from town from now on. They may have already put two and two together. We don't want to attract any attention. Let's get back to the campsite."

CHAPTER 19

Attack in Idaho and Golf House

When they got to the campsite, James and the team were loading weapons in the back of the van.

When they loaded everything, they sat down and prepared some of the food Mickey and Veronica brought back to the site.

"How did it go, James?" asked Mickey.

"As planned, Mickey," he answered. "We rented a four-person jet. We'll land at Weiser Municipal Airport and be back here by dawn. Simple."

"Four-person? Who's not going?" asked Mickey.

"You, Marie, and Ronnie are staying here. You guard the camp," said James.

"Well, that sucks!" said Mickey.

"I see. You don't want to stay alone with two beautiful women all night?" laughed Alyssa.

"Shut up, Aly. You know what I mean!" said Mickey.

"I know, but all we need is four people, and both ladies are a bit under the weather. You get to guard them. Let them get some rest."

"I guess I have no say in the matter."

"That's right, bro," said James as he gathered the paper plates, cups, and plastic utensils and threw them into the fire.

"We're going to leave soon and head to the airport. Let's go over what you guys can do while we're gone. I was kidding about you watching over the ladies. We need you to hit Grant's golf course house. If we do this simultaneously, he'll think we're everywhere. He'll blow his stack. We need to be in two places at the same time. It's not winter now, but all indications show that Grant's staying at his downtown apartment. It's closer to the factory, and he's trying to keep an eye on things there."

James pulled out the map they had downloaded and printed out. James pointed to the map and the surrounding area of the golf course house.

"Mickey, if you and Marie enter the area from this location," he said, "you can enter the house and make sure no one is staying or guarding it. If someone's there, secure them, get them out and torch it. Do your best to obtain total destruction. While you're there, we'll be in contact with you, and if possible, we'll hit the drop point terminal in Idaho simultaneously."

"If Marie is up to it, we can do it," said Mickey assuredly. "Are you up to it, Marie?"

"You bet I am!" she said. "What do you want us to do if someone's there?"

"There will be a good chance that Steinheim will have some elite guards there. Let Marie guide you since she may know the men and their strengths and, more importantly, weaknesses.

"I know you don't want to hear this, but if Marie recognizes someone, take them out. If you don't, they will still be here to attack later. We don't want that. Got it, Mickey?"

"Yeah, I guess that makes sense," answered Mickey.

"If it's anyone else, you can secure them with ties, move them outside, and torch the place," said James. "Aly, let's get going. We have a ways to go. Shorty, Stretch, load up!"

They all got into the vehicle and left Mickey, Marie, and Veronica at the campsite. Mickey waited for the phone call telling him that Alyssa was on the approach to the Weiser Municipal Airport. Mickey got the call around dark that evening.

Marie and Mickey drove to Grant's golf house and waited down the road from it, waiting for instructions from Veronica at command camp. It was dark, and they kept the lights out in the vehicle. Finally, they got a call saying the team was pulling up to the facility outside Caldwell, Idaho. Mickey and Ronnie got out and made their way to Grant's golf house.

As the map showed, it was right at the edge of the eight-hole of the golf course. Mickey worked his way around the side next to the golf course while Marie stayed outside of sight to the driveway entrance. All the lights were off inside the house, but they remained in the shadows of the moonlight. The house was two-story with wood siding painted a rustic brown to fit in with the rest of the homes along the road to the country club building. Mickey went up to the house and hid behind one of the bushes against the house. He placed a small explosive underneath a first-floor window so the explosion would go inside the house and cause more damage. Marie entered the garage's side door and placed an explosive charge next to the gas water heater and furnace. After placing the charge, she called Mickey, and he came around the side and followed her inside the house.

Since they didn't expect anyone to be home, they only had holstered sidearms. They crept through the house, room by room, to ensure no one was inside. As Mickey walked almost silently up the stairs, Marie followed from behind. They both heard the footsteps simultaneously, and they each drew their weapons. A large dog lunged at Mickey from the top of the stairs. Mickey fell backward as the dog connected with Mickey's arm and sunk his teeth into it. The dog crunched down on his forearm, and they both rolled down the stairs into Marie and hit the floor. The dog began shaking his head, trying to tear into Mickey's arm, while Marie constantly began pounding on the dog's head with the butt of her pistol. Finally, the dog loosened his grip and fell over with his skull crushed. He quivered, moaned a few times, lay on the floor, and died.

Mickey sat up and lay against the wall as his arm bled over the floor next to the dog.

Marie said, "Mickey, are you okay?"

She sat on the floor beside him holding her pistol pointed at the top of the stairs.

At the top of the stairs was another dog. In the moonlight, it seemed like a creature from hell with his teeth bared, growling, and eyes glowing with hatred toward the two people that had just killed his partner. It slowly started down the stairs, one step at a time.

"Yeah, he didn't hit anything crucial, like an artery or anything, but I'm bleeding like a fountain. Let's hurry and get out of here," he answered.

Marie, let off two shots from her silenced pistol. After the two pops from the gun, the dog dropped on the top steps of the staircase.

Marie got up and started up the steps. As she went up, she spoke softly to Mickey, "I'll make sure no one else is here and see if they have any bandages to fix you up before we leave."

Mickey sat holding his hand on the wound to slow the bleeding while Marie went from room to room on the second floor. He heard her opening doors and rummaging through drawers. He knew she was looking for first aid items for him. Finally, she came back down the stairs and announced that all was clear. She had a small bag in one hand and still held her pistol in the other.

As Mickey got up, he heard a low noise from above and saw the silhouette of a man with a gun. As the man raised the gun to fire, Mickey shot the man in the chest. The man dropped the gun, grabbed his chest, and fell into the rail, crashing through it and falling to the floor next to Mickey."

"Where did he come from?"

"I don't know. He just appeared at the top of the stairs," said Mickey.

Marie turned the man over and looked at his face. "Glad you saw him. They call him the Phantom. I don't know how I missed him when I was checking out upstairs, but he has an uncanny habit of appearing and disappearing. His real name is Oden Salinger. Those were his dogs, but I'll tell you more about him later. How's your arm?"

"It hurts. And I'm still bleeding like a waterfall."

They went outside and called Veronica to convey the message that charges were set and the house was clear.

As they got back into their vehicle, Marie drove while Mickey wrapped rags around his arm to stop the bleeding. She drove to the road outside the country club golf course. When they got onto the road, they blew the charges and watched the flames in the rearview mirror as the house exploded. Mickey set the charges to ensure the exterior walls would burn, and the charges Marie set would blow the gas line, and the house would be a total loss. It would also cover up the blood and carnage that had taken place with the man and his dogs on the stairs.

As Marie drove, she talked to Mickey to keep him from passing out. "Hey, Mickey. Are you still with me?" she asked.

"Yeah. I'm here."

"Sit up. Talk to me. Don't pass out on me now!"

"I'm not. I'm okay."

"You sure? You saved my bacon back there. I should have known that Oden was here as soon as we saw those dogs. I've only met him a couple of times. He uses one of those silent dog whistles to train his dogs. You still with me, Mickey?"

"Yes. I'm still here," he said, getting agitated with her.

"Hang in there. As I was saying, Oden trained those dogs, and they can move around very quietly. I don't know how I missed him. I guess he was hiding somewhere in a corner and didn't come out until he knew we were downstairs. If you hadn't seen him, we'd both be dead," she continued.

"Thank you for the background on Oden, but right now, I don't care. I'm trying to stop bleeding all over the car."

"Are you sure that dog didn't sever an artery? There sure is a lot of blood everywhere."

"I'm sure. A little blood goes a long way. It's just so messy. We'll never get all the blood off of everything," he said.

"It's a rental. Let the rental company clean it up," Marie said. "Are you still coherent?"

"Yes. I'm alive and fully awake. Now leave me alone and drive, Marie! Just take us back to the campsite."

Alyssa launched a drone over the site to get some infrared interior views. As she did this, Shorty, Stretch, and James made their way to the facility, being careful to stay out of sight of passersby on the road leading to it.

When they got to the facility, it was about two hundred feet away from the road and protected from view by a line of tall trees and undergrowth. This made their job easier to keep hidden. It had very little in the way of security. There was no fence or guard gate. They could almost walk right up to the building. The only problem was once inside the tree line, it was an open field. They could be seen over a hundred feet away, with only tall grass to cover them. It was dark, but the sky was clear, and there was moonlight, so they kept close to the ground, using the tall grass as cover.

Aly called them over the earbud communication units. "Guys, infrared views show there are eight men inside. Six are in the same area. Don't know if anyone is armed. They aren't carrying any weapons like rifles or automatic guns. They may have side arms.

"Wait, don't move. Second-floor tower. Left side. I'm sure it's used for machinery that powers other equipment inside the main building. Something's in there. It's giving off a heat signature, but I can't tell if it is machinery or a person. It isn't moving. Right tower has something also. It's moving, and he has some kind of long-barreled gun. I can't tell. I got it. It's a machine gun on a tripod. That place is heavily armed. If you decide to engage, do it carefully.

"Shorty, are you close enough to take him out?"

Shorty answered immediately. "Yes. I'm close enough, but if the guy in the other machinery tower has a gun also, we need to take him out at the same time so he doesn't get a fix on my location and return my fire."

"I agree. James or Stretch, do you have a line of sight on the left machinery tower?"

"I don't, but I can fire several rounds into the window there, giving Shorty enough time to move. Then he can do the same while I move," stated Stretch.

"The problem is, when we start shooting, it will alert the ones inside," added James.

Aly said, "I can direct you to where they are if you breach the building."

James suggested, "Give me a few minutes to get a bit closer, then Stretch and Shorty can open fire. While that fracas is happening, I'll make a run for the door at the loading dock."

"Sounds good, James. You call it when you're ready for us," called Shorty.

James crawled slowly toward the edge of the tall grass that hid them. He wanted to move the grass as little as possible to avoid being seen even in the moon's low light. It took him fifteen minutes to move forward to the outer perimeter of the grass.

"Okay, guys, lay down some cover fire for me. I'm heading for the loading dock," called James over the comm unit.

The firing started. Shorty took out the guy in the right tower because he was easily seen through the window with just a glint of moonlight. Stretch couldn't see inside the left tower window, but he fired at the window. When the bullets hit and shattered the window, he saw a man sitting inside next to a machine gun. Stretch took him out also. After that short barrage of gunfire, all was silent.

Aly's voice was the first one they heard over the comm units. "Good work, men. James is on the loading dock behind some crates. No movement from the men inside the towers on either side of the building. Others inside are moving around. Shorty and Stretch move in now while there's confusion inside."

Both men got up, ran to the loading dock, and took place behind boxes on the opposite side of large sliding doors of the dock area. That way, they could create a crossfire if it was necessary.

A voice came from inside the building. "Who's out there?"

James called out, "Come out with your hands up!"

"Who are you?" the voice called out again.

"Not your concern. Just come out," answered James.

"Over our dead bodies!" the voice answered.

"Have it your way. You can come out and live or stay inside, and you die. Your choice!" said James.

"What do you want?" the voice called out.

"We want your drugs and any weapons that you're shipping."

"If we give them to you, our boss will kill us. Either way, we'll be dead men."

"You have our word. We'll let you live if you come out," called James.

"Yeah, right. You expect us to believe you. You won't even tell us who you are!"

"If we told you, then we'd have to kill you. Just come out and live!"

James said softly into his come unit. "Aly, are there any other doors to this place?"

"Yes. On the left side back corner of the building. As a matter of fact, someone is headed toward that door as I speak."

Shorty heard Alyssa over his comm unit and immediately got up and headed toward that door to head off that person. As he rounded the side of the building, he saw the door open slowly. He continued running toward it as a head popped out and began looking around.

Shorty raised his gun and aimed at the man. When he did, the man froze in place.

"Drop your gun, and I won't shoot. If you make a move, I'll blow your head right off your shoulders. If you move back inside, I'll shoot through the door, and you still die."

Shorty heard a soft thud as the man's gun hit the concrete pad by the door.

"Good man. Walk out slowly with your hands up. Will the door lock when it closes?"

The man shook his head, "No."

"Let the door close quietly," Shorty said.

The man held the door and let it close.

"Now, sit on the ground and put your hands behind your back."

The man sat down as directed. Shorty then trussed him up like a cow at a roping contest. He put duct tape on his mouth.

When this was done, Shorty called into his comm unit. "Any other doors I need to check out, Aly?"

"While you were doing that one, Stretch got the other one. You can go inside and head to the upstairs area. There should be a stairway inside the door. There's one man left upstairs. Secure that area without bloodshed if you can take him alive. If not, do what you have to do," Aly answered Shorty.

While Shorty and Stretch were entering the building from the rear, James was having an insidious conversation with someone inside, keeping their attention.

"I don't know what I can do to assure you that we won't kill you if you come out," called James.

"I don't know either, so I guess we have a stand-off here," he called back.

James, Aly, and Stretch could hear Shorty's conversation with someone else inside.

"Look, man. I've got a gun aimed at your head. If you put that gun on the table and turn around, I won't shoot. If you don't, I have no choice but to put a hole in the middle of your skull and splatter your brains all over that wall," said Shorty.

There was silence from Shorty for a few moments, then he said, "That's smart. Now, sit down on the floor, face down. Do it...now!" Shorty insisted.

The others on the comm units heard a zip from a tie and duct tape tearing. Then Shorty told the man to get up and head for the stairs.

James continued talking to the voice. "We know there are eight of you. Two men were in the second-floor tower equipment rooms, but they're dead now. We have the other two men captured. They'll live because they followed instructions. We sincerely want you to do the same thing."

Stretch and Shorty came around the opposite side of the building. Shorty was pushing the two men he had captured. He pulled the tape off of each man's mouth.

He marched them up on the loading dock. "Now call out your names to the man inside," said Shorty.

"It's Bill," he called.

Shorty nudged the other man with his gun butt. "I'm Larry."

"Hear those men? They're alive and well. Do you hear me?" called James.

"That doesn't mean you won't shoot us anyway when we come out," he called back.

"Here's what we're going to do. We're going to set fire to the building from the back inside, cutting off your escape. You can come out this door unarmed and live. So, you choose to die in the fire or come out and take your chances with us."

James motioned for Shorty and Stretch to go to opposite sides of the building, go inside, and set fire to the building.

James moved the two prisoners away from the building to protect them from the fire. When he pushed them away, he zip-tied them together and bound their feet so they couldn't run.

When he was back at the loading door, he heard several explosions coming from the back of the building.

"Hear that, guys? That is the sound of my men throwing hand grenades and setting the building on fire. Now your only escape is this huge sliding door right before you. You have a few minutes before the smoke and fire reach your area. I'll sit here and wait for you."

Soon Stretch and Shorty came back around the building smiling.

Stretch spoke up, "Man, I love grenades. I wish we could use them more often. If we had a way to get to the guys inside, we could disable them with flash bang and smoke grenades."

Shorty turned to Stretch, "Yeah, but explosions are a lot more fun than smoke and noise."

They waited.

Ten minutes passed, and they saw wisps of smoke coming through cracks around the door and a small window off the side of the wall.

Shorty lit up a cigarette and started to smoke. "It won't be long now. They'll be coming out. Be on the lookout for guns."

James looked at him, "I didn't know you smoked, Shorty."

"Oops, you caught me," he said.

"Bad habit," said James.

"I know, and you ain't my daddy neither, so you can't tell me what I can and can't do on my own time."

"You're on company time now," James said.

"So, sue me."

They heard a noise as the door slowly opened, and smoke billowed out, and men started coming out, coughing and choking with smoke.

They counted the men as they came out. One was still inside.

James said, "We know that there's one man left inside. Come out now!"

One man walked out. Both hands were at his side, with a pistol in each hand.

Shorty and Stretch raised the weapons at the man.

James said to him calmly, "Drop the guns. Do not raise your arms. Drop the weapons by your side, NOW!"

The man answered, "I know you'll kill us anyway, so you can go to hell with me." The man raised both arms to fire the guns.

Shorty and Stretch shot the man in the head, dropping him in the middle of the doorway.

His coworkers started to run as James called out. "Stop! If you run, we'll hunt you down and shoot every one of you."

Two men continued to run. Stretch shot both, each in a leg, and they dropped, screaming in pain.

James shook his head. "You people just don't listen, do you?"

"Okay, guys, stop the bleeding, bind them together, and call an ambulance. Don't mention the fire department. Let the ambulance call when they get here. Now throw a couple more grenades inside to ensure total destruction of the building and its contents. Then let's roll out. Move, men!"

All three men bound wounds, secured the workers with zip ties, and duct tape so they couldn't leave that area.

As they started to leave, one of the men called out. "Who are you, and why are you here? What did we do to you?"

James turned to answer the man, "You ask a stupid question like that when you sell drugs to kids on the street. You sell guns on the street to potential terrorists and kill anyone that gets in your way. And you have the nerve to ask such a stupid question as that?

"Who are we, you asked? We are the mongooses. People like you and your bosses are evil snakes. A mongoose kills snakes. We didn't kill you tonight because we promised we wouldn't, but the authorities will find out what you're doing here, and you will go to jail. You can tell your bosses that we hit you tonight because you deal with Grant Littleton in Florence, Oregon. One by one, we'll take down all of his dealers, inventory transfers, and suppliers then he'll go to prison. If he tries to stop us, we'll kill him also. You make sure someone lets him know who we are and why we were here tonight. Do you hear me?"

The men just looked at him as James and his men walked into the darkness of the night, lit only by the light of the fire glowing from the burning building behind them.

As they walked out of earshot of the workers, Shorty walked up beside James and asked him, "James, you called us mongooses. I know that a mongoose is an animal that kills poisonous snakes, but isn't the plural of mongoose, mongeese?"

"No. The singular of goose is goose, and the plural of goose is geese. The singular of a mongoose is mongoose, but the plural of mongoose is mongooses," answered James as he continued walking.

"You sure about that?"

"Positive. Look it up."

Then they hiked back to the oversight truck with Alyssa and her drones. It was all over in less than 30 minutes. They had a one-hour drive back to Weiser Municipal Airport. They loaded the plane and left the equipment truck they rented where they had parked the aircraft. They were back at base camp by sunrise the following day.

Mickey and Marie had gotten back several hours before James' team had arrived back at base camp. Both missions were a success. But Mickey knew he needed to see a doctor for some stitches for the bite on his arm, so Veronica took him to a hospital in North Bend, about fifty miles away. They knew that they had to get far enough away so that when the story got out about the fire, and the two dogs that were killed, the hospital wouldn't connect them with it. People get dog bites all the time. This dog bite was no different, they hoped. After several hours and 25 stitches later, Mickey and Veronica left the hospital. They stopped by a pharmacy and got a prescription filled for antibiotics and some painkillers, and they stopped to get something to eat.

"Mickey, why didn't you say you were hurt before you got back to camp?" Veronica said as she ate a sandwich.

"It wasn't necessary. I was okay. I assumed that you would have worried about me."

"And you were right, I would have worried."

"See, I avoided getting you upset. I knew that all I needed was a few stitches and some antibiotics, just like we got. You can't get upset when someone gets hurt. It breaks concentration and could jeopardize the mission."

"Didn't you get upset when I got injured?" Veronica asked.

"Yes, I did. And yes, it affected my performance, so I now understand how important it is to stay focused. I took one for the team, as the expression goes."

"I see. When do you think this mission, as you call it, will be over?" Veronica asked.

"A few days more, I guess. When do you have to go back to work? I'm sure that you can't stay on vacation forever."

"I have over thirty days of vacation. I told them I needed one week but put me down for two, just in case I needed more time."

"How do you think this will affect your outlook and experience as an officer?"

"I honestly don't know. It'll affect me for sure, but exactly how, I don't know."

"We better get back. That little nap I took when Marie and I returned to camp didn't help me much. I was in a lot of pain. The pills we got a while ago are beginning to kick in."

They got back to camp just in time to listen to the last of the latest recordings of Grant's ranting about the fire at his second home, and he was given a report about what happened in Idaho last night.

"What happened to my house?" he screamed. "It has to be the same ones that burned down hill house. I bet it was. They're cold-blooded killers. They shot two of my men in cold blood. I'll personally watch them die a slow, horrible, painful death when we find them. What about the guy that was supposed to be guarding it? Where did he go?"

"He was found dead in the fire. So were his dogs," said Roger.

"I thought that Steinheim was the best. He said the ones he recommended were as good or better than the crew attacking us. How did this happen?"

"Don't get so upset, Grant. Insurance will cover it. You can build it back better than ever."

"Not yet. Insurance won't pay until the police investigate the fire's cause. And they are taking their sweet time about it. Now a second one. I may never get the insurance money. At least not for months. I had a lot of money tied up in the inventory in the Idaho drop terminal. Insurance doesn't cover drugs and guns, Roger. Someone is trying to put me out of business."

Mickey and the others turned and gave each other satisfied smiles.

"We didn't have anything to do with what happened in Idaho. They can't hold us responsible for that!" Grant said.

Roger shook his head. "You better think again. Whoever was there says that you're to blame, and they're spreading the word to everyone in the network. They're saying you are poison and cutting you out of the loop."

"They can't do that! I need that business to keep going. What money we make on the food distribution and sale of those products is not enough to keep us afloat. Even the school loses money each month."

"You need to make some calls, maybe even an in-person appearance to soothe some ruffled feathers. They lost the entire building loaded with a street value in the millions of drugs and weapons. You need to do some damage control, Grant. You won't have a business within a few more weeks, maybe even days of this. They might even try to kill you themselves if they think you're to blame," Roger suggested.

"Who are the mongooses?" Grant asked.

"They are furry little animals that…."

"I know that. You said that whoever did this said that they called themselves the Mongooses. What is that?"

"I don't know, but you better be concerned about the guys you deal with. I said they might try to kill you."

"Why would they do that? They wouldn't do that! They know how much of an asset I've been to the supply chain. I've made this supply chain what it is. I've helped clean up people's messes and kept things quiet for years. They wouldn't kill me!"

"You better clean up this mess, or we'll both end up dead. I'm just as deep in this thing as you are, Grant. I'm leaving town until you find out why and stop this. You better make peace with these people."

"Roger! Now isn't the time to leave! You can't leave now."

"Wanna bet? I like living! You're the cause of all this crap. You just won't own up to it. Everything was going fine until you had that girl killed. That's what started all this crap!"

"What girl?"

"Valerie, something. I don't know her last name."

"She has nothing to do with this!" said Grant.

"Too many coincidences are happening. One of the police detectives, named Veronica Morgan, listed it as a possible murder and started a full-scale investigation. Then some rich guy shows up from out of town to claim the body. Nickolas Oswald, the guy that was shot in the raid, the son of that bakery and coffee shop owner in town, says they're spending a lot of time together. She goes on vacation and drops out of sight. It all sounds suspicious to me," explained Roger.

"Why wasn't I told about all this?" Grant asked.

"I tried to tell you something was wrong when that new girl enrolled just days after Valerie died."

"You mean that little tart, Marie Alvarez? Or Sanchez, or whatever her name is?"

Marie interjected a comment into the team's silence, "There he goes calling me a tart again!" she fell silent.

Roger continues talking, "Yes, her. I told you something was off, but you didn't listen to me. And I didn't tell you more because I didn't put it together until they returned and got her at hill house! More crap happens every single day. You still look like a monster with your face still all swollen and bruised like that."

He reached up and touched his face. "Yeah, I know. And it still hurts. Who is this rich guy that showed up to claim her body?"

"I don't know."

"Well, find out. Can't you do anything without my help?"

"I've got people looking into that as we speak. That might give us some insight as to who they are. The only one we can definitely identify is the girl. We know she was in the military and was part of some black ops group. That's all we know."

"I know all that stuff. I know all about that Sanchez girl. I want to know about the people she is working for. That's why we went to the Sultan and ordered some professional people, but they aren't doing anything but getting killed and letting my property burn down. Find out, and put more people on it! Get me some answers! Now get out of my office."

Roger walked out the door and slammed it behind him. Grant Littleton just sat at his desk, gently running his hand over his face and grimacing when he touched a sore area.

Mickey stepped out of the vehicle, and everyone followed except Aly, who continued watching, fast-forwarding the video, and moving from one camera to another, trying to find something they might need or could use against Grant and his crew.

"I think it's time to wrap it up, don't you, Mickey?" asked James.

"Yeah, I guess it is. We've completed what we set out to do. We've got the recording of Grant and Roger admitting to having Valerie killed. The bonus is we closed another case. That is, we also found the person who killed Ronnie's father. It's time we take them down and leave town. How're we going to do this, James?"

"We go in just before Grant leaves, take all the workers and secure them, and wrap it all up in a neat bow for the authorities."

Later, they gathered around the fire, which they all hoped would be their last one here. James started explaining the plan for their final attack on the facility.

"Okay, we move just outside the loading dock area. Same place we've been to several times before. We shut down the power, and Aly had control of the alarm system, so she shuts that down, also. We don't want to be interrupted by the police." He laid the building floor plans on the ground in front of himself.

He pointed out to everyone, "This is where we enter the building. We split up here and search the entire building. When we find someone, we'll get them to tell us where the weapons and drugs are located in the building. We may be able to recognize them from similar markings they used in the past. We get everyone out of the building as well as any illegal items. We pile them in the loading area, just like we did the last time. We secure everyone. Aly will make copies of all the recordings we have of the admission of their crimes, including admission of the murder of Valerie and Ronnie's father. We leave them where the authorities can get them. Then, we'll let Mickey shoot a few RPGs into the building to burn it down. We gather our stuff and leave."

"Not until I kill everyone that laid a hand on me!" spoke up Marie.

"I'm not going to make any orders concerning the killing of anyone. Try not to do it. If you must return fire for self-defense, then I'll consider it justified," said James.

Mickey stood but said nothing. Veronica looked up at him, then leaned against him with tears in her eyes.

She said softly into Mickey's ear, "I can't condone the murder of anyone, but if Grant Littleton and the man that shot my Daddy are killed, I'll say a prayer of thanks."

"Where are we going to meet up?" asked Stretch.

"When we leave tonight, we leave for home. We'll meet in a few days at Mickey's place in Bridgeton. Until we meet tonight at the facility, this is our last meeting."

Everyone got up from the fire circle and went to various places to be alone for the last time.

Marie and Alyssa moved off toward the command truck. Stretch and Shorty moved upstream to be alone like the best friends they were. Mickey and Ronnie walked into the forest for their final walk in the woods. James just sat at the fire's edge and poked at it with a stick left to his thoughts. He took out his cell phone and called his wife, Darcy.

Mickey and Veronica talked as they walked along a path in the woods near the stream.

"I guess this is it, Ronnie," said Mickey.

"It doesn't have to be, Mickey. Why don't you come to my house for a few days when this is over?" said Veronica.

"Are you sure you want me to do that? At this point, we have a lot of past crammed into a few days, and most of it is pure bad memories."

"I would love you to come and stay for a few days. We haven't had a single day of rest or relaxation. I know you have a life to return to and a company to run, but you can spare a few extra days," Veronica countered.

"We'll see, Mickey said, and he bent down and kissed her. She returned his kiss.

Farther upstream, Stretch and Shorty were talking.

"Hey, man. This has been a real trip, hadn't it? We've had more injuries on this mission than on others in a long time. Marie was caught and tortured, Mickey got chewed up by those dogs, and Ronnie was shot. It's been interesting, to say the least," said Shorty.

"Yeah, it has been. And to think that we've been against a bunch of amateurs, not even trained soldiers. At least until the last couple of days. Too bad about Hemingway and Oden. They were pretty good guys. I guess as mercenaries, our loyalties lie to the one that strokes our paychecks. A stroke of bad luck for us. We've either gotten soft, or those guys got really lucky," answered Stretch.

"Sometimes, this life sucks. One day you fight beside a guy, and the next day, you shoot him."

"Yeah, I'm going to call my girl, and we're going to go out to celebrate like this was a real mission. Not some little rinky-dink bunch of losers out there."

"How's she doing, by the way?" asked Stretch.

"She's doing good. She keeps asking me to marry her, but it wouldn't be fair to a girl to get hitched up with a guy like me."

Marie and Alyssa talked inside the back of the command truck.

"How are you feeling after the beatings you took? They worked you over pretty good, didn't they?" asked Alyssa.

"I'm alright. I'm still a bit sore, but the bruises will take a while to clear up. They didn't do any serious damage to me or break any bones. So, all in all, I'm good, I guess. They weren't professional interrogators, or they probably would have done serious damage."

"Yeah, I suppose you're right," commented Alyssa.

"Hey, Dee," said James into the phone. "How are the kids?"

"They miss you, James," Darcy answered. "When will you be coming home?"

"We go out for the last roundup tonight. We'll be leaving on Alyssa's plane sometime late tonight or early morning," he told her.

"Is this another secret mission?" she asked.

"Yes, and no. Mickey had a few things he needed help with, and the team cleared it up."

"Was it dangerous?"

"You know that I never discuss details of a mission, even one that involves your brother."

Darcy knew that James never discussed what he did when he was on a mission. He never talked about work because he didn't want to worry them.

CHAPTER 20

Final Attack on Grant's Factory

When it was almost time to leave, they gathered up all the gear and buried all their trash. They left the place as they found it, except for a small pile of cold ashes where they had their campfire. They got in the vehicles and headed toward the school facility.

When they got within a few blocks, Aly parked the command truck on a side road with a dead end and one old, dilapidated house.

The others pulled up beside her, parked, and got out. It was dusk but not a lot of traffic on the road. Aly stayed inside the truck but got her drones out and ready to launch. They gave Veronica an assault rifle they had checked her out on back at camp.

Each had an assault rifle, a side-arm automatic pistol, several flash-bang grenades, and regular explosive grenades. They carried the usual zip ties and duct tape. Mickey also took a rocket launcher over one shoulder, and his rifle slung over the other. In addition to their rifles, Stretch and Shorty also carried a couple of small remotely triggered explosive charges. Marie carried a load comparable to the others.

They stayed off the road as much as possible to avoid being seen by passing cars. When they got to the school, they moved into the field beside one of the multi-story buildings where Mickey and James had placed the surveillance cameras. It was about an acre in size with unmowed grass, allowing them to lay down and remain unnoticed by average passers. They fanned out in a line in the field, watching the men work on the dock, loading and unloading boxes with a forklift. Mickey took off the rocket launcher and laid it beside him on the ground. He wouldn't need it until they were ready to leave. He didn't need it when they breached the building.

They heard James whisper over the earbud comm units, "Aly, you copy?"

"Copy loud and clear. Drone's overhead. I can see multiple figures. One looks like it's in Grant's office. That is probably him. I'll tag him and try to monitor his movements for you."

"That's the one I want," came Marie's voice over the comm unit.

"Same here," said Veronica.

"Ditto," came Mickey's voice.

James' voice came over the air, "S &S, can you flank the loaders outside and capture them without gunfire?"

"We'll try," came Shorty's voice, "but we can't guarantee no gunfire."

James said, "We need to take them quietly so the ones in the building don't know we're here."

"Our rifles don't have silencers. Our side arms do, so we'll have to use them, but we can do that," said Stretch.

"Do it," said James.

James saw gently moving grass on each side of the grassy field, and they knew Stretch and Shorty were moving forward to the fenced area. They were on opposite ends of the fence in a few minutes, cutting the fencing material to crawl through. Shorty jumped up on the left side, and Stretch jumped up on the right end of the dock.

One man looked up and reached for a gun at his side. Shorty put a bullet in the middle of the man's head. He fell back and knocked over some cans making a clanging noise. When he fell to the floor, the workers looked in his direction.

They saw Shorty standing there with a gun pointed at them. When they began reaching for their weapons, Stretch called to them from behind. "I wouldn't do that if I were you. I've got a gun aimed at your back. The first man to move toward his weapon gets dropped, just like your friend over there."

They all froze in position. Stretch holstered his sidearm while the men were facing Shorty. Shorty did the same when he told them to turn around and face him. They marched them down the dock steps and over to the chain-link fence. Shorty and Stretch made the workers put their hands behind their backs and zip tied each man to the fence.

"Well, hello, Stacks," he said to one of the men guarding the dock workers.

He turned to look at Stretch. "Hey, man. I heard that we might be coming against you guys."

"Yeah, we knew that Grant hired Steinheim, and he had brought in some heavy hitters. I didn't know that you were one of them," Stretch talked as he zip-tied the man.

"Yeah, Gordy's over there," he said, nodding his head toward one of the other men. He lowered his voice and added, "Be careful. You remember he always has a knife in his belt."

"Thanks for the heads up. I remember. A bit for you, we have orders to kill if you make a move. Just letting you know. I'd hate to take you down," said Stretch.

"Thanks, Stretch. I'll behave. If you can, tell Gordy the same for me."

"You bet," he answered as he pulled the tie as tight as he could.

He moved from man to man, zip-tying each man. When he got to the last man in line, he said to the man as he pulled his hands together, "Hey, Gordy. Fancy seeing you here."

The man didn't move but said softly, "Is that the little butthead I know as Stretch?"

"Yeah, it's me. Don't move and cooperate, or Shorty will shoot you."

"How you been?"

"Keeping busy. I see you're working with Steinheim now," he said as he put the man's hands together and put on a zip tie.

"I hate the man, but he offered us a bonus when he discovered that you, Shorty, and Alyssa were on this job. He also hates Alyssa and will be glad if she gets killed."

"Really? I didn't know he didn't like her," he said.

"Yeah, he's got a thing for her, and she won't give him the time of day. So, we are supposed to take her out if we get the slightest chance."

"Sorry, you won't get the chance, and I was serious. Shorty will shoot you if you make any move. And by the way, don't move, but I have to take the knife out of your pocket."

"Okay," he said without moving.

As Stretch began to move away, he asked Gordy, "How many did Grant hire, other than Steinheim?"

"Just the four of us, and you guys got Hemmingway and Oden. So, you got us all."

Stretch said to Aly, "Did you hear that?"

"Yeah, we got all the hired guns. You trust what Gordy just said?"

"Yes, I do. We are enemies on this job but brothers in the trade. I trust him, but I also trust him to kill me if he gets loose."

"Got it. That's six down and twelve more to go, guys," came Aly's voice.

While doing this, James, Mickey, Veronica, and Marie went inside. Mickey brought his rocket launcher also and propped it against the wall on the loading dock.

Aly's voice came over the comm unit. "Someone's coming down the hallway into the loading area. Someone needs to cut the power now."

"Copy that," said Mickey as he ran back outside to the power box. He ran to the place where James had cut the fence. He crawled through and pulled the lever down, and the building went blank.

"No one is moving right now. Maybe they're waiting for the power to come back on. It's an excellent chance to get inside and find cover while they're confused. They saw the emergency light on the wall light up as they went in. Mickey took out his silenced pistol and shot them out. The others did the same with the lights near them.

Now in almost total darkness and armed with infrared goggles, they knew they had a definite advantage. Marie headed toward Grant Littleton's office with Veronica close behind. Shorty and Stretch waited for instructions from Alyssa.

"S&S, you head for the back room straight ahead of you. There are four men back there. There are other heat signatures back there, and nothing is moving. I'll give you better directions as you go.

"Mickey and James, you go to your right. That's where you found the other weapons and drugs. That would be an excellent area to investigate. There are four heavily armed men in there and one more. I don't know what he has. Nothing big. It could be a sidearm, probably guarding whatever's there," Aly directed.

Everyone shot out the lights as they progressed.

Aly's voice crackled over the comm units, "Marie and Ronnie, two figures, are making their way to Grant's office. Be careful. I can't see any large weapons."

Marie and Veronica waited until Alyssa told them that all three were in Grant's office.

They went down the front hallway to Grant's door. They stood on each side of it, and Veronica nodded for Marie to open it. When she did, both women stepped inside.

"Hello, Mr. Grant," said Marie as she leveled her gun at his stomach. His face looked bloated and contorted under the dim glow of the emergency light. She smiled at him with the satisfaction that his face was a product of the beating she had given him the last time she was here. All three men glared back at the two women now holding automatic rifles at them.

"And who are you, and what do you want?" said one of the men.

"I was about to ask you the same question," said Marie, "but I recognize you. You are one of the men that beat me at hill house. Your name is Ernest. And I also know you, Roger," she said.

"How do you know me?" he asked. "I've never even seen you before."

"I'm Marie Sanchez!"

"We've met. We know each other, don't we?"

"I remember you!" he said to her. "You're the one that burned down hill house and escaped."

Veronica just stood there but said nothing. She wanted to pull the trigger and blast Grant Littleton apart, but she was a cop, and cops didn't shoot people unless it was in defense of another human being. She was trembling, not in fear but in rage. She was standing in front of the man that had had her father murdered.

"Who is she?" asked Grant, pointing to Veronica.

"She's Veronica Morgan. You had her father and Valerie Green killed," said Marie.

Veronica still stood in silence. She remained motionless.

Marie spoke, "Would you like to go outside with us, gentlemen?"

"No, I would not!" Grant answered.

She walked around the desk, got up in his face, and said, "I am telling you to go outside! Now move."

"I will not move from this room," he said firmly.

She stepped back a couple of feet, looked him straight in the eyes, and kicked him squarely in the groin. He grasped his groin with both hands and bent forward. She then clasped her hands, stretched her arms out, swung them up in a huge arc, and gave him an upward blow to his face, knocking him back against the wall. Blood spurted everywhere.

She turned to the other two men. "Would you boys like to help him outside?"

Ernest and Roger helped Grant get up and moved him toward the door. As they moved into the hall, Veronica grabbed Ernest's shoulder.

She held him back as the other two and Marie headed to the door.

"Where's Amir?" she asked.

"I don't know. Amir was supposed to be in the back with some others guarding the inventory," he stammered.

She caught up with Marie and said to her. "You take them. I'm going after Amir."

She heard shooting and stopped as she turned and headed back to Mickey and James' area. She heard Mickey calling someone.

"Come out, and we'll let you live!" he said.

"Not going to happen," was the answer she heard.

"Don't be a fool. No one has to get hurt here!" called James.

"We have some heavy artillery here. You're outgunned," said Mickey.

"Either come out, or we'll be forced to use them. Believe me, you can't win!" called James.

"Nope," came the answer. Veronica raised her gun waist-high, aiming forward, and stepped into the door opening. She saw Amir. She recognized him from the videos that she had watched back at base camp.

Mickey and James were crouching behind some tall boxes. She saw Amir as he stood and pulled the pin from a hand grenade. She knew if she hesitated, he would throw it toward the boxes, and the explosion would kill all of them. She pulled the trigger of the automatic rifle and sprayed the area at Amir. Blood stains blossomed from his chest. He looked down at the blood, dropped the grenade, then fell to the floor.

She called out to Mickey and James, "Stay down. He dropped a grenade."

She moved to the side and against the wall and braced for the explosion. She heard the clink as it hit the floor, and then the grenade exploded. Smoke and flames belched out through the opening. She hoped that Mickey and James were okay. A few moments later, they both walked out covered with dust.

She rushed to Mickey and hugged him. "You're okay, thank God."

"Let's get out of here, so we can see better," he said as they all walked briskly toward the door.

"I went back there looking for Amir," she said. "Ernest said he was back here."

"That was Amir. He was afraid that he would be deported. So, he refused to give himself up."

"I'm glad. I'm not sorry that I killed him," Veronica said as they walked.

"You're sounding more like Marie every day," Mickey said as they walked out to the pavement at the loading dock.

Aly came over the earbuds. "That about wraps it up. I'll come on down there and bring the recordings. Why don't you have someone bring out some of the guns and drugs they have inside."

"Will do," answered Mickey.

In another half an hour, they had brought out five crates of guns and two cases of drugs mixed in with other cooking ingredients. Everyone that was still alive was zip tied to the fence. They put a stack of video recordings on top of the guns and drugs. Aly had moved the command truck to the loading area, and the team got inside. They called the Florence police, and as Mickey got into the Humvee, he got out, put the rocket launcher onto his shoulder, fired it through the open door on the dock, and watched the inside of the building explode into flames. Mickey looked over at Grant, who had vomited all over himself and passed out from the pain in his groin area, got in the Humvee, and James drove away.

CHAPTER 21

Mickey Goes Home

The following morning, everyone got into the van with the equipment, and Mickey and Veronica took everyone to the airport.

"We did good. Didn't we, everyone?" said Mickey.

Alyssa, Stretch, and Shorty sat silently, looking out of the van's side windows. To them, it was just another job.

"I got the person that killed Daddy," said Veronica.

"And we got justice for Valerie," added Mickey.

"Yeah, Amir actually killed your dad and Valerie, but Grant ordered the kill. I wanted to kill Grant myself. So, I didn't get the justice I wanted," said Marie.

"Marie, you didn't want justice. You wanted revenge. Besides, the people that actually beat you are dead," said James. "Grant will go to jail for the rest of his life."

"Revenge or justice are different words for the same thing. I wanted to look into his eyes as I pulled the trigger to kill him," she said angrily with gritted teeth.

Alyssa said, "Listen. Mickey, Ronnie, and Marie all had personal reasons for wanting those people dead. It was just a job for my team, meaning Stretch and Shorty. We are sorry you didn't get everything you wanted, but we took down some very bad men and hurt their network. So, we feel good about the outcome."

James turned to them. "Yes, Ronnie got closure for her father, and Mickey got justice for Valerie. Marie, I promise Grant will pay with his life for what he had done to you."

"You mean….," started Marie.

"Yes, my dear friend, I've already put out the word to take care of it," answered James.

"I wanted to take care of it myself, but I appreciate it, James," she said and sat back in the seat.

Veronica spoke up, "If Grant talks, he'll name me as taking part in this last raid, and that will end my career. Maybe even put me in jail also."

James then turned to Veronica. "You are now an honorary member of this team. We take care of our own. Trust me, Grant will never say a word about you."

"You can't stop him, James!" she said.

"I said, trust me," he stated and turned back to face the road, and silence resumed the rest of the way to the airport.

They loaded the weapons onto Alyssa's private plane and took off. Mickey and Veronica watched as the plane took off and turned toward the East Coast and Virginia.

Mickey called a number James had given him to get instructions on where to leave the Humvee for pick up. He was told to leave it in the airport short stay lot, and it would be picked up, and they took a cab back to her house.

When they got back, they each took long showers to clean off the dirt and grime of the past couple of weeks. That night they stayed at her house to just relax and rest.

Mickey turned on the television to watch the news. The newscaster was reporting from the location of the Culinary Institute of Oregon and Factory.

"In the late hours of last night, a group of marauders attacked the Institute and manufacturer of the country's most elite gourmet food products, which were shipped all over the United States.

"They set fire to the building, and at this time, the owner of the school and factory is claiming he was framed for selling guns and drugs. The police have called the FBI, DEA, and several other government agencies to help with the investigation. It is alleged that firearms and drugs were planted on the property.

"Grant Littleton had sworn complete ignorance about what was taking place in his own plant. He has pledged to clear his name and restore this business. The FBI has taken an entire truckload of weapons and drugs to be analyzed at one of their labs. They also say that they have recorded videos and audio of other crimes. If Littleton is convicted of these crimes, he will spend the rest of his life in prison."

Mickey reached over and pushed the mute button on the remote. "I was wondering if we were going to pull it off. It seemed that someone was getting injured at every turn. How are you doing, by the way? It's only been a bit over a week."

"I'm doing a lot better. I can take a few more days, but I need to call in to the captain and tell him that in a few days, I'll report for duty. Mickey, why don't you stay here?" She asked as she snuggled closer to him.

"You know I have to get back. I have a business to run. Pop can do it, but he wants to retire, and I want him to have some wonderful carefree retirement years."

"I don't want you to leave." She snuggled closer.

"I have to. I can stay a few more days to look after you and ensure you'll be okay. You still have a ways to go to heal completely."

"You're going to stay with me, aren't you?"

"Of course, if you want me to stay here."

She reached over and picked up the phone and dialed the police station, and asked for her captain.

"Hello, Captain Kramer," she said.

"Good to hear from you, Ronnie. How's the injury doing?" he asked.

"What do you mean, Captain?"

"You know darn well what I mean. You called in days ago and said you needed some time off. Strange coincidence that there is a lot of destruction going on at the same time you took off. And after the investigation of the incident at our hospital, some people say the person brought in for emergency surgery due to a gunshot wound in the shoulder was you?"

"What do you want me to say?"

"Right now, I don't want you to say anything. Keep your mouth shut. I have my suspicions but no proof. What happens from here will depend on what Grant Littleton says in a pending plea deal," the captain said.

"You want me to lie or admit to everything?"

"Neither. I want you to keep your mouth shut. I don't believe for a minute that you have been home relaxing doing nothing. You are in this up to your eyeballs, but there is no proof yet. As a matter of fact, keep out of sight until this either comes to a head or is over. Got it, detective?"

"Got it, Captain. And thanks."

"Don't thank me yet. Just don't come back to work until I tell you. You are on official vacation until that time."

She disconnected and put the phone on the table, and turned to Mickey. "He knows I was in on all of it."

"No, he suspects. At this point, he knows nothing. And that is good. It is all suspicion, and legally, that doesn't mean a thing. Are you sleeping in your parent's old room or the one you grew up in?"

"I moved to my parent's room a long time ago. At first, when they were gone, I stayed in my old room, but I decided that I needed to move on, so I moved into their room."

"Did you buy new furniture?"

"No. I haven't moved that far ahead, but someday I will," she mused.

"Why not tomorrow? We can go to a furniture store in town and buy a new bedroom suite for the master bedroom. You're about to enter a new chapter of your life. We found your father's killer. Now, remember him, but move on. He'd want you to do that."

"Yes, maybe you're right. Okay, we'll both go furniture hunting tomorrow. Now, I think it's time for bed. Are you going to join me?" she said coyly.

"Not if you mean what I think you mean."

"I meant exactly what I said. Will you join me in bed?"

He leaned over, took her hand, and led her up the stairs. When he got to the master bedroom, he turned and kissed her lightly on the lips, then turned, winked, smiled, and said, "Good night. Sweet dreams. I'll see you in the morning."

He walked toward her childhood bedroom and quietly closed the door.

The next morning, Veronica came downstairs sleepy-eyed in a pullover shirt and jeans. Mickey was at the stove cooking breakfast.

"Good morning, sleepy head. How do you like your eggs?"

"Scrambled. Are we going furniture shopping today?" she asked as she poured a cup of coffee.

"Yep."

"Why do you care so much that I get new stuff? Especially if you aren't going to join me in it?"

He looked at her and said, "Because you need to move on. Your parents wouldn't want you to stagnate in the past."

"You don't know them, so you can't say that," she said, taking a careful sip of the hot brown liquid in her cup.

"I can say it. No good parent would want their grown daughter to stand still in time. Remember the good times. Enjoy the memories, but don't wallow in them. Live. Love. Learn. And move on with life. You can start with bedroom furniture," Mickey said as he stirred her eggs to scramble them in the pan.

"Okay," she said, reaching over and picking up a piece of bacon and putting it in her mouth.

They ate and headed for the furniture store downtown. After wandering from store to store, she told Mickey that she had never picked out furniture before.

"When I went away to college, Mother and Daddy helped me pick out dorm furniture. Let's face it. A dorm room isn't exactly where one tries to make a decorative furniture statement. When I moved back home, I didn't change anything, so I didn't have much experience picking out furniture or interior design."

Mickey helped her pick out something that might make her feel at home but eclectic in style.

After shopping, they drove around in the Jaguar. "Mickey, how long can you stay?" she asked.

"We've already talked about this. I told you, a few more days, then I have to get back home," he said.

"If you're the CEO, can't you run it for a while from here? You did say that you have people working for you. Can't they handle it?" she asked.

"Sure, they can take care of things for a while. Pop's there, and he's capable, but it wouldn't be fair to dump it all on him. I need to get home."

She leaned over and whispered in his ear. "I want you to stay here."

He kept his eyes on the road. "I'll stay a few more days, and then I must leave."

She sat back in the seat and pouted.

He wanted to stay, but he couldn't. He had his family and a business. He had to go home.

The next few days went by quickly, and they enjoyed each other's company by riding around in her dad's cars and eating in some of the best restaurants in Florence. They drove around the countryside and looked at the scenery. They laughed, they got to know everything they could about each other, but it was time for Mickey to leave.

They sat watching the television on that last evening and turned on the news. The newscaster was showing the burned-out hulk of the school and bakery factory. When Mickey turned up the volume, he heard the anchorman say, "Grant Littleton was killed today in the county jail while waiting to be arraigned on multiple charges of drug distribution and various gun trafficking. It was rumored that he was trying to arrange a plea bargain for a lesser sentence. He was willing to give names, dates, and specifics on the gang who had attacked his business. Littleton claims a mercenary team had killed and burned down the building. Since he is now deceased, there is no knowledge of any allegations, and the case will be closed by the police department based on the assumption that it was a rival criminal element trying to take over his business. No further investigation will be made."

Mickey and Veronica just looked at each other and smiled. They knew the whole story, that it was not a rival criminal element and that all guilty parties were now deceased or gone.

"That pretty well ends the situation here. Case closed. James told you to trust him," said Mickey.

"I guess I'll be getting a call from the captain saying I am free to come back to work."

"I hate to say this, but I guess it's time for me to go home. I'll leave in the morning. I need to call Marie to let her know that justice has been served for her also," Mickey added.

Tears flowed down Veronica's face. "I want you to stay, but I understand. Your life is in Virginia. Mine is here."

Mickey moved over closer to her, "I have to go home. You'll always be in my mind and in my heart. I'll never forget our time together."

The following morning he began packing his clothes, and Ronnie walked into the bedroom. She was still wearing flannel pajamas, and he was fully dressed. He was getting the clothes out of the dresser and laying them on the bed. She silently picked them up, folded them, and placed them into the suitcase. She was crying again as she packed his clothes.

Mickey didn't know what else to say. He felt like crying, also, but men don't cry. Yes, he knew they did, but not in front of others, especially a woman. He continued until all the clothes were on the bed and put in the suitcases. He took one, and Veronica took the other, and they proceeded downstairs and outside. She continued walking around the house to the back, and Mickey followed her.

As they walked toward the back of the house, Mickey talked.

"You know that the network isn't shut down. We have a copy of all Grant's customers and suppliers. At some time, we may need to take them down, don't you think?" said Mickey. "If we don't do that, it'll be like a game of Whack-a-mole. They'll keep popping up in a different location."

"I didn't think of that, but I see your point. Maybe someday we can meet and take them down," she answered as she continued to the back of the house.

When she got to the garage, she slid the door open, put the luggage into the trunk of the Jaguar, and turned to take his other suitcase.

"One last ride, I guess. Are you driving me to the airport, or do I get to drive it one more time?" he asked. "Either way, you need to go back inside and get dressed. They won't let you into the airport in pajamas."

She took the suitcase without a word, placed it in the trunk beside the other, and closed the boot lid. She pulled him close, looked into his eyes, and looked into his soul one last time. She put her arms around his neck, reached up to him, and kissed him passionately. As she did so, she slid the keys into his pocket, backed away from him, and wiped away her tears.

"I'm not going with you to the airport. I'm staying here. You take the Jaguar."

"Whoa, Ronnie. I can't take your car. It was your father's favorite thing. You said so yourself."

"No, Mickey. Momma and I were his favorites. His cars came second to us. You helped me find his killer, and now I must move on. You will take the car to remember me and our time together."

"I don't need this car to remember you. I'll always remember you," he said, trying not to choke up.

"You have my heart. Now you will take my car. Go, Mickey Ray Christianson. Drive it home, all the way to Virginia, and think of me all the way. I will love you forever."

They kissed again. Mickey got into the Jaguar, started it up, and drove toward Virginia.

The Landlord's Stay
at the Spa

Prologue:

Finally, the world was great again. Everything was going fine. Mickey drove with the top down and the wind in his hair, listening to old 1960s music blaring from the radio in his 1963 Jaguar XKE. It was a gift to him from Detective Veronica Morgan of the Florence, Oregon Police Department for helping find her father's killer and bringing the man to justice.

A couple of days ago, Mickey and the Mongoose team had wrapped up a case in Florence that solved several murder cases in the beautiful little West Coast town in Oregon. In addition to finding Veronica's father's killer, they had solved the murder of Valerie Green, his ex-fiancée, and several other cases.

Yes, Mickey was in a good mood. He was on his way home to Bridgeton, a medium-sized town midway between Williamsburg and Richmond, Virginia. He'd been on the road for several hours on the third day, and he decided to stop for a short break and have a relaxing lunch at the restaurant advertised on the roadside sign.

Pulling off the interstate at the next exit, he headed toward the Woodside restaurant. Driving into the parking lot, he noticed it was crowded with cars, which usually meant the food was good.

Inside, as he stood waiting for the Hostess, an attractive young Asian woman entered, looking around the room, hoping for a table. When the Hostess arrived, she asked them if they were together.

"No," answered Mickey.

"I'm sorry, Miss," she said to the Asian woman. "We only have one available table. If you don't mind, another one should be ready in five to ten minutes."

Mickey turned to the woman and said, "Miss, if you don't mind, I certainly don't mind sharing a table with you."

She smiled and answered, "That is very kind, but I wouldn't want to intrude."

"It wouldn't be an intrusion. It would be my pleasure," he said, bowing slightly and gesturing with an open palm for her and the Hostess to lead the way.

The Hostess led them to a table in the back corner of the room. Mickey stood while the lady moved to the back of the table in the corner. As she sat, she again scanned the room. Mickey sat on her left side so as not to block her view.

The Hostess placed the menus in front of them and announced that Betty would be their server.

As she continued to scan the room, she turned to Mickey and introduced herself, "My name is Aya. Thank you for sharing your table with me."

"It's my pleasure, Aya. My name's Mickey," he answered.

"Well, Mickey. I've been here many times, but I've never seen you here before," she said.

"I'm just passing through. I'm heading home. If you've been here many times, apparently, you're from around here," Mickey said.

"Not really. I'm here to meet a couple of clients."

"That explains why you keep looking around the room. You must be expecting them to arrive soon."

"Oh, not exactly here. Down the road a bit. We have a meeting area. I am here just for lunch. Then I will drive to the exact meeting spot. I just like to be aware of my surroundings."

She was a beautiful young Asian woman in a business suit and long flowing hair, which captured the eyes of every man in the room.

Her dark eyes sparkled as she talked, suggesting an easy, comforting atmosphere. Mickey felt drawn in by her deliberate gestures and mesmerizing soft voice.

The server, Betty, came and took their order, and Mickey began to talk as the server walked away. As they spoke, three Asian men entered the restaurant, looked around, spotted Aya, and started walking to their table. They stopped and stood side by side, completely blocking the table from view to others in the restaurant.

"Good afternoon, Aya. I thought that was your car in the parking lot—a pink Lamborghini. I'm sure you look good in it. We've been looking for you," the Japanese man said, standing to Mickey's left when they stopped at the table where Aya and Mickey were waiting for lunch.

She looked at Mickey, rolled her eyes, and pushed her long hair back over her shoulders. "What do you want, Giichi?" she asked the man.

"I want you to come with me. Now," he answered.

"Can't you see that I am having lunch with a friend?" she said sarcastically.

"Tell your friend that you must leave now," he said as he looked at Mickey. "We'll have someone drive your car so you can ride with us."

"I don't want to leave, so go away," she said, looking up at Giichi standing across the table. The other two men stood to Giichi's left side.

The man looked at her with a crooked smile.

"You will come with us, young lady. This is a crowded restaurant, and we don't want to cause a scene," he said, patting a bulge in his coat. The other two men also patted matching bulges under the coats.

Mickey looked at the bulge and knew instinctively what it was. He had just met this young lady and had no idea why these men insisted she go with them. But he felt very uncomfortable about the situation, so he prepared himself to act if necessary.

"And who are these men, Aya? They look like an oriental version of Moe, Larry, and Curly," Mickey said.

The man looked at Mickey and spoke, "Little man, you mind your own business."

Mickey bit his lip and looked up at the man as he assessed the situation and all three men. "If you don't mind. We're having a nice quiet meal. You and your stooges may leave now."

Again, the man looked at Mickey. "I told you to mind your own business!" he said more firmly.

"I told you to leave us alone. The lady doesn't want to go with you. I suggest you leave. If you don't, I'll ask someone to call the police."

Aya looked at Mickey with a grave expression. "Please, Mickey. Do not get involved with my business. These are dangerous men, and they are now leaving."

"Not without you. Aya, I will tell you once more and drag you out of here by the hair, dead or alive if I must. But you will go with us," he said as he pulled his coat back, exposing the holstered handgun.

Some woman at the table to their left screamed when she saw the man's gun.

"Even if I go with you, I will probably end up dead, so you can go to the depths of hell. I do not care," Aya seethed.

The man unsnapped the strap holding the gun and started to withdraw it. At that moment, Mickey launched up from the table, sending his chair flying backward. With a fork in his hand, Mickey drove it into the man's gun hand and lunged his shoulder into the man's stomach, sending him falling to the floor. The other two men stepped back, knocking tables over, and reached to draw their guns.

Mickey saw their actions and moved toward them, driving his body toward the middle man's midsection and sending him to the floor also. Mickey grabbed the third man's gun hand and pushed it away from his gun. Mickey then withdrew the weapon from the man's holster and shot the second man in the chest. He then dropped the gun, knocked the third man to the floor, and started pummeling him in the face until he passed out. Mickey turned to the first man, Giichi, as Aya had called him.

Still lying on the floor and with his bleeding hand, the first man withdrew his gun and shot Mickey. Mickey fell to the floor, hitting his head on the corner of the table as blood flowed from his side.

People began jumping out of chairs and diving for the floor when they saw what was happening. They turned over tables and hid behind them. Another woman screamed as the entire restaurant became a crowd of terrified people running for cover wherever they thought they would be safe from flying bullets.

The first man was still holding the gun in his bleeding hand when Aya jumped up and kicked the man as he attempted to get up. He fell back down as Aya took another stance indicative of a person trained in martial arts. The man slid back out of her range and started to get up slowly again. She moved forward, kicked the man again in the head, and rocketed herself on top of him, driving her foot into his abdomen multiple times until he fell again.

When she saw the man didn't move, she ran to Mickey, who was also unconscious, and ripped up part of the table cloth and wrapped it around Mickey to slow the bleeding in his side. She then called for someone in the restaurant to help put Mickey into her car so she could get him medical aid. As two patrons came and started taking Mickey outside, Aya made a call on her cell phone.

"Hello. This is Aya. Send a medical helo to the landing pickup area. Also, send someone to take care of the restaurant's owners and calm them down. We don't want any repercussions from the authorities. Do it immediately."

She disconnected the call and went to the parking lot to help the men load Mickey into her car.

If you haven't read the first books in the Landlord series, take a few moments to look at these:

Book 1. The Landlord's Inheritance
This was Mickey's first adventure and the one that started it all.

Book 2. The Landlord and the Wheelchair Child
Mickey thinks that all is well until he finds a little girl all alone in one of his apartment complexes. He has to help this little girl find her parents.

Book 3. The Landlord's Dead Body
When construction starts at one of his new projects, new CEO Mickey Ray Christianson must find out who killed and buried this young lady in the middle of his project.

The entire Landlord's series is available at amazon.com, barnesandnoble.com and terryjoegunnelsbooks.com.

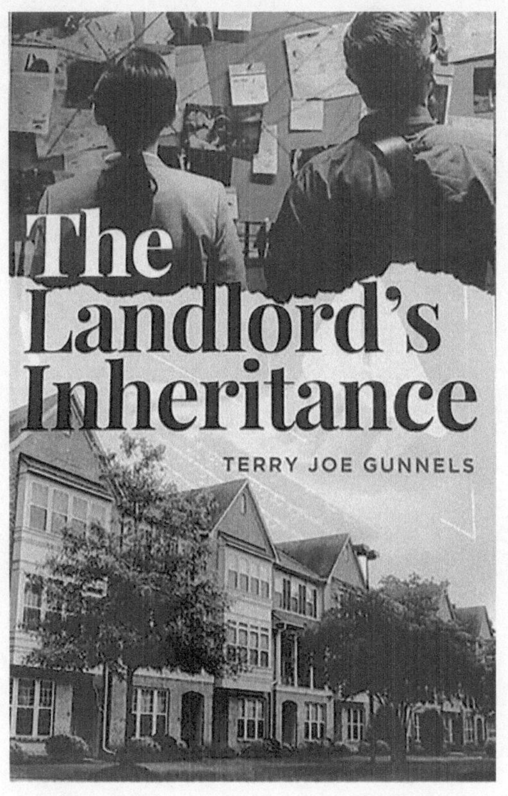

Siblings Mickey Ray and Darcy Jean are informed that the automobile disaster that caused the death of their Mother and their Father's multiple injuries including brain damage was not an accident but an attempted murder. The local police seem ambivalent, and their aunt comes in with a forgotten Power of Attorney signed by their Father, Daniel, and tries to take control of the Real Estate holdings. The brother and sister team begin a power struggle and are physically threatened by unknown thugs which results in Mickey's girlfriend's disappearance which she is presumed dead and Darcy Jean in hiding. James, Mickey's best friend, a disfigured Ex-Military Black Ops operative, assists in the hunt to put a stop to the "takeover".

Simple Detective Work, Internet Research, Adventure, Action and Suspense with a Sprinkle of Romance, and a Fast-Paced, Explosive ending are included in this book of intrigue.

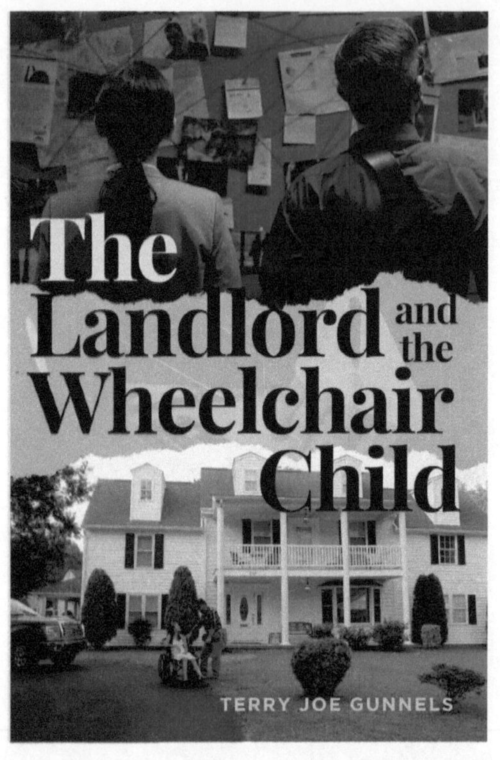

Landlord Mickey Ray Christianson is walking the grounds of his apartment complex late one afternoon, and he sees a little girl in a wheelchair sitting all alone. He sits down beside her and begins talking to her. He then finds out that her mother left her, intending to return. When the child's mother doesn't return, Mickey has the gut feeling that something has gone awry and calls his sister, Darcy, to run a background check on her parents. After Darcy gets permission from the Department of Child's Services to take custody of the child, Carrie, Mickey Ray, and his best friend, James, go hunting for Carrie's parents, assuming they were kidnapped. With help from some of James' past Black Ops teammates, a find-and-rescue operation takes place. After a suspenseful mission and a lot of action, Mickey reunites Carrie with her parents.

I hope you like Mickey and James' newest adventure as they dive headfirst into helping this little child. It is suspenseful to the very end.

After many months of preparation, construction has begun on a new Apartment complex. On the very first day, a worker with a backhoe, digs up a body of a young lady. After the police identify the victim, it turns out that Mickey Ray Christianson and his sister Darcy Jean went to school with the her. The victim, Betty Duncan was single, pregnant and lived with her mother in one of their apartments, so Mickey and his best friend and brother-in-law, James Bower set out to find her killer. They start with the obvious suspects, the baby daddy. Along the way, Mickey connects with one of his old school-mates and thinks he is falling in love with her. After tracking down several leads and dead ends, the case is solved with a huge twist for Mickey and all involved.

I hope this one keeps you on the edge of your seat as it did me as I wrote it. Believe it or not, I didn't know "who dunnit" until the very end!

A picture of the Author and one of his collectible autos.

The entire Landlord's series is available at:
    amazon.com
    barnesandnoble.com
    terryjoegunnelsbooks.com